The Proof of the Pudding

BERKLEY PRIME CRIME TITLES BY RHYS BOWEN

Royal Spyness Mysteries

MASKED BALL AT BROXLEY MANOR
(enovella)

HER ROYAL SPYNESS

A ROYAL PAIN

ROYAL FLUSH

ROYAL BLOOD

NAUGHTY IN NICE

THE TWELVE CLUES OF CHRISTMAS

HEIRS AND GRACES

QUEEN OF HEARTS

MALICE AT THE PALACE

CROWNED AND DANGEROUS

ON HER MAJESTY'S FRIGHTFULLY SECRET SERVICE

FOUR FUNERALS AND MAYBE A WEDDING

LOVE AND DEATH AMONG THE CHEETAHS

THE LAST MRS. SUMMERS

GOD REST YE, ROYAL GENTLEMEN

PERIL IN PARIS

THE PROOF OF THE PUDDING

Constable Evans Mysteries

EVANS ABOVE

EVAN HELP US

EVANLY CHOIRS

EVAN AND ELLE

EVAN CAN WAIT

EVANS TO BETSY

EVAN ONLY KNOWS

EVAN'S GATE

EVAN BLESSED

Anthologies

A ROYAL THREESOME

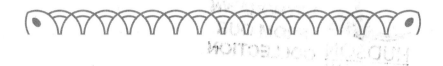

The Proof
of the Pudding

RHYS BOWEN

BERKLEY PRIME CRIME
New York

BERKLEY PRIME CRIME
Published by Berkley
An imprint of Penguin Random House LLC
penguinrandomhouse.com

Library of Congress Cataloging-in-Publication Data

Names: Bowen, Rhys, author.
Title: The proof of the pudding / Rhys Bowen.
Description: New York: Berkley Prime Crime, 2023. |
Series: Royal Spyness mysteries; 17
Identifiers: LCCN 2023026686 (print) | LCCN 2023026687 (ebook) |
ISBN 9780593437889 (hardcover) | ISBN 9780593437896 (ebook)
Subjects: LCSH: Rannoch, Georgie (Fictitious character)—Fiction. |
Women spies—Fiction. | Aristocracy (Social class)—Fiction. |
LCGFT: Cozy mysteries. | Novels.
Classification: LCC PR6052.O848 P76 2023 (print) |
LCC PR6052.O848 (ebook) | DDC 823/.914—dc23/eng/20230609
LC record available at https://lccn.loc.gov/2023026686
LC ebook record available at https://lccn.loc.gov/2023026687

Printed in the United States of America
1st Printing

I'm dedicating this to my children's spouses:
Tim, Tom and Meredith. Always loving, always helpful.
I have the best in-laws ever and couldn't love them more if they
were my own. And I compliment my kids on their good taste.

The Proof of the Pudding

Chapter 1

JUNE 25, 1936
EYNSLEIGH, SUSSEX

Excited and nervous about the impending arrival. Oh golly, I hope it goes well. I hope Queenie behaves herself and doesn't make things too difficult.

You have probably heard that Darcy and I were expecting a baby in August, but that wasn't the arrival I was nervous about at that moment. It was still sufficiently far away that I was not considering the implications of childbirth. Every time I thought about the baby, I imagined holding him or her in my arms and seeing that adorable little face looking up at me—maybe with Darcy's blue eyes and dark curly hair. I had pushed images of the actual delivery and what that meant into the dark recesses of my mind. Actually I knew little about it. One isn't educated in such matters at school. Mummy had once said it was absolutely the worst thing one could imagine and she decided on the spot that she'd never do it again, but then Mummy did tend to be overdramatic about most things.

The arrival that was concerning me more at the moment was that of our new chef, Pierre. We had been living at Sir Hubert Anstruther's lovely Elizabethan house called Eynsleigh for almost a year now. Sir Hubert is my godfather and one of my mother's many husbands. As he spends most of his time climbing mountains, he invited Darcy and me to move in. It was a lovely invitation and we jumped at it, since we were both penniless and had been looking at ghastly flats in London.

After a rocky start we had loved living there. I've always been a country girl at heart, having grown up in a castle in the Scottish Highlands (my father being the Duke of Rannoch). It suited me well to look out on acres of parkland and to walk my dogs every morning. There had been a servant problem when we moved in, but luckily the former housekeeper, Mrs. Holbrook, had agreed to come back and take care of the place so that it now ran like clockwork. We had acquired a housemaid and a footman/chauffeur, a personal maid for me and a gardener, all of whom were local folk and most satisfactory. But the one thing we still didn't possess was a proper cook.

So far our only cook had been my former maid Queenie. Yes. That Queenie. Those of you who have been following my exploits might remember that Queenie was a walking disaster area. When she was my lady's maid she ironed my one good velvet dress and burned off the pile; she lost my shoes on my wedding day. In fact there were more disasters than I could now recall. I kept her on because she had been jolly brave on occasions and I knew full well that nobody else would ever hire her. However, as it turned out, she was not a bad cook. So she had taken over the kitchen at Eynsleigh and so far she hadn't burned it down. However, her cooking was limited to dishes that she knew from her Cockney upbringing, so we tended to eat a lot of suet puddings, toad-in-the-hole, shepherd's pie. Hardly the sort of elegant fare that one would expect at an upper-class household. One could not really entertain local gentry and serve them spotted dick.

Darcy had been pestering me to find a proper chef but I had put it off. I'm not very good at hiring servants. However, recently two things had happened: we had received a letter from Sir Hubert to say he had finished climbing everything in the Andes and would be coming home in time for the impending birth, and we had just returned from Paris, where I had met a chef in need of employment. Pierre had been acting as a waiter when I met him, unable to find a job as a chef in the competitive market of Paris. So I offered him the job at Eynsleigh. This was a bit of a risk, as I hadn't actually tasted his cooking. But I decided that anyone who had been to a culinary school in France would know how to cook better than Queenie. Frankly I didn't think he'd take the job, as he was an avowed communist, but he'd agreed and would be arriving shortly.

There was only one problem, and that was Queenie. When she heard I was bringing in a French chef she got very upset. She didn't want no foreigners cooking foreign muck in her kitchen, she said. She was hurt that her cooking wasn't good enough for me. She thought I liked her cakes and biscuits. I seemed to tuck into them readily enough!

I did, I told her. She was good at baking and her cakes were delicious. But when Sir Hubert came home he would want to hold dinner parties. There was no way that Queenie would be able to create a multicourse meal for twenty, was there?

She agreed that she'd probably find that a bit beyond her, especially if they wanted fancy muck like that cocky-van she'd had to cook at Christmastime. Then she told me she wouldn't mind so much if I got in a proper English cook, a nice lady like that one we had worked with in Norfolk. But not some foreign bloke who was going to boss her around.

"If he comes, then I quit," she said.

Oh golly. That did put me in a bind. I wouldn't actually be sad to see her go, in many ways, and she could now probably get a job as a cook in someone else's house, but then she changed her mind. "I'll just go back to being your lady's maid," she said. "You can tell that Maisie girl that she can go back to dusting and sweeping, or she can be the scullery maid in the kitchen and wait on the foreign bloke."

Then she stomped off, making the ornaments on the shelves jingle and rattle as she passed. She was a hefty girl and she always walked as if she were an advancing army. I went through into the drawing room, hoping to find my grandfather there. He had been staying at Eynsleigh for a while following another attack of bronchitis, and I had persuaded him to come and be looked after. He had taken a lot of persuading, as he felt ill at ease in a great house, especially with servants waiting on him. It was quite out of character for a former Cockney policeman. And in case you are wondering why I had a father who was a duke with a castle and a grandfather who was a Cockney, I had better explain that while my father was Queen Victoria's grandson, he had married my mother, who was a famous actress and beauty but came from humble beginnings (which she now chose to forget).

He had been reading the local newspaper when I entered the room. He looked up and saw my face. "What's wrong, ducks?" he asked. "Your face looks like you could curdle milk."

"It's Queenie." I sank into the armchair opposite him.

"What's she done now?" He looked amused. "Forgotten to put the toad in the toad-in-the-hole?"

I sighed. "She hasn't done anything, except for making it quite clear that she will resign as cook if I bring in Pierre from Paris."

My grandfather continued to smile. "Well, that's not the worst thing in the world, is it? I don't think she'd be too great a loss. And didn't you tell me that those relatives of Darcy's thought a lot of her? She could go back to work for them."

"That wasn't all she said." I gave another sigh. "She said she'd just have to go back to being my lady's maid and I could get rid of Maisie." I gave him an imploring look. "What am I going to do, Granddad? I don't want her as my maid. I like Maisie. She's sweet. She's efficient. The only thing wrong with her is that she won't leave her mother, which makes it hard for me when I travel, but I'm not going to be going anywhere with a new baby, am I?"

"Then you have to be honest with Queenie," he said. "You tell her that you are quite satisfied with your current maid and have no plans to replace her." He reached across and patted my knee. "You are the boss, after all, ducks. You show her who's in charge."

"I know," I said. "I'm just not good at ordering servants around. I know it should come easily to people like me, but it never has. My sister-in-law, Fig, thinks nothing of bossing everyone, but I always feel guilty."

"You're too kindhearted," he said. "You get that from me. Although your mum don't seem to mind bossing everyone around either, does she?"

I had to laugh at this. "She certainly doesn't," I said. "She makes the most of being the dowager duchess, even if she isn't officially entitled to call herself that any longer."

Granddad frowned. "Well, that's one of the things she'll have to give up when she marries that German bloke, won't she? She'll be plain old Frau. And I won't be going to the wedding, that's for sure. Not to some Kraut. I think she's making a big mistake, don't you?"

"I do, actually," I said. "I quite like Max, but I don't like what's going on in Germany these days. You should have seen the Germans I met in Paris, Granddad. When Mummy went shopping she had a minder—a terrifying woman who watched over everything she did."

"Nothing good ever came out of Germany," he said. Rather a sweeping statement, as I happened to like quite a few German wines and composers. But Granddad was biased, as his only son, my uncle Jimmy, whom I had never met, had been killed in the Great War. "I don't know why she wants to marry this bloke. She's quite happy living in sin with most of them, isn't she?"

"It's Max," I said. "He's very prim and proper and wants to do the right thing."

"She'll regret it, you mark my words," he said, wagging a finger at me. "When she becomes Frau whatsit she'll have to give up her British nationality, won't she? And then she won't be able to leave even if she wants to."

"Oh golly. You're right," I said. "I wouldn't want to be trapped in Germany right now, even if she will be one of the favored few."

Granddad gave a sigh. "Not that she'll listen to any of us. She never has done so up to now. Is she coming over for the birth of your baby?"

"She promised to."

He chuckled. "I can't see her being any use as a grandma. Never lifted a finger to take care of her own child, did she? I think she was back in the South of France right after you were born."

I thought about this. I had few recollections of my mother, certainly none from the days when I was in the nursery. It was Nanny who took care of me, who tucked me in and sang to me. Thank heavens she was a kind and loving woman, or who knows how I would have grown up. I planned to be much more involved with my own child.

Granddad folded his newspaper. "So when's this Froggy bloke arriving?" he asked.

"By the end of the week."

"And would you want Queenie to stay on in the kitchen, as his helper?"

"That would be ideal," I said. "I can't expect a proper chef to do all his own preparation and cleanup."

"So you'll be reducing Queenie to scullery maid?"

I stared out of the window, watching the trees in the park dance in the stiff breeze. Why did life have to be so complicated?

Chapter 2

Today is the day. Pierre is arriving. I was expecting to have a few
days to sort things out with Queenie, but I got a telegram
yesterday to say he was catching the boat train and asking for
someone to meet him at the station. Not exactly the humble
servant, then, who would be prepared to walk the miles from
the station if they couldn't hitch a lift on a farm cart. If I can't
control Queenie, how am I going to manage with him? I'm
beginning to wonder if this whole thing isn't a big mistake.
After all, spotted dick isn't so bad, is it?

Darcy was up early when Maisie brought my morning tea. When
Queenie had been my maid it was never certain that morning tea
would arrive at the right time, slopped into the saucer, or at all. But
Maisie was as punctual as clockwork, and good-natured too.

"Good morning, my lady. It's another lovely day," she said as she placed the tray on my bedside table before going across to draw the curtains.

Darcy came from his dressing room, trying to tie his tie as he walked. He paused in front of the dressing table mirror and finished the job. He looked exceedingly handsome, as usual. I watched him, wondering how such a dashing man could have chosen me. He caught me looking at him and winked, making me blush.

"This girl's certainly an improvement on the last one, isn't she?" he asked. "Well, that's a stupid thing to say, because anybody with two legs and two arms would be an improvement."

He saw my face fall. "What on earth's wrong?"

"Oh, Darcy. I'm not quite sure what to do," I said. "You know the new chef is arriving. Queenie says she's not going to work with some foreign bloke and she'll go back to being my maid."

"I don't see what's so hard about that." Darcy patted my shoulder as he walked past me. "Tell her you already have a satisfactory maid and she's welcome to stay on in the kitchen or find employment elsewhere."

"But that's the trouble," I said. "Who would want to employ her? I know she's not a bad cook, but she does have more than her fair share of mishaps."

"We can send her back to my aunt," Darcy said. "They actually liked her."

"I suppose so." I swung my legs over the side of the bed and reached for my teacup. "I'm just not sure I want to get rid of her. She saved my life once, you know."

"I know. Never mind. You'll figure it out. You are mistress of a great house now. You have to step into the role."

I took a gulp of tea. "I suppose so," I repeated.

"I'm off, then," he said.

"May one ask where?" With Darcy it could be anywhere—France, South America . . . He didn't officially work for the British government, but he did a lot of undercover, hush-hush and dangerous sort of stuff, which he enjoyed and I worried about.

"To see a man about a dog," he said with a conspiratorial smile. So annoying.

"Darcy! That's what you always say!" I glared at him.

"Oh, all right. To see a man about a dog in London."

"London?"

He gave me a cheeky smile. "Would you rather if I said I was visiting my mistress in Mayfair?"

I smiled too. "I know for a fact you don't have a mistress in Mayfair. She'd be too expensive to keep." I paused, hoping for more. "Is this for your work? Government stuff?"

"Georgie, you know I can't tell you that."

Alarm bells jangled in my head. "They won't be sending you anywhere far away, will they? You promised you'd be home for the birth."

"I won't be going far away, I promise." He bent to give me a peck on the cheek. "Be back for dinner, unless anything comes up." He paused. "If there is any dinner, that is. The new chef won't know how anything works and Queenie will have stormed out."

"Don't say that," I said. "I'm absolutely dreading it."

"Just teasing, old thing. I'm sure it will all be fine."

Which shows you just how clueless men can be.

I DRESSED, TAKING a deep breath before I came out of my bedroom. As I opened the door I heard the patter of tiny feet on the floor. No, not those tiny feet and actually no longer so tiny, as the two puppies came bounding toward me, tongues lolling out, tails wagging madly. I intercepted them before they knocked me over—they were getting quite big but still thought they were adorable balls of fluff.

"Naughty," I said. "You know you're not allowed upstairs!" This was because they chewed anything they could get their mouths on, especially shoes.

They stared up at me with adoring eyes. "But you know how much we love you, and when we heard you moving around we had to come and greet you," those eyes seemed to say. As usual I couldn't be cross for long, and they danced beside me as I made my way down the stairs.

No appetizing smells greeted me as I entered the dining room. The sideboard was bare. No bacon. No kidneys. No eggs. Nothing. I rang the bell. Phipps, our footman, appeared carrying a toast rack filled with toast.

"Sorry, my lady," he said, "but Queenie said she ain't cook no more. Mrs. Holbrook is boiling you an egg right now, and I'll bring the coffee up."

"Oh dear. Thank you, Phipps."

He didn't return my smile. In fact there was a hostile look in his eyes. "If you don't mind me speaking my mind, your lady, I think it was downright mean of you."

"What? Bringing in a French chef?"

"No, not that. Of course you needed a proper cook. I meant the way you're tossing out poor Maisie. I know she's not wanted to travel with you on account of her sick mother, but that's not a reason to give her the sack like that when she's been a good worker."

"Give her the sack?" I frowned.

"That's right. She's upstairs right now packing her things and crying her eyes out."

"But I never said anything. She seemed quite cheerful when she brought my morning tea."

"That was before Queenie came to her and said that you wanted her to be your maid again now so Maisie could clear off. She said the mistress was chucking her out on account of the fact that she wouldn't travel with the family like a proper lady's maid."

"Queenie's got a nerve!" I put down the piece of toast I had selected. "I never said anything of the sort and I have no intention of sacking Maisie. I'd better go and find her right away, and have a word with Queenie. She's become really difficult. Thank you for telling me, Phipps."

I hurried up the main staircase and then along the hall and up a second stair that led to the servants' bedrooms. I climbed this one a little more slowly on account of the extra weight I was carrying. I now had an impressive bump in front. I wasn't sure which room was Maisie's, but it was easy enough to find as I could hear the sound of crying coming from it. The door was half open. I tapped and walked in.

She had a small suitcase open on her bed and was in the process of emptying drawers. I put a hand on her shoulder, making her jump with alarm.

"Maisie, my dear," I said. "It's all right. Don't cry. You're not going anywhere."

She looked up at me with tear-stained cheeks. "But Queenie said you didn't need me anymore. She said I was never going to be a proper lady's maid if I didn't go wherever my mistress wanted. She said she'd been all sorts of wicked, foreign places and never complained and now she was taking her old job back."

"Queenie had no right to say that," I said. "She will not be taking your job, Maisie. You do it very well and I'm pleased with you. Besides, I'm not going anywhere with a new baby, so we don't have to face that problem for quite a while."

I saw the hope come into her eyes. "So I don't have to leave?"

"No, you don't. I want you to stay as my personal maid."

"Oh, thank you, my lady. I'm ever so grateful." I thought for a moment she was going to hug me. "I don't know what my mum would do without the money I give her. She has an awful lot of doctor's bills."

"So that's settled," I said. "Dry your eyes and get back to work."

"Yes, my lady." She gave me a damp smile and started putting the clothing back in her chest of drawers.

I went down the stairs carefully, as my balance wasn't what it used to be, then through the baize door and down another flight of stone steps to the kitchen. I was greeted by two exuberant puppies, delighted to see me, but no sign of Queenie. Mrs. Holbrook appeared as I stopped the dogs from jumping up and petted them.

"Oh, my lady. Is everything all right? I don't know what's got into Queenie. She was quite bolshie this morning and said she wasn't your cook anymore."

"She's upset because I have a French chef coming, Mrs. Holbrook, and she's behaving badly."

"Do you want me to have a word with her, my lady?"

"I'm going to have a word with her myself, Mrs. Holbrook. I'm most disappointed in the way she's behaving. Do you know where she is?"

"I haven't seen her all morning. Can she have left without giving us notice?"

"Who knows." I shrugged. "With Queenie anything is possible."

"It's a shame," she said, "because I think she was doing quite nicely as the cook. Not too many disasters, if you know what I mean."

"I do know." I smiled at her. "Send her to me if you find her."

"I will. You go back to your breakfast and I'll bring up a boiled egg in a jiffy as well as some more toast. I expect that first lot is cold by now."

We searched the rooms downstairs, then I went back up. No sign of her in the dining room. I was going to return to my breakfast when another thought occurred to me. I went back upstairs to my bedroom, and there was Queenie, rearranging my clothes in the wardrobe.

"Queenie, what are you doing?" I demanded.

"Putting everything back in its proper order, missus," she said. (You'll note that she had never learned to call me "my lady." It was "miss" until I married and now had moved on to "missus." I was never quite sure whether this was deliberate or she just wasn't too bright).

I took a deep breath. "Once and for all, you are not my maid. I have a perfectly good maid called Maisie, and you had absolutely no right to tell her she was sacked. You are lucky I don't sack you on the spot for your impertinence. But let's get one thing straight: you can stay on in this household as assistant cook and hopefully learn some skills from a trained chef, which will help you to get a head cook's job in the future, or you can give me your two weeks' notice and look for another position."

"Then that's what I'll be doing," she muttered. "I'm not having no foreign gentleman telling me what to do. I tried that once and I didn't like it. And you'll be sorry when I'm gone."

With that she flounced out of my bedroom. Oh dear.

$\mathcal{C}$hapter 3

JUNE 30
EYNSLEIGH

I do hate upsets, and I can't help feeling uneasy about Queenie.
    Still, she knew that her position was only temporary until we
    found a trained chef, didn't she? And she must realize that
    she is not qualified to cook more than the simplest dishes.
    It's stupid, but I shall miss her if she goes. I wonder if she's
    bluffing.

I finished my simple breakfast but found I couldn't settle to anything as we waited for the arrival of Pierre.

"Am I doing the right thing, Granddad?" I asked. "It seems to have upset the entire household."

"You're doing what's expected of you, my love," he said. "You know Sir Hubert will be back soon, and he told you last time he was here that you should be looking for a good cook and he'd pay.

Well, you've been taking your time and he'll be disappointed if you don't have a proper cook in place."

"You're right," I agreed. "I have been putting it off for this very reason. I didn't want to upset Queenie."

"If you ask me, that girl has been a pain in the neck since you first took her on," he said. "I'd send her back to Darcy's aunt and good riddance."

"I know, Granddad," I said. "The problem is that she's been so brave and loyal and not complained when I took her to outlandish places like Transylvania. So I feel sort of responsible for her. But as you say, she did enjoy being with Darcy's aunt and uncle. Only then I'd have to look for another assistant cook, and I hate hiring servants."

"It will all sort itself out, you'll see." He smiled. "Mrs. Holbrook will find you a girl if you need one. She's a good woman, isn't she?"

I sensed that my grandfather was sweet on her. He had that wistful smile whenever he spoke of her. "She is. And I hope she will stay on for a while. I know she's at the normal retirement age."

"She likes being useful and needed. I know how she feels. It's sad when you realize that nobody wants or needs you anymore and all you're fit for is the scrap heap."

I reached out and took his hand. "Granddad, you are very much wanted and needed around here. I value your company."

"That's very nice, ducks," he said, "but it's not as if I have anything useful to do, is it?"

"Then we'll find you something. Darcy and I have been talking about getting the home farm up and running again. Start with some chickens and maybe a pig or two."

This made him chuckle. "As if I know anything about pigs!"

"You could learn."

"What's that they say about not teaching an old dog new tricks?" But he was still smiling.

I glanced out the window as I heard a noise in the driveway. But it was only the postman on his bike.

"I wonder what time Pierre will be arriving," I said. "He said he'd telephone from the station to be picked up."

"Let's hope it's before dinner, or we'll all die of starvation," Granddad said.

"Golly, I hope I haven't made a mistake in hiring him," I said. "I've never actually tasted his cooking."

"You haven't?" He looked up now, frowning. "You got a recommendation from somebody, then?"

"Not exactly." I found I was chewing my bottom lip. Something I used to do as a little girl when I was nervous. "I met him in Paris. He was working as a waiter but he told me he was a qualified chef, only he couldn't find a job in Paris. So I offered him the post with us. I thought anyone who qualified as a chef in Paris had to be better than Queenie."

"Maybe he couldn't get a job for a good reason."

"Oh golly. Don't say that. He is a poet. And he is a passionate communist. Let's hope he doesn't make it his mission to poison all the aristocracy."

QUEENIE, OR SOMEBODY, managed to heat up yesterday's soup for lunch. It was probably too much to wish that we'd have cakes for tea. I took the dogs for a long walk and had just returned when they dashed to the front door, barking madly.

"Holly! Jolly! Get down! Quiet, you brutes." I tried to grab them. They were six months old and still very much playful puppies with not a mean bone in their bodies, but they were now quite large and could be alarming to a visitor. Luckily Phipps appeared and opened the door as I held their collars. Outside stood Pierre, red-faced and sweating, holding a large suitcase.

"*Mon dieu,*" he said, eyeing the dogs suspiciously. "I thought I would never reach this place." He said this in French as he came in and deposited the suitcase on the marble floor.

This was not the time to tell him that the servants' entrance was on the ground floor at the side of the house.

"I thought you were going to telephone us to send someone to the station," I said, also in French.

"That was my intention," he said, walking forward as he examined the staircase, the portraits on the walls, and the suit of armor. "But I met a man at the station who said he was driving past your house, so I thought it would save you sending someone to pick me up. Alas, I did not realize that it is such a distance from the gates to the house, and on such a hot day . . ." He paused to mop his forehead.

The dogs were now straining to get at him, to cover him with slobbery kisses. But he backed away. "These animals, they are dangerous?"

"Only to people we don't like," I replied. "No, they are still young and very friendly." I turned to Phipps. "Take the dogs and shut them in the scullery for now, Phipps. This is our new chef, Pierre. I will show him to the kitchen and his quarters."

Pierre watched as the dogs were dragged away.

"Now, if you will follow me," I said. "I did not ask you how good your English was. You will need to communicate with the other servants."

"I am speaking . . . leetle bit," he said. "My American friends. They try to learn me."

"Then I hope you will work hard to pick it up quickly. I speak French but I don't think anyone else in the house does." I indicated his suitcase. "Come along, then. Follow me."

He picked up the suitcase and followed as I led him down the hallway.

"Ees very grand," he said in English.

"Yes. Very grand. But your part of the house is this way." I pushed open the green baize door and went down the stone staircase that led to the kitchens and the servants' area.

"This will be your domain," I said. "The kitchen is here."

He looked around. From his expression I couldn't tell whether he approved or not.

"Ees big," he said. Then he frowned. "But old. Not modern."

"No. Not very modern. This house was built in fifteen eighty-something."

He walked around, running a finger over surfaces like a visiting maiden aunt. I hoped he wasn't going to be temperamental. He had seemed so pleasant and easygoing in Paris.

"And your room will be through here." I left the kitchen, went past Mrs. Holbrook's little sitting room, and opened the door to a bedroom. It hadn't been used since the last chef left, as Queenie had kept her bedroom on the top floor. The curtains were drawn and it smelled musty. Pierre regarded it with horror.

"No, no." He waved his arms. "This is not possible. I cannot sleep here." He reverted to French. "It is dark and smelly. I cannot live underground. Only rats and bats like this sort of place." He turned away. "Now you see why I am a communist. You live in a place of great grandeur, but your servants, they must live in holes below the ground. This is not right."

I had to agree with him. It was not the most appealing of rooms. But I wanted to make sure that we did not start off on the wrong foot, with Pierre lording it over the household or expounding his communist ideas to the rest of the staff.

"Pierre, I hope you remember that I gave you a chance when I offered you this job," I said, reverting to French. "You wished to be a chef but you could find no chef's position in Paris and you had to act as a waiter. A humble waiter, Pierre. I am taking a chance on you. I have not even sampled your cooking. Who knows, maybe you are not good as a chef and that was why you could not find work."

I saw his face flush with indignation. "I am a very good cook," he said. "You will see."

"I'm glad to hear it," I went on. "Here you will not find the work hard. You will be cooking mostly for myself, my husband, and later my godfather, who owns this house. You will be able to try out new dishes and earn a reputation. Make the most of this."

He nodded with enthusiasm. "Oh, madame, I am happy for this chance. Yes. But you must understand that I am also a poet, yes? I have the soul of a poet. I cannot live in darkness and gloom. My soul would shrivel and die."

"Very well," I said. "We will arrange for a room on the top floor with the other servants. Those rooms are not as big, but you will have plenty of light. But first I should introduce you to Mrs. Holbrook. She is the housekeeper and she is in charge here. A very nice woman."

As I spoke I went to knock on her sitting room door. Nobody answered and I guessed that she was probably taking her afternoon nap. Instead I went through the kitchen to the servants' dining room on the other side. This was where I expected to find one of the maids, who could make up a room for Pierre on the top floor.

I was right. Maisie was there, along with the housemaid, Sally. They were both doing some mending and scrambled to their feet as they saw me. They eyed Pierre with interest.

"Ladies, this is Pierre, the new chef," I said. "You will address him as 'Chef' and I expect you to help him improve his English."

"Yes, my lady," they muttered in unison.

"And he wishes to have a room on the top floor with the rest of you. So, Sally, would you please go up, find a room for him and make up the bed."

"Yes, my lady." She bobbed a little curtsy and scurried off, giving Pierre a cheeky little smile as she passed. I hadn't considered before that a good-looking Frenchman might be throwing the proverbial spanner into the works in the house.

"And, Maisie," I said, "would you go and find Queenie and tell her that I want her to start showing the new chef where everything is in the kitchen. And we'd like some tea in the drawing room at the usual time."

"Very good, my lady." Maisie looked dubious, if not downright scared. I suspected she wasn't happy about tackling Queenie, who might seem like a formidable presence to a small and delicate girl.

I turned to address Pierre. "I don't know how much of that you understood, Pierre. The first girl, Sally, has gone to find you a room and make your bed. The second girl, Maisie, is my personal maid and she has gone to find Queenie, who has been the cook until now."

I said this in French. He nodded. "This woman will now be my sous-chef?" he asked.

"I'm not sure. She is undecided as to whether she'll stay on or not. She is a decent basic cook but has no knowledge of haute cuisine. If she stays I hope you can teach her."

"I will do my best, my lady," he replied.

I heaved a sigh of relief. He had recovered from the long slog up the driveway and was going to make an effort to fit in. We both looked up at the sound of footsteps clattering down the stone stairs. Queenie appeared, red-faced and puffing.

"You want me to show the foreign bloke around my kitchen?" she demanded. "I ain't going to—" She broke off as she caught sight of Pierre. Her mouth dropped open. "Cor, missus," she said. "He ain't half handsome!"

$\mathcal{C}hapter$ 4

I think things may work out after all.

Queenie continued to stare at Pierre.

"Queenie," I said. "This is Pierre. If you choose to remain in this household you will help him in the kitchen. You will address him as 'Chef.'"

Queenie took a step toward him and stuck out her hand. "Whatcha, mate," she said. "I'm Queenie. Bonjour."

A smile spread across Pierre's face as he took her hand. "Ah, you speak my language."

"I picked up a bit of the old parley-vous when I was with the missus in the South of France," Queenie said.

Wonders would never cease. That Queenie, who had never

managed to master the English language, had picked up any French was a miracle.

"This is very good," he said. "You will show me everything I need to know, *oui*?" He put what I considered to be a lot of meaning into this sentence. Queenie blushed scarlet.

"*Oui, oui,*" she said and burst out laughing at what she had just said.

"This is funny?" He frowned.

"Wee-wee," she repeated. "It's what we say when kids take a piss."

This was beyond his English comprehension.

"We don't want to teach Chef bad words, Queenie. Why don't you show him around the kitchen until his room is ready?"

"Bob's your uncle, missus," she said.

Pierre was frowning again. "This uncle," he said. "Who is he? What is the importance of him? He lives here with you?"

"It's an English saying, Pierre. Or rather a strange saying from the people of London. Nothing to do with uncles. It just means she agrees with me and she'll do what I ask."

Pierre shook his head. "No uncles? Then why . . ."

"Queenie has her own way of speaking, I'm afraid."

"'ere, I can speak proper if I want to," Queenie said. "Come along, ducks. Follow me."

Again Pierre frowned. "There are some ducks here? *Canard?* Yes?"

"No ducks. Another English expression. Like calling you a friend."

"Ah. So a friend is also a duck, *oui*?"

I could see this soon could get complicated. "I'll leave you to show him around, then, Queenie."

And I escaped to the drawing room.

Miraculously tea arrived at the right time, on a tray, with matching cups and saucers, watercress sandwiches, and a good selection of biscuits. This, I told myself, was going to work out well. Queenie was clearly going to pull out all the stops to impress Pierre. Now all I had to hope for was that Pierre could impress Darcy and me.

Darcy arrived home shortly after five. I was out on the lawn with Granddad and the dogs, enjoying the warm sunshine. The dogs bounded up to the motorcar as it came up the drive and leaped up to Darcy as he got out.

"All right, you mad brutes," he said, laughing as he fended them off. "Down. No jumping." He headed across to me. "Really, we have to take these creatures in hand, Georgie. They are impossible. We must train them."

"I've tried," I said. "They are like unruly children. They will do what I tell them when I'm actually working with them. They know how to sit, how to stay and come, but only if they want to. I'm hoping they'll grow up and get lazy like other Labs."

Darcy picked up a ball and threw it far into the park. The dogs rushed after it.

"So did the new chef arrive?" he asked. "Did Queenie stalk out in disgust?"

"The answer to the first is that yes, he has arrived. But a minor miracle has happened. Queenie took one look at him, commented that he was very handsome and immediately decided to stay."

"Is he very handsome?" Darcy asked.

"You could say so. Dark and Gallic-looking. Brooding, like a French poet."

"I'm not sure about leaving my wife alone in the house with a handsome Frenchman," Darcy said, his eyes teasing mine.

I patted my round stomach. "I'm hardly in a position to seduce or be seduced," I replied. "Besides, I already have one dark and handsome man. That's quite enough."

Darcy took me into his arms and gave me a little kiss. "Not long now," he said. "I'm dying to know if it's a boy or a girl, aren't you?"

"I am," I said. I hesitated. "Will you be disappointed if it's a girl?"

"Of course not. Plenty of time for a boy later. Although maybe if we end up with ten girls . . ."

"Ten? I'm not going through this ten times," I said. "If you want ten children, you have them."

"That's what your grandma said when she had your mum," Granddad said, looking up from his lawn chair. "She said if we wanted another one it was my turn."

"That would definitely keep the population down, if men had to have the babies, wouldn't it?" I laughed with him.

"So will we get a taste of Pierre's cooking at dinner tonight, do you think?"

"I doubt it. Give the poor chap time to settle in," I said. "Besides, I rather expect Queenie will want to show off her own skills to him. We may end up eating rather well."

"That's good," Darcy said. "I was a bit worried that your godfather would come home and be served beans on toast."

※

DINNER WAS A thick vegetable soup, followed by leg of lamb with all the trimmings.

"Blimey." Darcy looked up when Phipps served it to him. "It's not Sunday, is it? Or Easter?"

"I'm as surprised as you are," I said. "I'd no idea we even had a leg of lamb. And it's actually perfectly cooked too. Maybe Pierre took over right away."

Then the dessert course arrived and it was treacle pudding (that is a steamed suet pudding with golden syrup; rather delicious, but definitely not haute cuisine). This proved that Queenie had created at least part of the dinner. This was good news either way: she had cooked an excellent meal, proving she could if she tried, or she had already learned to work alongside Pierre.

"Ask Queenie to come up to the dining room, Phipps," I said as he served us the cheese board.

"She's not in disgrace again, is she?" he asked.

"Not at all. I just want a word with her."

She appeared as we were drinking our coffee, a rather smug look on her face.

"Queenie, we're dying to know," I said. "Who cooked the meal tonight? Was it a joint effort?"

"Not on your nelly, missus. It was all me. Pierre said he'd need time to learn how everything worked, so he'd watch me. Well, I wasn't going to let him think that the English don't know how to eat well. So I decided to cook the leg of lamb Mrs. Holbrook had got in for Sunday, and I'd already made that soup for our lunch tomorrow. So all I had to do was to whip up the pudding. He was most interested, I can tell you. I don't think he'd ever seen a suet pudding before. But he approved of the leg of lamb. He said English people must be rich to be able to afford so much meat. I told him no, any family can afford a Sunday joint. Even families like mine down the East End."

"Congratulations, Queenie. You've done us proud," Darcy said, making her beam at him adoringly. "I can see we can look forward to good meals in the future between the two of you."

As Queenie returned to the kitchen, he turned to me. "You see, you were getting into a state over nothing. It's all going to run very smoothly."

$\mathcal{C}$hapter 5

JULY 1
EYNSLEIGH

I am so relieved. Queenie will work hard to impress Pierre, and he
seems amiable enough. Everything will be running smoothly by
the time Sir Hubert gets home.

The next morning I was about to start my breakfast when Pierre
appeared in the dining room.

"Madame, I must speak with you," he said. He looked perplexed.

"Of course. What seems to be the trouble?"

"Madame—I am expected to cook this breakfast?" he asked.
"These animal parts and fishes and God knows what else?"

"It's our normal breakfast," I said.

"But a chef, he does not do the breakfast cooking. His job is to
create the perfect dinner, *oui*? For breakfast the baker bakes the

croissants and baguettes and we take the jam and voilà. *C'est tout.*
That is the reasonable breakfast, not this orgy of food. It is not
healthy to wake up the body with so much food. You will die an
early death."

"I'm afraid this is how it's done in England."

He gave a despairing shrug.

"Maybe we can leave the breakfast to Queenie," I said. "It will
be good for her to be in charge of something. She is inclined to be
lazy, so you must make sure she works properly."

"She seems most agreeable," he said.

I didn't like to say that was because he was a man and good-
looking. I didn't want him to get ideas.

"Was there anything else, Pierre?"

"Yes, madame. My uniform. I was told by Mrs. Holbrook to
look in the uniform cupboard and I would find something suitable,
but no—there are only aprons. A chef does not wear an apron. I
must have a proper jacket and hat. These are the requirements of
my profession."

"You didn't bring a jacket with you?"

"No, madame. It is up to my employer to decide if she wishes
the white jacket or the black jacket."

I took a deep breath. "Very well, Chef, we will have to see where
we can purchase such a jacket for you. Are there places that sell
such things?"

"I do not know how things are done in your country," he said.
"I only know that I cannot prepare meals for you without a suitable
jacket."

"Perhaps we could buy some fabric and have one made locally,"
I said, but even as the words came out I remembered what my ball
gown had looked like when the gamekeeper's wife had tried to rep-

licate what I had seen in a women's magazine. Not exactly a pretty sight. Then I had a brilliant idea. "I will call my friend in London. She has a chef. She will know."

He gave me a beaming smile. Really, Queenie was right. He was exceedingly handsome. He went off, satisfied, and I telephoned my dear friend Zou Zou (aka Princess Zamanska), praying that she'd be at home and not off in her little plane to some remote part of the world. Her maid answered and immediately Zou Zou herself was on the line.

"Georgie—is everything all right?" she asked in a breathless voice. "It's too soon for the baby, surely?"

"Everything is fine, Zou Zou," I said. "I just need advice. I have finally found a French chef, but I have no jacket for him and he tells me it is the responsibility of the employer to provide his uniform."

"Quite right," she said. "Clever old you to find a French chef. They are much in demand."

"So I thought you might know where one can buy a chef's jacket."

"Darling, I had my tailor run one up for Robert," she said. "It looks marvelous. Mind you, he is a stunning-looking man in the first place."

"But I don't have a tailor, Zou Zou."

"Then let him come up to London and send him to mine."

I had to laugh. "Nor could I afford your tailor, darling."

"My treat," she said. "Tell him to say that Princess Z sent him."

"Zou Zou, I can't have you treating me all the time. It's not right," I said.

"Don't be silly. I enjoy it. I have no family anymore after they were all slaughtered. You and Darcy are the closest thing I have to family now. My life would be extremely dreary and dull without you."

"Dreary and dull?" I chuckled. "Where were you flying to when I last spoke to you?"

"Casablanca, darling. I found it quite dull, apart from the oranges." She paused. "Anyway, I now consider you my family. I enjoy playing at fairy godmother."

"Which reminds me, Zou Zou," I said. "Darcy and I wondered if you would be the baby's godmother."

"You darlings! I should love to," she said. "Oh, what fun."

"Only you're not to spoil him or her."

"Don't be silly. You know I'll spoil the little darling rotten. Have you chosen a name yet?"

"We've toyed with several but haven't come up with the perfect one. Darcy says we should look at the child first and see which name fits."

"If it's a girl I demand that one of the names is after me."

"Of course. What are your names? I've only ever known you as Zou Zou."

"Alexandra Maria Olga Ludmilla Iga," she said.

"I'm sure Alexandra would be perfect," I said quickly, not wanting a daughter called Ludmilla or Iga. Or Olga for that matter."

"That's settled, then. Send the chef up to me and I'll have my Robert take him to my tailor. On one condition."

"What's that?"

"That you invite me to your first dinner party once he's cooking for you."

"Of course we will." I took a big breath. "I haven't exactly had experience with dinner parties, but Darcy says that now we have a chef we should start entertaining. Sir Hubert will be back soon and he'll want to entertain his friends."

"Oh yes, the famous Sir Hubert. I met him briefly at your wedding. Quite a charmer, if I remember correctly."

"My mother thought so, but he kept going off to climb mountains."

Zou Zou chuckled. "Thrown over for a mountain peak. No, Claire would not like that. How is your dear mama? Still with the silent Hun?"

"She is. About to marry him, I'm afraid."

"Big mistake. As one who escaped from an authoritarian regime I should tell her that she does not want to find herself stuck there."

"Then you tell her. She won't listen to me."

A voice spoke in the background. "Already?" Zou Zou said. "But I'm not dressed. Tell him to wait in the sitting room."

She came back to the telephone. "Darling, I must run. My accountant is here and I have to talk about what to do with all that lovely money. Wasn't it clever of my late husband to have transferred all his assets to Switzerland before he was hacked to pieces by angry peasants?"

With that she hung up.

I relayed her message to Pierre and he looked impressed when I mentioned she was a princess, even though he professed to be a communist. "And one more thing, madame," he said. "I have made a list of items that I need to prepare food for you. The kitchen is quite lacking in basic spices and condiments. When I visit the tailor in London you agree that I should find the right place to buy these?"

He handed me the list. It took up two pages. I stared at it. It was in French with that strange handwriting style that I can hardly read, and those I could read I had no idea how to identify. "Yes, I suppose so," I muttered. "Of course. If you need them. Are these all necessary?"

"Of course. Any good kitchen must have them."

"What is this one?" I pointed.

"Saffron. Essential for bouillabaisse."

"And this?"

"Garlic, madame. Can you believe there was not a single clove of garlic in the house? Nor shallots. Only big coarse onions. And herbs . . ."

"Have you checked the kitchen garden?" I asked. "I am sure the gardener can find you herbs and will be happy to plant anything you need and grow garlic and shallots for you."

That at least pacified him. "Ah. So I can expect fresh vegetables from the estate?"

"Of course. Tell the gardener what you would like him to plant if they are not already there."

"Very well, madame. I shall only need to buy the spices, then. And some kitchen tools. And more bowls. And a bain-marie . . ."

Heavens. I had no idea what a bain-marie was. It was Mary's bath. And I didn't know who Mary was. I hoped Sir Hubert knew that a chef might be expensive. Darcy and I certainly couldn't afford him. But I gave him the house checkbook and off he went to London. I reported the encounter to Darcy that evening.

"Are you sure he's not taking advantage of an inexperienced employer?" he asked.

"I have no idea. If a chef tells me he needs certain items, I suppose we have to believe him."

Darcy sighed. "Being a homeowner is complicated, isn't it?"

"Horribly. I think I'd rather live in a cottage in Ireland with no staff."

"There's always the lodge on my father's estate." He smiled at me.

"Don't tempt me." I looked up as Mrs. Holbrook came into the room.

"Telegram, my lady," she said and held out a silver salver.

"Oh golly." I associated telegrams with bad news. Granddad was right here. It had to be Mummy. . . . I tore it open.

SAILING TOMORROW ON THE HMS
CARINTHIA. ARRIVING JULY 12.
HUBERT

Chapter 6

JULY 3

EYNSLEIGH

Now we're expecting another imminent arrival! Sir Hubert is
   coming home. We received a telegram. I'm just praying that the
   new chef works out and that Sir Hubert finds the house in
   order. I don't know why I'm worrying. He's the kindest man.
   But I don't want him to be disappointed.

As far as we could tell, Pierre did not attempt to cook until his uniform arrived. He had come back from the city with two large car-
rier bags from Harrods and explained that various larger items
would be delivered. When I saw the check he had written I decided
it would be less expensive to dine out. And we still hadn't seen
whether he could cook! I worried that the uniform would not arrive
before Sir Hubert and I'd have to explain that I was paying a French
chef who wouldn't actually do any culinary work.

Queenie came to me complaining that it wasn't fair that she had to cook breakfast. "He gets to have a lie-in in the mornings!"

"He is the head chef, Queenie," I said. "And besides, I thought you'd like to be in charge of one meal. Pierre doesn't know about English breakfasts. He can't cook kidneys or kippers. So that's why it's up to you."

I saw the change of expression come over her face. "Bob's yer uncle, then, missus," she said. I gave a little smile as she left. At least it was easy to pacify her.

Miraculously the uniform arrived before Sir Hubert. Pierre modeled it for me. He certainly looked dashing—a double-breasted white jacket and the traditional tall chef's hat. And that evening a delicate green pea soup was served to us.

"*Potage San-Germain*, my lady," Phipps said. "That's what chef told me to call it."

And after it some kind of fowl in a rich, sticky sauce. Delicious. Then to follow it, light meringue with berries. When we were seated with our coffee I summoned Pierre.

"What was the meat that we were eating?" I asked.

A worried look crossed his face. "You do not like?"

"I like very much. I just couldn't identify it."

"It is friend, my lady. Breast of friend à l'orange. With the orange sauce."

"Friend?" The thought of my cook roasting one of my friends and covering them in orange sauce was an uneasy one.

He grinned. "Yes. Is *canard*. You call this friend, yes?"

"Oh. Duck." I started to laugh. Darcy looked confused.

"You tell me ducks is same as friend, *n'est-ce pas?*"

"Not exactly." I was trying to control my laughter. "In the dialect that Queenie speaks, from the East End of London, they call people ducks as a term of endearment."

"This is very strange." He shook his head. "I would not insult anyone by calling them a duck."

"So the dinner was duck à l'orange?" Darcy asked. "It was very good."

"Thank you, my lord," Pierre said.

"Unfortunately I'm not my lord," Darcy explained. "Not until my father dies. You can just call me 'sir.'"

Pierre looked confused now. "But she is 'my lady'? Madame Holbrook told me I must call her this."

"Yes. She's more important than me." Darcy shot me a grin. "She's related to the king. So you must behave well or she'll have your head chopped off."

Pierre frowned then understood what Darcy was saying and laughed. "Me, I do not believe in kings," he said. "One day there will be the revolution."

"But until that day, please go on cooking for us," Darcy said, "because the food was really good tonight."

I went to bed feeling relieved and satisfied. Sir Hubert would not be disappointed in my choice. Unfortunately the rich meal did not agree with my current condition and I suffered from heartburn all night. A small price to pay for eating well, and it wouldn't be long now before I'd be back to my normal shape.

AFTER THIS THE house was in a flurry of activity. Sir Hubert's rooms were aired and cleaned. Menus were discussed for his first night home. Phipps went to the station to meet him and we stood as a welcoming committee in the front hall. He bounded up the steps looking tanned and fit.

"Well, what a lovely welcome," he said, opening his arms to me. "And look at you, my dear. Positively blooming. How long to the big day?"

"Three weeks. But you are looking marvelous."

"I'm feeling fine now," he said. "I'm pretty much recovered from that fall on Aconcagua. I dislocated my shoulder holding on to the rope but I was able to pop it back in and climb down using the other arm." He shook hands with Darcy and even kissed Mrs. Holbrook on the cheek. She went very pink as she escorted him to his suite. I was holding my breath as we went in to dine that evening. I was just praying that Pierre would continue to produce small miracles and that Queenie would not somehow sabotage them.

We were in the salon, having our sherry before dinner, when Mrs. Holbrook approached me. "My lady. The chef would like a word," she whispered.

Full of foreboding, I followed her. Pierre was waiting by the kitchen door.

"I am sorry, but this is too much, my lady." He looked as if he was about to cry.

"What's wrong?" I asked.

"It is that girl," he went on, the words tumbling out in French. "I have tried to be patient with her. I was patient when she threw away the chopped dill because she thought it was carrot tops. I was patient when she fed the duck fat I was saving for larding to those brutes of dogs. But this is too much." He waved his arms expressively. "She opened the oven door to see if the soufflés were ready!"

"And?"

"They were not ready. They have sunk. They are ruined. What am I going to serve as a dessert?"

"I'm sorry, Pierre," I said. "How annoying for you. Perhaps some simple strawberries and cream would suffice."

"Perhaps." He sounded doubtful. "And another thing, my lady. I do not wish to complain, but this girl, she is attracted to me."

"You're an attractive man, Pierre."

"I know this. I know the women they like me. But she throws herself at me. Always beside me. She stands in the way when I have to pass her so that I have to brush against her. It is not right."

"No," I agreed. "It is not right. I will speak to her."

"Thank you, my lady. I cannot cook with such distractions. And another thing—those dogs! It is not sanitary to have dogs in the kitchen. Such naughty dogs too. They are big. They jump up to the table and steal the meat I am preparing."

"Oh no. Of course that's not right. We must make sure they are shut out of the kitchen. We'll have them upstairs with us. It's time they were better trained anyway."

"Thank you, my lady." He gave a little bow. "Now I must get back to my kitchen. I hope this girl has not interfered with any other part of my dinner."

In spite of Pierre's worries, the dinner exceeded expectations: cream of leek soup followed by scallops in their shells and then beef bourguignon. The strawberries and cream were actually perfect, followed by some good Stilton cheese. Sir Hubert put down his fork. "My goodness. What a meal. That was a feast fit for a king. After several months of living on corned beef cooked in a bully tin, it was almost too much for me. Where on earth did you find someone who can cook like that?"

"In Paris. Where else?" I tried to toss off the remark but then added, "I was lucky to meet him when I was there earlier this year."

"My dear girl, you are to be complimented," he said. "Absolutely superb." His face lit up. "I know. We must have a dinner party. The neighbors will descend on us anyway when they know I'm back. We'll invite everyone. I'll draw up a list and you discuss menus with the chef. We'll knock their socks off, won't we?"

"How many people were you thinking of?" I asked cautiously.

"The table seats thirty, I believe. Let's come up with names and we'll go from there."

I swallowed back the word "golly." I didn't want to admit I was terrified at playing hostess for thirty people. For four people, actually. And with Queenie in the kitchen, there was always the chance of disaster. I did speak to her the next morning. I scolded her for ruining the soufflés.

"I was only trying to be helpful. I thought he'd forgotten them," she said defiantly.

"In future let Chef give you his instructions," I said. "And don't throw anything away without asking him." As she went to stomp off indignantly, muttering, "It was my kitchen first, who does he think he is, the ruddy king of England?" I called after her. "Oh, and Queenie, one more thing. I believe you are attempting to flirt with the chef. Please don't do this. It takes his mind off the cooking."

"What that man wants is a good woman," she said. "It's not right he should be all alone in England."

"I don't think you're his type, Queenie."

"He'll come around. When he sees what I've got to offer."

I couldn't think what else to say. She was smirking now as she walked away.

That morning I sat down with Sir Hubert to discuss the guest list.

"We must invite all the neighbors or they'll be put out," he said. "Lord and Lady Mountjoy. You know them, don't you?"

I nodded. "I was presented at court with their daughter."

"And Colonel and Mrs. Bancroft. You must have met her. She runs the Girl Guides and the Women's Institute and everything else. Poisonous woman, but we'd never hear the last of it if we didn't invite her. And the vicar and his wife, of course. He's a good man. And the Turnbulls—he farms the land adjoining ours."

He listed several more people, some of whom I had met. "And a couple of friends of mine whom I'd love to catch up with. "Freddie Robson-Clough. Must have him. Do you know him, by any chance?"

I shook my head.

"Famous explorer. Been to the most remote of places. He and I did an expedition together to Nuristan. Fascinating. I climbed a mountain and he mingled with the inhabitants. Nearly got both of us killed, but a wonderful time."

I didn't think this would be my definition of a wonderful time.

Sir Hubert pondered for a while. "How many does that make? We need one more." Then he waved a hand excitedly. "And you know who else we'll invite? Sir Mordred Mortimer. He counts as a neighbor, doesn't he?"

When I looked puzzled he went on. "Surely you know who he is?"

"The name's familiar but . . . isn't he a writer? He writes those frightening books about murders and hauntings and things. I tried to read one once. It gave me nightmares."

Sir Hubert chuckled. "They sell awfully well, I gather. People love to be scared. Well, he lives not too far from here. He'd make a fascinating dinner guest."

"If you think so," I said. Vicars and farmers were alarming enough for me without adding a celebrity.

"And, of course, feel free to invite your friends too," he went on.

And so the invitations went out. Most people accepted. Sir Hubert was the sort of man people wanted to meet. I invited Zou Zou and suggested she might want to stay for a few days. She said she'd be delighted. The only one who turned me down was Granddad.

"Oh no, my love," he said. "I'm not sitting at a table with all the posh folk. Not for all the tea in China. I'll take my meal with Mrs. Holbrook."

I did understand his point. I discussed menus with Pierre. "Let's keep it simple, just in case," I said. "Things that can be prepared in advance?"

He suggested a consommé with spring vegetables and herbed croutons followed by dover sole volute followed by a crispy roast chicken served with potatoes au gratin and asparagus and to finish a tarte tatin. That did not sound exactly simple to me. He commented that not all the neighbors might be used to food that was unfamiliar to them. Knowing the British suspicion of anything foreign, I agreed with this. I also suggested that he give Queenie something specific to do that would keep her out of trouble. He agreed with that immediately! "I will assign her to consommé. I have shown her how it should be prepared, so I think I can trust her with it." He ended this statement almost as a question.

Zou Zou arrived, armed with presents, of course. Various items for the nursery this time as well as champagne to celebrate the arrival. "I can't wait to meet the little darling," she said.

"Me too. I'm anxious to get it over with now. It's not very convenient walking around with a barrel sticking out in front."

"Don't worry. Your figure will return immediately," she said. "I have a little man who can give you exercises." She looked around, then added in a soft voice, "Between us girls, your godfather is rather gorgeous. I think I might want to know him better."

Oh gosh. Somehow I didn't think that would go down well with Mummy. In spite of not wanting him herself, I didn't think she'd want anyone else to have him either. I was glad she wasn't here.

The silver was polished, the table was laid. Everything looked splendid. I could not fit into any of my normal evening clothes so I had to improvise a little with a large fringed silk shawl, but the result was not too bad. As Darcy said, I looked pregnant and there was no hiding it. The hour arrived and we went down to meet the guests. Colonel and Mrs. Bancroft were the first to arrive. She entered the room complaining that the lack of rain was ruining their tomatoes. The other neighbors appeared soon after and immediately started exchanging local scandal. Sir Hubert's fellow explorer, Mr. Robson-Clough, arrived, clearly out of place among us normal people, and hardly said a word. Zou Zou looked stunning, as always, in a slinky black evening gown, and was turning the full force of her charm on Sir Hubert. He looked rather like a deer caught in the headlights. Poor Darcy's father, I thought. We had hoped those two would make a match of it, but his stupid pride had held him back from proposing to a rich woman.

"Are we all met?" Sir Hubert asked.

"Only your famous Sir Mordred isn't here yet," I replied.

"Good God, you haven't invited that awful man, have you?" Mrs. Bancroft exclaimed.

"But he's fascinating," Lady Mountjoy replied. "And I adore his books. So absolutely creepy."

"The man is no good Christian," Mrs. Bancroft snapped. "You

wait. He's probably brought a whole host of demons or evil spirits with him."

"I do hope not," the vicar replied. "I doubt there will be room for them at the table." He looked across at me and winked.

"The man has a damned fine garden, so I've heard," Colonel Bancroft said. "Of course, he can still afford the gardeners. You should have seen our garden when we were out in India. We employed a whole team of women on their hands and knees with little sheers to cut the lawns. Didn't have lawn mowers in those days. Of course, they were glad to be employed rather than starving. Untouchables, you know."

Darcy shot me a horrified look. "Should we perhaps go in to dinner?" he asked.

At that moment Phipps ushered in another guest.

"Sir Mordred Mortimer," he said.

And a tall, thin man with long silver hair swept into the room.

Chapter 7

**Golly! What a strange and terrifying person. Darcy thinks it's all
for show. I jolly well hope so.**

Sir Mordred Mortimer clearly wanted to live up to his name and
reputation. He was dressed entirely in black except for the white
handkerchief in his dinner jacket, and a black velvet cape hung
from his shoulders. It flew out as he strode forward. If he'd tried to
hang upside down from the rafters or repose in a coffin I don't
think I would have been surprised.

"Ah, so you are our hostess," he said in an accent that was so
frightfully clipped and posh it made the royal family sound like
barrow boys. "How kind of you to invite me, my dear. Mordred
Mortimer at your service."

I held out my hand. He took it and kissed it. Of course everyone clustered around, wanting to meet him owing to that strange fascination with celebrity (except for Mrs. Bancroft, who was glaring at him and standing well away).

I had to admit he was a fascinating creature. He must have been at least fifty but his face was unlined, with cold blue eyes. When he looked at you it felt quite uneasy, almost as if he was reading your mind. He had been placed beside me at dinner and he was definitely an interesting companion. He told me how he had bought the house he now lived in ten years ago because it was called Blackheart Manor and he couldn't resist. "Where else should a person like me live?" he asked. Also, he added, it had a poison garden.

"A what?" I sounded startled.

"A poison garden, my dear. You know—a garden composed of only the most deadly plants in the world. I could kill everyone at this table if I wanted to with a few seeds or berries."

"How horrid," I said.

"But so fascinating." Those blue eyes sparkled with amusement. "I've made poisons my study, of course. I've used some of the more exotic ones in some of my books. But the truth is, my dear"—and he covered my hand with his own slim white one—"if you really wanted to kill someone, you could do it with no trace. So easy. Ordinary household substances. No need for exotic poisons. But then that wouldn't sell books, would it?" And he laughed.

Lord Mountjoy, seated across from us, had overheard this. "I say, Mortimer," he said, "did I not read that you are holding an open house for the public to tour your gardens?"

"I am indeed," Sir Mordred said. "There has been so much interest I thought it was only fair. And it will raise money for my charity too. Good news all around. My readers get a peek at my life and the orphans in South Africa benefit."

"We absolutely have to come," Lady Mountjoy said, glancing at her husband. "I'd be fascinated to see a poison garden."

"Aren't you taking a bit of a risk, old chap?" Sir Hubert asked. "Hundreds of people milling through a garden full of deadly plants. You're not worried that someone could help themselves or at least get ideas for future dark deeds?"

Sir Mordred chuckled. "Since many of the plants are easily available by the wayside, I don't think there is much danger. Deadly nightshade, you know. Hemlock. All growing beside the road. Yew trees in every churchyard. It just happens that the man who designed the garden in the eighteen hundreds took the trouble to assemble the plants in one place."

He took the roll beside his plate and broke off a tiny piece with his long, elegant fingers before popping it into his mouth. "I must add," he went on, "that the chap also created a physic garden, full of plants that can heal all maladies. Kill and cure. Fascinating, isn't it?"

"I'd be most interested to see these gardens," the explorer, Freddie Robson-Clough, said. I think these were his first words all evening. He flushed red when people turned to him. "I have studied botanical healing. Most interesting. In fact once in Bulgaria . . ." He never managed to finish this as Mrs. Bancroft interrupted him with her booming tones that had made generations of Cub Scouts and Girl Guides get in order.

"So you'll be letting in the general public on this open day? All and sundry? Aren't you worried about vandals? We've had to deal with them ourselves, you know, haven't we, Charles?"

Colonel Bancroft nodded. "Damn people claiming they have a right-of-way footpath across my back paddock. I told them you can't walk past my house like that. You can see in our windows from that so-called path. The memsahib might be in a state of un-dress."

I saw Darcy's mouth twitch as he repressed a smile at the thought of anyone wanting to see Mrs. Bancroft in a state of un-dress.

"Hooligans, the lot of them," Mrs. Bancroft went on. "The lower classes have become too uppity since we returned from India. It was the Great War, you know. Letting young men see there was a world outside their village. Now they think they are equals. Whatever next."

She took a large slurp of soup and we went back to eating.

The dinner lived up to my hopes. Every course was delicious. No disasters. When it was over everyone thanked us profusely and said they couldn't remember eating a better meal. As they were about to leave Sir Mordred drew me aside. "My dear, that was a remarkable meal. I must compliment your chef."

"Thank you. He is rather good, isn't he? I found him in Paris."

"Paris, eh? Has he been with you long?"

"No, only a few weeks."

"How's his English?"

"Not too wonderful yet, but he seems willing to learn and he does cook so well."

"Indeed he does." He moved closer to me. "I hope you won't think me impertinent, but might I meet him and compliment him in person?"

Darcy had moved over to join us. I was glad because Sir Mor-dred's closeness was making me feel a little uneasy. "Yes, of course," I said. "I'll have him brought up to meet you."

We waited in the foyer until Pierre, still red-faced and dishev-eled from cooking, appeared.

"Is something not good, my lady?" he asked.

"On the contrary, Pierre. The dinner was perfect. Everyone said it was the best meal they could remember eating."

He beamed. "I am most glad."

"And, Pierre, this gentleman is a famous author. Sir Mordred Mortimer. He wanted to meet you and congratulate you in person."

Sir Mordred stepped forward, holding out his hand. "Well done, young man. I hear you have just arrived from Paris?"

"*Oui*, monsieur," Pierre said. "I have only been here little while."

Sir Mordred glanced at me, then turned to Pierre. "I hope you don't think I'm being too forward, but I have a proposition to make to you."

A proposition? I tried not to let my face show any alarm. What sort of proposition did this man have in mind?

"You see, I am planning to host an open day at my house near here. Open to the public. You know they've been dying to see it for ages. All my fans. My publisher thinks it will be a splendid idea to launch my new book. And during dinner I came up with a marvelous idea. Why not finish the day with something extra special?" He gave a dramatic pause—spreading his hands before going on. "Why not have a banquet for the favored few and maybe a celebrity or two thrown in—those who are willing to pay a hefty sum for the privilege?" He gave that thin little laugh. "But you know, my chef is not up to it. He's getting older and slower. So I wondered if I might entice this young man to come and cook for us, if you would let me borrow your chef for the evening, Lady Georgiana?"

He turned those piercing blue eyes onto me.

"Well, yes, I suppose so, but it would be up to Pierre," I said. I could see he had not understood most of the conversation, so I relayed it briefly in French. Pierre's eyes lit up.

"So what do you say, young man?" Sir Mordred asked. "I'd pay you well and you'd be given carte blanche to serve whatever you chose, no expense spared."

I translated.

"Yes, I could do this. If my lady can do without me for one evening." Pierre looked across at me.

"Naturally you and your husband must come to the dinner as my guests, Lady Georgiana," Sir Mordred said rapidly. "And I'd love to give you a personal tour of my poison garden first. Absolutely fascinating. You would not believe how the most innocent-looking of plants are the most deadly."

The baby gave a big kick, reminding me. "How soon is this event to be? Because as you can see I have an upcoming event of my own, after which I shall be out of commission for a while."

"Of course. My congratulations, my dear. The child is due when?"

"The beginning of August. "

"Well then, that would work splendidly. My open house is on July the fifteenth."

"All right," I said. "In that case we'd love to attend."

"Then it's all settled. Splendid. Perhaps you can bring this young man over to take a look at my kitchen first, meet my chef, discuss the menu. Let's make it a showstopper, shall we? Dishes you wouldn't get anywhere else. It will be the event of the year, you'll see." He turned to Darcy and shook his hand, then took my hand and kissed it again. "And now I must take my leave of you. À bientôt, then. Until we meet again."

Then he sailed out of the front door, his cape billowing out behind him.

Chapter 8

Well, we survived the dinner party with no huge disasters. A
miracle! And everyone seemed to have a good time. Pierre was a
resounding success and has been asked to cook for a very fancy
banquet. I don't quite know what to make of Sir Mordred
Mortimer. He rather frightens me, but then I think that is his
intention. I certainly don't want to read one of his books!

"Blimey," Darcy muttered, using one of Queenie's favorite words.
"Is that chap for real, do you think, or is it all a marvelous act?"

"I suspect he's living up to the persona of what people might
expect of a Sir Mordred Mortimer."

"Is that his real name, then?"

"I don't know. He told me he inherited the Mortimer title and
estate, so I suppose it must be."

"I'm glad we're normal," Darcy commented.

"Am I free to go now, my lady?" Pierre asked, reverting to French.

"Oh, Pierre, of course you are," I said. "Thank you again for the marvelous meal. And I hope that you did not feel pressured into cooking this banquet for Sir Mordred?"

"No. I am excited for it," he said. "There will be people from high society there?"

"I'm sure there will. He's a rather famous author."

"It will be good for my reputation, then?"

"I would think so, but I hope you won't be leaving us anytime soon."

"Oh no. I like it here. The work is easy, except for that woman. She makes the cow eyes at me and she unbuttons the top of her uniform. What is she thinking?"

"She is hoping you'll notice her charms, I expect."

He shook his head. "She thinks she has charms?"

"I think you had better invent a fiancée at home and tell her you are already engaged."

He grinned. "This is a good idea. I will try it." He gave a little bow to us. "I bid you bonsoir, then, my lady." He switched back to English. "And good night, Mr. O'Mara."

And he headed back in the direction of the kitchen.

Darcy put an arm around my shoulders as he steered me back into the drawing room. "Well, you should feel proud of yourself," he said. "The evening went flawlessly. They were all quite impressed, even that Bancroft woman."

"I'm rather amazed myself," I said. "The food was awfully good, wasn't it?"

"You've found us a gem," Darcy said. "The Bancroft woman

warned me that we'd better keep quiet about our chef or he would be lured away by someone with more money but less breeding." He shook his head. "And now we've agreed to let him cook a banquet for the rich and famous. Probably a very silly move."

Sir Hubert was sitting on the sofa with Zou Zou, apparently showing her some photographs. "And this is the Hindu Kush," he was saying. "Had a bit of a run-in with the local inhabitants there."

"You have led such a fascinating life, Hubert," she said. "I do hope you're going to write your memoirs."

"How about you?" he said. "Your life seems to have been equally fascinating. Are you writing your memoirs?"

She gave an enchanting smile. "Oh no. I couldn't name names. Too many dubious relationships, I'm afraid."

"Sounds like Georgie's mother." Sir Hubert looked up as we came to sit opposite.

"Oh, I don't think I can compete on that front," she said. "Georgie's mother is the ultimate femme fatale, isn't she? Still gorgeous even though she must be in her forties now."

"You're quite a stunner yourself, old girl," Sir Hubert said.

"Flatterer!"

They exchanged a long look before turning their attention to us.

"A memorable evening, Georgie," Sir Hubert said. "Well done."

"I really had little to do with it, apart from smiling at people and listening to their stories," I said. "I didn't cook or even lay the table."

"But you were the gracious hostess. You kept that Mordred chap fascinated all evening."

"Only because he wants to borrow my chef," I said. I perched on the chair across from the fire. "He's come up with the idea of having a banquet after his open house and he wants to borrow Pierre."

"Goodness, I hope he has a big table," Zou Zou said, chuckling. "Everyone will want to stay for a banquet."

"Not if it costs twenty guineas a head," Darcy commented, sitting on the arm of my chair. "It's only for the favored few."

"Then we'll have to attend, Hubert," Zou Zou said. "I'm dying to see inside his house, aren't you?"

"Not at that price."

"Then it's my treat. I want to go and I need an escort. Do you think he has strange oak chests and secret doors all over the place?"

"And a coffin or two, I shouldn't be surprised," Sir Hubert said, laughing now. "The chap is a complete charlatan, I expect. Probably his real name is Bob Smith and he's the son of a butcher."

"No, he really is a Mortimer," I said. "He told me his branch of the family was quite humble but he'd inherited the title and the estate from a third cousin. He said it was a complete shock. Quite out of the blue."

"Why didn't his father inherit?"

"Parents died in India during a cholera epidemic. Family trust sent him to school," I said. "He was pretty much on his own from the age of fourteen, one gathers."

"Does he live alone now?" Zou Zou asked. "There was no mention of a wife, was there?"

"No. He didn't mention any family. He's the sort of man who would live alone, don't you think?"

"Darling, who'd want to marry him? He's quite creepy, isn't he?" Zou Zou smiled. "Do you think his blood is green? And that funny affected way he talks."

I stood up. "I don't know about you, but I'm exhausted. Being the gracious hostess is quite tiring when one is pregnant."

Zou Zou took my hand. "You did splendidly. Now, go and have a good sleep."

Darcy escorted me up the stairs to our bedroom.

"I hope I won't dream of ghouls and vampires," I said.

"Don't worry. I'll protect you." Darcy drew me into his arms and I rested my head on his shoulder. I was feeling quite content until he complained. "It's getting harder to put my arms around you. You'd better stop expanding!"

"It's your fault I'm like this." I gave him a playful slap.

I SLEPT WITH no bad dreams and awoke to Maisie standing beside me with my cup of tea.

"It's another lovely morning, my lady," she said. "Aren't we having a good summer so far?"

"Don't jinx it, Maisie," I said. "It has to stay fine for Sir Mordred Mortimer's garden party."

"They were talking about him this morning, my lady," she said. "They said he was like something out of a film. Not quite real."

"He was certainly strange, Maisie," I said. "Did Pierre tell you he has been asked to cook for a banquet at Sir Mordred's house?"

"Pierre's not awake yet, my lady. He worked awfully hard last night."

Maisie went off to run my bath. I got up, bathed and went downstairs. All was quiet. I decided I should take the dogs for a walk. "Holly? Jolly? Walkies," I shouted. No dogs appeared.

I poked my head into the kitchen. "Queenie, where are the dogs?"

"Don't know, missus. I ain't seen them for a while."

I went back upstairs, into the morning room, where Granddad was already up and reading the newspaper. "I hear you had a good old blowout last night," he said.

"It went very well."

"You're becoming the proper posh hostess, aren't you?" he smiled. "Who would have thought that my little girl would start taking after her great-grandma. Not my mum, you understand. She worked in a pub. No, I mean the old queen."

"Golly, I hope I don't turn into Queen Victoria," I said. "She was an awful hostess. When she finished eating everyone else had to have their plates whisked away whether they were done or not. People hated eating with her."

"I meant her confidence," he said. "That air of being in charge. Too bad the current king doesn't act that way. He's not at all regal, is he?"

"He's a nice man," I said. "Very kind and funny, and to be fair, he never wanted to be king."

"But he's supposed to be running the country and where is he?" Granddad said. "Off on a yacht in the Med with some woman, so they say."

I knew who that woman was, of course, but the British public still did not. Her name was Mrs. Wallis Simpson and she believed that she was going to marry my cousin Edward. Since the king cannot marry a divorced woman I didn't see how that could happen, but she was a determined person who always liked to get her own way. We'd have to wait and see, but I didn't think the outcome could be good.

I heard barking outside. I looked out of the window, and there was Sir Hubert with Zou Zou. They were walking together, laughing, as Sir Hubert threw a ball for the dogs. Oh dear.

Chapter 9

JULY 20

EYNSLEIGH

The birth is suddenly becoming rather real. The weather is hot and
sticky and I can't get comfortable wherever I sit or lie. I shall be
glad when it's over.

Zou Zou has gone back to London. I'm relieved in a way. Of course
she and my godfather do make a lovely couple, but I have always
hoped secretly that he and Mummy will get back together one
day. I'm sure he's still in love with her and I suspect she still has
feelings for him. It's just she loves Max's money. But how can
one like living in Germany right now?

Everything was in place for the arrival of little O'Mara. At least I
hoped it was. Having no wise female relative to advise me, I'd had
to rely on Zou Zou and Mrs. Holbrook, neither of whom had had
children. When Maisie was asked, she said that her mum always

shoved the newest baby in one of the drawers of the dresser until it was big enough to climb out. At least we had a proper cot and bassinet and, thanks to Zou Zou, enough clothes to change its outfit three times a day. Not being the most practical of women, she hadn't provided any nappies, but I had bought those. I'd also bought white wool and knitting needles, but I hadn't even managed to finish the one shawl I'd started. I reasoned it was the middle of summer and the child wouldn't need too many clothes for a while.

Darcy stood with me, admiring the nursery. Fresh curtains were hung at the windows. There was a bright braided rug on the floor and the large teddy bear that Zou Zou had bought sat on the shelves. In one window was the lovely rocking horse that Sir Hubert had ridden as a boy, and I remembered riding it too when I had lived here as a small child. I eyed it fondly.

Darcy slipped an arm around my shoulders. "It's hard to imagine that in a couple of weeks there will be a squalling baby lying there, isn't it?"

"I hope it won't squall too much. I'm going to have the bassinet in our bedroom to begin with so that I can feed the baby when it wakes."

Darcy frowned. "We should really think about hiring a nursemaid. I'm sure it's expected of us. You grew up with a nanny and so did I."

"But I would rather have had my mother," I said. "Although Nanny was very nice."

"And I suppose my mother was quite involved with us," Darcy said. A wistful look came over his face as it often did when speaking of his mother, who had died when he was a child. "She was a very warm woman. I remember her reading me bedtime stories. All the same, you don't want to be changing nappies and things, do you?"

"Maisie indicated she'd quite like to help look after the baby," I said. "She won't have that much to do as my lady's maid if I'm tied to the house for a few months, and her mother has had nine of them, of whom she's the oldest, so she has a good idea what to do."

"Let's see how that works for now, then," Darcy said. He steered me out of the room and we made our way downstairs.

"Let's hope the baby doesn't decide to come early," I said. "I'm dying to see Sir Mordred's house and garden, aren't you? And the dinner sounds as if it will be fabulous."

"It should be at that price," Darcy said. "Lucky we are invited guests. The others will all be nosy parkers who want to take a peek at his estate."

"Rich nosy parkers."

He chuckled.

"He'll make quite a bit of money from this, won't he? The open house all day and then this banquet at night. And I shouldn't think he's short of cash, the way his books sell."

"He's donating the money to charity, I think," I replied. "At least he mentioned something to that effect."

"Oh well, he's a better fellow than I thought, then."

"I'm supposed to be taking Pierre over to Sir Mordred's house to see the kitchens and meet his chef," I said. "I should probably do that sooner rather than later so Pierre has a chance to buy all the exotic items for the menu."

"It's going to be exotic, is it?"

"He didn't specifically say exotic, but he told Pierre no expense would be spared."

"Oh." Darcy looked disappointed. "I thought you meant things like monkey brains and grilled pangolins."

I made a face. "How disgusting. I hope it's not going to be anything too outlandish. My stomach rebels these days and I'd hate to have to make a dash from the dinner table in front of all those people."

"Just politely refuse anything you don't think you can eat," Darcy said. He gave me a peck on the cheek. "I must be off, then. I've a meeting with the Foreign Office at two."

"Don't you dare let them send you anywhere at this moment."

He smiled. "I've made that quite clear, my darling. I'll be here to hold your hand, I promise."

And off he went. I just hoped he meant what he said. If His Majesty's government called upon him, would Darcy be able to say no? I thought about this as I went down to retrieve Pierre and take him to Sir Mordred's. His Majesty's government—always working, always trying to do the right thing when His Majesty himself, my cousin David, still behaved as if he hadn't a care in the world. What would the British public say when they finally learned about his affair with a married woman? Surely he couldn't keep her a secret much longer, not when she had every intention of marrying him next.

I MUST HAVE driven past Sir Mordred's estate, the aptly named Blackheart Manor, many times before, but from the road one would not know it existed. Thick woodland grew up to a high redbrick wall. There was no nameplate or anything to indicate that a house lay beyond that wall. We almost drove past the tall wrought-iron gate. Phipps was acting as chauffeur. He got out and tried the gate, but it wouldn't open. Then we noticed there was a discreet box beside it. He pressed a button, words were exchanged with someone in the house, and the gate opened, slowly and mysteriously. We drove in, past those tall gateposts, and then through a stand of tall trees that crowded close to the drive, their branches reaching across the road to create a tunnel of deep shade. Then the drive curved around, and we came out of shadow to see beautifully manicured lawns in front of us and, beyond, a large stone house. It had the appearance of being really old, lacking the elegance of later buildings—no pillars or statues. In fact in many ways it looked more castle than house, built on the remains of a fortified keep. The windows were tall and narrow. There was even a round turret at one end and battlements along part of the roof. It did not give an immediately friendly appearance, in contrast to those gorgeous gardens around it. Roses were in full bloom in beds and over arbors, herbaceous borders packed with every kind of summer flower. Such a strange mixture, I thought—the menacing and the inviting. I wondered if this was a metaphor for their owner.

As we pulled up in front of the house a young man in an open-necked shirt and white shorts came out and stood waiting for us, holding his hand over his eyes to shield them from the bright sunlight. He was pale and skinny with longish hair and a slightly unkempt look to him. I thought Sir Mordred must be very lax about his servants if he let them dress like this on a hot day. The man came over and opened the car door for me before Phipps could come around.

"Hello," he said, still blinking in the light. "I suppose you must be Lady Georgiana. I've been charged to wait for you and make you welcome. The old man is on the telephone with his publisher at the moment."

I got out of the car. "Do you work for Sir Mordred?" I asked.

He laughed at this. "Not unless I have to," he said. "He's my father. I'm Edwin Mortimer."

"Oh, I'm so sorry," I said. I felt myself blushing. "I did not realize your father was married. He never mentioned a family."

"He only does when it suits him," Edwin replied. "Most of the time we're invisible and unimportant." He paused, pushing back a lock of hair that had fallen across his forehead, making him look absurdly young. "Not the greatest family man. It goes against his image. Actually it no longer matters as we're not at home much. I'm down from Oxford for the summer and Sylvia's now married and living in a flat somewhere with that ghastly husband of hers. Serves her right."

"And your mother?"

A spasm of pain crossed his face. "My mother died when we were very young. So far my father hasn't chosen to fill the vacant position. Between ourselves I don't think he likes women very much, but she was an American heiress. Lots of lovely cash. How could he resist?"

I shifted uneasily, glancing up at the steps and wishing we could go inside. Pierre had come around to join me.

"This is my chef, Pierre," I said, happy to change the subject. "I've brought him to inspect the kitchen and meet your chef."

"Oh yes. We've heard all about him," Edwin said. He nodded to Pierre. "You want to watch it or he'll try to lure you away. A very persistent man, my father. He likes to get his own way at all costs." He started toward the steps. "Well, come on in, then. I'll show you around."

"Your father doesn't have a butler?"

"He does, but he's older than the hills and can't manage steps anymore. He came with the house when my father bought it ten years ago. Ogden. That's his name."

We entered through an arched doorway into a large gloomy

foyer. The walls were paneled in dark oak and an oak stairway ran up one side to a gallery above, from which banners hung. Before my eyes could adjust to the darkness I took a step back to look up at the banners and uttered a little scream as a figure rose behind me, an axe held in menacing fashion over my head.

"Sorry, I should have warned you about Humphrey," Edwin said.

I put my hand to my heart, which was now thumping, as I saw that it was actually a full suit of armor, one arm raised and holding an axe.

"Ghoulish, isn't it?" Edwin said. "The décor came with the house too, including Humphrey here." He gestured to the suit of armor. "When we were younger we used to swear he moved about at night. You'd find the axe in different positions in the morning. And to say nothing of the ghosts . . ."

I smiled, having regained my composure. "If you're trying to scare me, you're talking to the wrong person," I said. "I grew up in a Scottish castle much gloomier than this one, and with its fair share of ghosts too."

"Golly, did you?" He sounded like me. "Of course, I'd forgotten. You're related to the royal family, aren't you? The new king's cousin?"

"That's right," I said.

"So you actually know him?"

"I do. Very well," I said.

"So what's he like?"

"As a person lots of fun. Kind. Generous. As a king, I'm not sure. I don't think he takes the job seriously. He never wanted it, of course. That's the problem if you're royal. You get stuck with duty."

"Do you suppose he'll now have to marry some dreadful foreign princess to produce the heir?"

I realized that he had heard nothing of Mrs. Simpson. "We'll just have to see, won't we?"

"Well, I'd better take your chef down to the kitchens, then," Edwin said. "No use summoning Ogden, as he takes half an hour to go down the stairs. It's this way." He motioned to Pierre.

"I should probably come too," I said. "Pierre needs help understanding English."

"Righto. Come on, then." He led me through the entrance hall and down a dark and narrow passage where more weapons hung from the walls. Through a heavy oak door and down a flight of stone steps to a kitchen that was half underground. High windows let in natural light but didn't quite manage to dispel the gloom. A huge range was on one wall, with a row of copper pans hanging above it. A young girl was standing at the center table, chopping some kind of vegetable. She took one look at us, her mouth open in terror, and ran into a back room. "Mr. Henman," she called. "The visitors is here."

"Coming. Coming." An elderly man shuffled out. He was wearing a chef's jacket, rather splattered with food stains.

"This is Lady Georgiana," Edwin said. "And this is Pierre, her chef."

"My lady," he said, giving me a curt little bow. Then he looked at Pierre. "So you're the one who's coming to take over my kitchen, then. Shove me aside like an old boot, eh?"

"Not at all, Mr. Henman," I said, because Pierre was still trying to translate "old boot." "He's coming to help you because clearly a banquet for thirty people is too much for one chef."

"If it's only for one banquet, all well and good, my lady. But I've been chef here for thirty years and I don't want the master getting any fancy ideas."

"I'm sure your master values you enough to realize that you'd find a banquet overwhelming."

I saw Henman weighing this speech, not wanting to admit that the banquet would be too much for him, but not wanting to find he had to cook it either. Finally he nodded to Pierre. "Well, I suppose I'd better show you what we've got and where everything is. I hope you won't be wanting too much of that fancy foreign stuff."

"It depends what your employer chooses for the menu," I replied.

"Can't he speak for himself?" Mr. Henman asked aggressively. "Cat got your tongue, boy?"

Pierre frowned. "Which cat is this? You do not want me to cook a cat, I hope."

"He doesn't understand too much English yet," I said. "You have to explain simply what you want."

"A bloody foreigner who doesn't speak English. That's all I need, begging your pardon, my lady," he muttered. "Come on, then. The larder's this way."

Edwin tapped me on the arm. "We'd better leave them to it. Come and have a sherry or something."

I followed him up the stairs. "So how does the food get up to the dining room? Do you have servants to carry it up the stairs?"

"Oh no. We've a dumbwaiter. Sylvia and I used to ride up and down in it when we first moved here. It's a fun house for kids in some ways. Great for hide-and-seek. Secret passages and all."

We emerged back into the main part of the house and Edwin led me through the foyer and into a long gallery. These walls were also paneled in oak, as was the ceiling, and in the center was an enormous fireplace, big enough to roast an ox—which obviously it had once done, as the stone above it was blackened. The tall, narrow windows were paned in leaded glass that distorted the view from the outside.

"Sit down," he said. "Sherry or whiskey?"

"Golly, it's a bit early, isn't it?" I glanced at my watch. It was only just past eleven.

"Never too early for a drink." Edwin poured me a glass of sherry then a large whiskey for himself.

"So you're at Oxford," I said. "What are you studying?"

"Philosophy," he said. "No bloody use to anyone."

"So what do you plan to do when you graduate?"

"As little as possible." He sat opposite me and stretched out his legs. "I don't actually have any calling to a profession. I'm sure I'd have no head for business. The law's too bloody boring. And I certainly wouldn't go into the army like my father. I can't see myself killing people—especially not the way wars are these days. All those poor blokes who died in the mud last time." He shuddered.

"Your father was an army man?" I must have sounded surprised because Sir Mordred had seemed like the least likely to serve in the armed forces.

"He was, strange to think," Edwin replied. "Son of a penniless junior branch of the family and his father already in the Bengal Lancers. He was born in India, you know. Came over to school when he was seven, poor little bugger. Actually it probably saved his life, as his parents both died in the cholera epidemic."

"So he also went into the Indian Army?" I took a sip of sherry.

"No. I think he'd been put off India for life. He joined a Guards regiment, hoping to guard Buckingham Palace and march around. But then the Boer War broke out and he found himself fighting Zulus in South Africa. Rather horrid and bloody, so one gathers."

"And then he inherited the title and all was well." I smiled.

"Not for a while. He stayed on in South Africa for a spot of diamond prospecting with a local chap."

"Oh. That was ambitious. Did he make a killing?"

"On the contrary. Nearly lost his life. The mine they were working caved in and they were both buried. Luckily he was still alive when he was dug out. The other chap wasn't. And they never found any diamonds worth anything either."

"Are you boring Lady Georgiana with my life history?" said a voice from the shadows, and Sir Mordred came to join us.

Chapter 10

I'm not sure what to make of Sir Mordred. Actually I think he's a
perfectly ordinary chap who enjoys playing a part. I'm jolly glad
I'm not living at Blackheart Manor, though. One of the more
depressing houses I've ever visited. Dark and damp and scary.
With all his money I can't see why he'd actually want to live
there. But I am dying to see the poison garden!

"Oh hello, Sir Mordred," I said as he crossed the room toward me.
"Edwin has been looking after me well and keeping me entertained.
One certainly couldn't be bored with your life history. Most color-
ful. Fighting Zulus. Digging for diamonds. I'm surprised you don't
write about South Africa since you were there for quite a while."

"Too many painful memories, my dear." He poured himself a
sherry and came over to join us. Today he was dressed in white

flannels and a cricket sweater and looked less alarming, apart from the long silver hair that curled over his shoulders. And those piercing eyes. "So your chappie is downstairs with old Henman, is he? Jolly good. Does he have ideas for a menu? I want this meal to be one that the guests will remember for the rest of their lives."

"He did an awfully good duck breast for us," I said. "That would be something the average English person doesn't have too often, wouldn't it?"

"That sounds like a good idea. If he does it well. We've had a remarkably good response. I've spread the word and we already have quite a number of sign-ups, including the famous actress Jill Esmond and her husband, Laurence Olivier. I rather think my publisher might have a hand in this, as there is talk of making a film version of my book *After Midnight*, and this Olivier chap would make an excellent vampire. Dark and brooding, you know. A little too handsome."

The way his expression changed made me wonder if he was actually attracted to other men as Edwin had implied. That would explain why he never remarried after his wife died.

"Oh dear," I said. "Perhaps we should not attend if the rest of the company is to be famous."

"Not at all, my dear. Frankly the rest of the company may well be boring beyond belief. The names don't mean anything to me, apart from your godfather and the charming princess. I suspect the others might be devoted fans of my books, dying to interact with me. We'll just have to see. But then, they will be paying twenty guineas for the privilege, so I have to make sure they get a slap-up meal." He stood up again. "Let's ring for your chappie and see what ideas he has for the menu."

He tugged on a bell pull. Slow footsteps could be heard and a stooped, white-haired old man came in. "You rang, sir?"

"I did, Ogden. Please summon the visiting chef."

"Very good, sir."

And the footsteps shuffled off again.

"Poor old thing. It will take him half the morning to deliver the message. I should really let him go," Sir Mordred said. "He should have retired years ago, but he's no family so I keep him on out of the goodness of my heart. He came to this house as a boy, can you believe. Worked his way up from boot boy. He remembers meeting Prince Albert." He suddenly turned to me and gestured excitedly. "Your grandfather, right?"

"Great-grandfather," I said.

"Splendid."

The way he said this gave me the feeling that Sir Mordred himself was rather struck by celebrity. I suspected he, not his publisher, had invited the film stars, and that I was being included as a token member of the royal family.

Contrary to his prediction, Pierre appeared shortly after. He was invited to sit and Sir Mordred peppered him with questions about the menu.

"I'm sorry. His English is still lacking," I said and translated for him. "Maybe we should continue in French."

"Sorry, but my French is as lacking as his English," Sir Mordred said. "I never was much good at languages. And don't ask Edwin either. He was a dashed useless student. Paid for an expensive school for nothing, didn't I? And had to bribe them to get you into Oxford."

"Well, you went to an equally expensive school and apparently you never managed to learn French either," Edwin said. "Touché, Papa."

"Impudent puppy. Go on. Bugger off." He waved an imperious hand.

"I can tell when I'm not wanted," Edwin said. He stuck his hands into his pockets and sauntered out of the room.

"Useless little bugger," Sir Mordred said. "God knows what he'll do with himself after Oxford. His idea of life is to go out drinking at nightclubs with his friends. Or visit someone's yacht on the Med. Of course, he's never had to work for a crust like I've had to." He swiveled toward Pierre. "Right, young man. Menu. What do you propose to dazzle my guests?"

Between English, French, and much gesticulating we managed to establish that he'd suggest starting with a crab mousse, decorated with caviar, followed by a cream of asparagus soup, then quenelles of some kind of fish, and for a main course perhaps venison.

"Venison?" I asked. "It's not the hunting season. I don't know where you'd find venison."

Pierre looked surprised. "But you have deer on your estate. I have seen them from the windows."

"You can't go killing one of my deer!" I heard the horror in my voice.

"Who would know? It's your land, is it not? And your deer. You can kill them when you wish."

"But these are exotic deer, Pierre. Sir Hubert brought the first pair back from the Himalayas years ago."

"Then they have bred well. If we eat one, then there will be another to take its place."

I supposed this was true, but I was rather fond of my deer and it seemed wrong to kill one of them.

"No, Pierre. No venison," I said.

He shrugged in that Gallic way. "Then what do you suggest? The boring roast beef, I suppose. Like all you English. No imagination."

"I thought your duck with the orange sauce was awfully good. It's not a dish that's on the menu often in England."

He frowned. "How many people again?"

"We're capping it at thirty," Sir Mordred said.

I translated.

"Duck for thirty—that is much work. To dismember and prepare all those ducks . . ."

"Maybe you could have Queenie help you prepare them?"

A horrified expression crossed his face. "How would she know how to prepare a duck? She will cut off the wrong parts."

"You can show her."

He shrugged again. "Very well, if you insist. And to accompany— the proper English peas. Queenie can shell them in advance."

"And for pudding?" Sir Mordred asked.

"Pudding?" Pierre looked horrified. "You wish me to make a pudding? What kind of pudding? Not the type that the girl makes with the suet and the raisins. The spotted dock?"

"Dick," I said. "No, Sir Mordred didn't mean that type of pudding. It's what we call the dessert course in England. Pudding. Afters. Anything sweet to follow the main course."

"Ah, the dessert." He nodded. "I understand."

"Do you have a favorite?" I asked Sir Mordred.

"We have a lovely crop of berries in my kitchen garden. Strawberries, raspberries, loganberries . . . Can we use those?"

Pierre nodded when I translated this. "I could make the small tartes," he said. "The fine pastry—the *pâte sucrée*, a layer of creamy custard, the *crème pâtissière*, the berries, and topped with the crème fraîche."

"That sounds very nice." Sir Mordred nodded with satisfaction. "And to finish? A savory?"

"What can be better than the good cheeses and fruits?" Pierre said. "A cheese board with the good Camembert and Roquefort and a bowl with the peaches and plums."

"And chocolate liqueurs to accompany the coffee!" Sir Mordred clapped his hands. "I get a special sort from Fortnum's. If this doesn't give them dyspepsia, I don't know what will. But they will damned well be getting their money's worth."

A thought had occurred to me. "What about your chef, Sir Mordred? I should not like him to think he was being ignored. Can we give him one or two of his specialties to create?"

"He's a lazy bugger these days," Sir Mordred said. "But he does do some rather good pastry."

"You said we'd be having a reception beforehand?"

He nodded.

"How about he makes some appetizers to hand around?"

"He does make bloody good cheese straws and curry puffs. And those little puff pastry things stuffed with shrimp. Yes. They'd go down nicely with champagne. A Dom Pérignon, I thought." He managed the ghost of a smile. "Splendid idea, Lady Georgiana. Well done." He patted my hand. His own hand was cold. He got up. "Right. I think we've done it. Come over whenever you want, Monsieur Pierre."

"So how will we arrange for the purchase of all the foodstuffs?" I asked. "Do you want Pierre to order them or would you rather your Mr. Henman orders from his usual suppliers?"

"Oh, I think Pierre should do his own choosing of items. It

would be an insult to expect him to work with food that might not be up to his standards."

Pierre nodded, looking pleased. "*Exactement*, monsieur. I will choose the best."

"And we haven't discussed his fee for the evening," I said.

"The event will certainly enhance his reputation in England, and he is already receiving a salary from you, Lady Georgiana," Sir Mordred said. For one horrible moment I thought he was going to insinuate that Pierre did not need to be paid. But then he went on. "But five pounds for his extra work, do you think?"

I relayed this to Pierre, who nodded. "*Bien*," he said. I couldn't tell from his expression if he was pleased or not. I stood up too. "We should not take up any more of your time. I'm sure you want to get back to your writing."

"As a matter of fact I am between books at the moment, which is why I decided upon this as the perfect time for my open house. There is much arranging to be done so that the day is an enormous success—and gets the publicity it deserves. But before you go I should perhaps show you the banquet room."

His feet tapped neatly on the stone floor, then he opened a door at the end of the gallery and we entered another long dark room. Again the walls were wood-paneled and this time hung with tapestries of pastoral scenes. An oak table ran the length of the room, adorned at the moment only with two rather extravagant candelabras. Light came in through thin arched windows and the floor was slate tiles. Not a very inviting space. It reminded me a little of Castle Rannoch, but then we had tartan carpet on the floor and fierce-looking weapons on the walls.

"It will look quite different when there is silver and china on the table, and candlelight sparkling," Sir Mordred said. "Do you like the candelabras? Magnificent, aren't they? I got them from a convent in Spain, along with the table."

When he saw my shocked expression he added, "Oh, I bought them, paid good money and the nuns were short of cash."

I eyed those candelabras, wondering how much more of this place had been bought from poor nuns in order to create the image Sir Mordred wanted.

He walked around the room, looking quite pleased with himself. "Maybe we'll arrange for a musician or two up in the minstrel gallery." I noticed then that there was a small gallery at one end of the room. "Quite the medieval banquet. I wonder if one can buy mead? A pity one can't serve swan." And he laughed. He then proceeded to show us the dumbwaiter, cleverly concealed in a sort of anteroom hidden behind curtains. "So the food comes up hot from the kitchen and final touches can be performed here before the plates are brought to the table," he said.

I relayed this to Pierre. He frowned. "You will have someone to perform the final touches out of my sight?" he asked. "How will this person know what the plates should look like?"

Sir Mordred gave a little shrug. "Very well. I understand that great chefs are temperamental. Why don't we ask Mr. Henman if he will be in here. You arrange a sample plate as you wish and he will decorate the others accordingly."

"If he does not object to this task," Pierre said cautiously.

"No. He'll be delighted to be useful," Sir Mordred said with great optimism. "Now perhaps I should also take Monsieur Pierre on a tour of the kitchen garden so that you can see what kind of fruits and vegetables are available. We grow most things here. No need to buy them."

We stepped from the darkness into the bright sunshine. Sir

Mordred fell into step beside Pierre. "So you have come from France because you wish to make your name working with nobility? Are there not plenty of noblemen in your country?"

"I came because I met Lady Georgiana and I liked her," Pierre said, having understood the gist of Sir Mordred's question. "And it is not my ambition to work with the nobility. In fact I am a communist at heart. I do not approve of nobility."

Sir Mordred laughed and clapped him on the shoulder. "Splendid. Splendid. That's the ticket. You'll be perfect, I'm sure."

"Ticket?" Pierre shot me a worried look. "What ticket must I have?"

"Another silly English expression," I said. "It means that it is just right."

"*Oui*, English is a very silly language," Pierre commented.

As we talked, we had been walking around to the back of the house, across a formal garden of topiary hedges and into an area of kitchen garden. I saw Pierre's eyes light up at the array of fresh produce.

"Oh *oui*," he said. "You have the excellent berries. And the asparagus and peas. And the fine peaches too."

"You must come and help yourself nearer the date. Choose only the best."

"And you have the artichokes!" Pierre looked ecstatic now. "I will add the artichoke with the aioli as a cold appetizer. *Magnifique*."

I had to admit that the garden was magnificent and told Sir Mordred. He smiled. "The gardens are my passion, you know. They were really the reason I bought this house. I always dreamed of owning a fine, lush garden like this one. I was intrigued by the poison garden, I do admit, but the rest of the grounds were so magnificent that I had to buy the place. It's quite a task to keep it all up to snuff, but I do employ the best gardeners. And I like to help out myself too. I have thirty varieties of roses in the front beds. And on that far side I have the exotic garden with plants from all over the world."

"And the poison garden—where is that?" I asked

"Ah, the poison garden." He gave a wicked grin. "It's behind this wall. I'll give you a brief look if you like, but you'll get the full tour when you come for the open house."

He opened a wooden gate in the wall.

"You don't keep it locked, then?"

"My dear girl, it's in a private estate with just me and my servants. Why should I need to keep it locked? I assure you my servants would never want to poison me. I pay them too well." And he laughed as the gate swung open. We stepped inside into a space of neat beds. I don't know what I had expected—strange exotic plants, but these looked remarkably ordinary. I even recognized some of them. "Oh, those are foxgloves," I said. "And lily of the valley?"

"Naturally. Both can be quite deadly. Even the most innocuous plants can kill. Remember even potatoes have poisonous parts. And rhubarb. And apricot pits are full of cyanide."

"Golly," I said. "It's lucky we're still alive."

"There are some more exotic ones, of course." He led me along a narrow path. "Castor beans. Quite a pretty plant, isn't it? All parts of it are toxic, but the seeds are the worst."

"But don't we take castor oil as a laxative? I'm sure my nanny used to give it to me."

"That's because the toxin works well in small doses. The same for many poisons. There is arsenic in some medicines, I understand. I've started to study up on the subject."

Again he must have noticed my worried expression.

"When one writes books like mine one has to get the facts right." Then he laughed and patted my arm. "I think that's enough for now. We don't want Pierre to be helping himself to the wrong sort of thing, do we?" He glanced back at Pierre, who hadn't understood this. "You will be getting the full tour on the day of the open house. And I can also show you the old books on herbal lore that I have acquired. I'm making it quite a hobby."

He ushered us out again, closing the gate behind us. We came around to the front of the house and I saw Phipps standing beside the car.

Sir Mordred took my hand. "I bid you farewell for now, then. I am much looking forward to the big event." He paused, chuckling. "But I suppose you have another event that you are looking forward to, even more than this."

"I do. Thank you for the tour. It's been most interesting."

"I have enjoyed spending time with you. A most charming young woman." He lifted my hand to his lips and planted a kiss on it. I was sharply reminded of my former suitor, Prince Siegfried, whom Belinda and I had nicknamed Fishface.

Chapter 11

JULY 20

LEAVING BLACKHEART MANOR

I'm not sure that I want to attend Sir Mordred's banquet. I came
  away from Blackheart Manor feeling rather uneasy. Maybe it
  was the casual way he discussed all those poisons. Maybe it was
  the cold, damp feeling and musty smell of the place. Or the suit
  of armor with an axe that moved. Maybe it was Sir Mordred
  himself. I can't forget the way he looked when he mentioned
  buying things from a convent—a look of triumph. Perhaps
  he really is as evil as the characters he writes about. Golly.
  I hope not.

Pierre sat beside Phipps in silence as we drove home.

"Are you looking forward to cooking this meal, Pierre?" I asked,
leaning forward from the back seat. "It appears there will be celebrities present. You'll make your name."

"That is true," he replied. "But this house, I do not like. It has a bad feel to it, *n'est-ce pas?*"

"I agree. I did not feel comfortable there."

He sighed. "I too do not feel comfortable. In fact I feel guilty that I can make a good living cooking for rich people who live this sort of life. As a communist, this all seems so wrong to me. That one person should live in such a great estate, when poor people are crammed together six to a room in the slums. How can that be right?"

"It's not right," I said. "But I don't know how to make it better. I only live in a great house because my godfather lets me live there. Before that Darcy and I were looking at the most horrible little flats in London. I might come from a royal background, but neither of us have any money, you know."

"Do you think it is right that one person should have many people waiting on him? Those old men, they should be retired by now, *non?* And yet they still work on while he sits and does nothing."

"He does write books," I reminded him. "That is work in its way. And apparently he pays those old men well. The problem with being a servant is that you have nowhere to go when you leave. Most of them would not be given a pension."

"When the communists take over the government, all will be given a pension," he said.

"We've seen what communism did in Russia. It made things worse for everybody. I'm afraid most people are not good at sharing. Those in power always want more for themselves and take it at the expense of others, don't they?"

"I suppose that's true," he agreed. He turned to me. "I think you are a good person, even though you are a lady."

I had to laugh at this. "So you'll spare me from the guillotine when the revolution comes?" I paused, watching his face. "I have to tell you, Pierre, that there will be no revolution in England. We British are far too sensible. We like a quiet life of moderation. So no communists and no Fascists. Most of us like things the way they are."

I thought about this conversation as I lay in bed that night. It was wrong that I had this big, beautiful house to myself while others lived in slums. But we were born to a certain situation, weren't we? My cousin didn't want to be king but was stuck with it. Only my grandfather seemed content with his little house in Essex and his gnomes in the front garden. But should I be doing more? Maybe like Sir Mordred I should take more interest in my kitchen garden and grow enough produce to share. After all, we were relying on Sir Hubert's generosity and it would be nice to be doing our bit to keep Eynsleigh running. Not that I knew anything about gardening or farming, but I could learn. It would be a new challenge while I was staying home with a new baby. This thought reminded me of something I had tended to overlook. In a couple of weeks I'd have a baby to look after. I'd be a mother. Golly.

PREPARATIONS FOR THE open house were in full swing. Pierre went up to London to buy ingredients he couldn't find locally. He ordered fresh crab and plaice to be delivered directly from fishermen on the coast. Phipps drove him over to Blackheart for a consultation with Mr. Henman. All seemed to be going well until, the day before the big event, Mr. Henman was taken ill. Some kind of stomach upset, we were told. He felt too weak to be able to participate. It occurred to me that he had never approved of Pierre coming to cook in his kitchen and this was his way of making a statement. But it left Pierre in the lurch.

"How am I to prepare all this food by myself?" he asked. "There is only the kitchen maid and she knows nothing."

"You can always bring Queenie with you," I suggested.

A look of horror flashed across his face. "Oh no. Not her, I implore you."

"But she does cook quite well, you've said so yourself. You can give her the simple tasks of preparation."

"But she also has the mishaps," he said. "She knocks over the sauce I have prepared. She ruins my soufflés."

"I don't think you have much choice, do you? It's Queenie or the kitchen girl from Sir Mordred's house, who you said knew nothing."

"Very well. If I must." He gave an exaggerated sigh.

Queenie was thrilled by the prospect. "Me cooking at a posh banquet, missus? Blimey. Fancy that. Wait till I write to my mum and tell her. And my dad. He was the one who thought I'd never amount to anything. He used to say I must be twins because one couldn't be so daft." A knowing look came over her face. "So Chef couldn't do without me, eh? I knew he secretly fancied me, even though he won't admit it. I'll bring him round. You'll see. I'll be ever so helpful at the banquet." She leaned closer to me. "He says there will be celebrities coming. Film stars."

"So I've been told."

"Blimey, missus. Do you think I can get their autograph? My cousin Florrie won't half be jealous."

It seemed that everything Queenie did was designed to score points against her family. But at least she was excited and willing.

"So you'll have to promise me you'll be extra careful and have no accidents. No setting the kitchen on fire."

"I don't set no kitchens on fire! Well, only that one time and that was because the tea towel was hanging over the stove. Oh, and that other time when we was visiting that lady over Christmas . . ."

"Promise me you'll be extra careful this time, then," I repeated. "It's the reputation of this household that you are representing. Our good name."

"Bob's yer uncle, missus," she said and went away happily.

LUCKILY THE DAY of the open house dawned gloriously warm and sunny. It had been a splendid summer so far and I was tanned and healthy-looking. I got out of bed and stood looking across the park, feeling quite hopeful and excited. I was going to have a lovely time with fabulous food, even if the baby was now so big that there was no room for food in my stomach. I'd just have to nibble at each of the courses.

I was on my way down to the kitchen to see how preparations were going and find out what time Pierre wanted to be driven over to Sir Mordred's when I heard the most horrifying and blood-curdling scream. It was so loud that it echoed up the stairwell. I ran down the last of the stairs and pushed open the kitchen door. Mrs. Holbrook was hot on my heels. I think even Granddad had heard it from the morning room and was coming too.

"What on earth is happening?" I demanded.

Queenie was standing at the kitchen table. A sack had spilled over onto it and the table was now alive with crabs, all scurrying to find shelter, bumping into each other and falling off the table. Queenie was pointing at them in horror.

"Look what he wants me to do!" she exclaimed. "When he said prepare the crabs I never thought the ruddy things would still be alive. I opened the ruddy sack and the bloody thing nearly took my finger off and then they all came running out!" She waved the offended finger at Pierre.

"Stop them, you silly girl!" Pierre shouted from across the kitchen, where he was stirring a pot on the stove. "Do not let them get away. Do not let those dogs eat them."

The puppies, I noticed, were certainly not going to eat any crabs that had fallen to the floor. They had backed away with a look of anxiety on their faces. Jolly was barking.

"Pick them up. Immediately," Pierre commanded.

Queenie made a grab for one, then screamed again. "It won't stop still."

"Oh, come on, Queenie," Mrs. Holbrook said. "Just avoid the claws. See?" She bent and picked up a crab, holding it by the shell with claws waving violently before dropping it back into the sack. I was going to volunteer to help but realized that with my current shape I couldn't bend down. So I watched in horrified fascination as they retrieved the runaways.

"You dogs are supposed to be retrievers," I said to the cowering puppies. "You were no help at all."

They looked at me with big helpless eyes. "We are trained to retrieve dead ducks," those eyes were saying. "Not things like this with all those legs."

"Well, they're back in the sack, but I ain't cutting up no live crabs. Not for all the tea in China," Queenie said defiantly.

"*Mon dieu.* You do not cut them when they are alive, silly girl," Pierre replied. "First you drop them in the boiling water."

"I don't want to do that neither," she said. "Poor things. What did they ever do to you?"

Pierre looked as if he was about to explode. "How am I going to make my crab mousse if this stupid woman does not prepare the crabmeat for me?" he demanded in French, raising his hands in desperation.

"Someone has to kill all of the meat and fish that we eat, Queenie," Mrs. Holbrook said, coming over to comfort her. "These crabs would not live long out of the sea. A quick end is actually being kind to them."

"Oh, I see." Queenie nodded. "Being kind, eh? Right, then." And she placed a giant pot on the stove and started to fill it with water.

"Thank you, Mrs. Holbrook. You saved the day," I whispered as we crept back up the stairs.

Mrs. Holbrook smiled. "She's a simple soul, isn't she? Good-hearted but not the brightest."

"I just hope that's not an omen for the rest of the day. She doesn't have to pluck the ducks, does she?"

"Oh goodness, I hope not. They're being delivered to the other gentleman's house. Let's just pray."

APPARENTLY THE CRAB preparation went smoothly after that, as I watched Pierre and Queenie setting off with covered dishes, presumably containing the crab mousse. I went upstairs to get ready. It had been a challenge to know what to wear, not only because of my current bulbous state but also because we were to be given that tour of the grounds first, which would make walking in evening slippers impossible. I had confided in Zou Zou, who had arrived the day before.

"Should it be evening wear, even though it starts late afternoon with a tour of the grounds?"

"Darling, I'm going to wear my evening pajama, whatever happens," she said. "One has to look right, and it is a banquet, after all."

She came up to examine my wardrobe, shaking her head over the pathetically few items. "Oh dear," she said. "You do seem to be lacking in the evening department."

"It didn't make sense to have a dress made for such a short time."

"Pity it's not a daytime event or you could wear the dress Chanel designed for you. What a fashion coup that would be."

I gave a despairing chuckle. "Zou Zou, you saw that dress. I couldn't walk in it."

"We could always cut the bottom off."

"Then it would be too short."

She frowned. "I wonder if I whisked my little dressmaker down from London whether she could whip up a simple evening dress for you. Let me try. May I use your telephone?"

She was gone down the stairs before I could stop her. I heard her saying, "Yes. Sussex. We'll pick you up at the station. I don't know. I'll ask her." She looked up at me. "Do you have a sewing machine in the house?"

"I don't think so, but Maisie's mother has one in the village. She's done some alterations for me." I came down the rest of the staircase. "But Zou Zou—you can't ask . . ."

"We'll have a sewing machine for you, Natalia darling. All you have to do is bring yourself and some suitable evening fabric. Not too flashy. The lady is in the family way. Color?"

She looked back at me. "Oh, green, I think. Or blue. She's a blonde."

She put back the telephone. "She'll be arriving later today. I hope you can put her up for the night."

"Zou Zou—how do you manage these things?" I asked.

She smiled. "I pay well."

BY LUNCHTIME ON the next day I had a dress to wear—a simple sheath in a misty blue. Zou Zou eyed it critically as the little dressmaker lady made a final fitting. "Wear your most sparkling necklace, darling. It will take the eyes away from the bulge. And you do have a pretty shawl to wear when we go outside."

And so I was dressed respectably, if not glamorously. I put on a necklace of lapis and pearls and my shawl with the silver threads through it. Darcy nodded approvingly when he saw me.

"You look nice."

"So do you." He looked dashingly handsome in his evening suit.

Granddad also said I looked a treat, so I was feeling excited and hopeful as Sir Hubert drove us to Blackheart Manor.

Chapter 12

I'm sure Pierre will do a splendid job this evening (although there is
a sliver of worry at the back of my mind that Queenie will be in
the kitchen with him). But I'm not sure I'm looking forward to
eating dinner in that dark and rather creepy dining room.

Blackheart was humming with activity as we drove through the
gates. This time they were wide open, bunting was draped around
them, and a big sign proclaimed *Open House Today. 5 Shillings in
Aid of South African Orphans.* We encountered a steady stream of
people now leaving, some on foot, some in cars. It seemed the public was being turned out so that we favored few could have the place
to ourselves. There were already several cars parked outside the
front entrance—Bentleys and Daimlers among them. We were wel-
comed by Edwin, dressed formally but not looking happy about it.

"Jolly nice to see you again," he said. "Ready for the bean feast, then? Let me escort you to the terrace, where things are kicking off." I introduced Darcy, Zou Zou, and Sir Hubert.

"I've read about you, sir." Edwin seemed suddenly animated. "You were the one who climbed K2 recently, weren't you?"

"That's right." Sir Hubert smiled.

Edwin had gone rather pink. "I'd love to try something like that. See the world. Do something that's never been done before. Instead I'm stuck at Oxford studying useless subjects."

"I was at Cambridge myself," Sir Hubert said. "Studying equally useless stuff. But we all have to do it before we can get out into the real world. Wasn't your father once in South Africa? Maybe he could arrange for you to go out there, see what the rest of the world is like."

"I've asked him but he doesn't seem very keen. He says he knows nobody there now. He has bad memories of the Boer War. And then his near-death experience didn't make him feel any fonder of the place."

"Near death? During the war, you mean?"

"No, after the war. He stayed on in the country for a while and tried his hand at prospecting, since he actually had no real prospects at home at that stage." He grinned at his own play on words. "He was digging for diamonds and there was a cave-in. He was buried in soft sand. The friend he was digging with was killed," he said.

"I've had some narrow escapes myself," Sir Hubert said. "One bad fall in the Alps. In hospital for months. But that doesn't put me off wanting to try more."

We came around the house to see the terrace was now decorated with bunting and small tables had been set up, each adorned with roses from the garden. Several young men in smart white uniforms were serving champagne and canapés. Either Sir Mordred had hired extra help for the evening or he had a bigger staff than I had seen before.

Even as I was considering this, Edwin leaned closer to me. "Some of my pals from Baliol, you know. Eager to make a few pounds." He winked at one of them—a handsome youth with a decidedly upper-class air to him.

"Champagne, my lady?" he asked.

Edwin nudged me. "The Honorable Skewes-Clarke," he said. "Loads of titles. Poor as a church mouse. And you'll find a motley crew of guests too. Not what you would call top-drawer."

Zou Zou touched my arm. "Oh no. There's that ghastly woman."

"Which one?" I scanned the crowd.

"The one at your dinner party who complained about everything. I thought she was terribly anti–Sir Mordred. Didn't she say his books were un-Christian and demons would accompany him to the dinner table?"

I spotted Colonel and Mrs. Bancroft. She was already tucking into the canapés.

"I expect curiosity won out over principles," Darcy commented.

"That's right. Everyone has been dying to see inside this place," Sir Hubert agreed. "Ah, there's old Robson-Clough. I must go and say hello to him."

I followed where he was indicating and saw an older man, standing a little apart from the group, I now recognized from my dinner party. He was wearing an ill-fitting and well-worn dinner jacket and looked clearly ill at ease. Mr. Robson-Clough, the famous explorer.

We followed Sir Hubert toward Mr. Robson-Clough.

"I wouldn't have thought this was his sort of event," I muttered to Zou Zou.

"Ah, but he's curious, like everyone else, darling. And he is an absolute expert on the healing powers of plants. He's written a book on the subject, you know. He claims he was cured of all sorts of horrid diseases when he was in remote places."

Before we could reach Mr. Robson-Clough Sir Mordred caught sight of us and came over, arms extended in welcome.

"Lady Georgiana," he said, a little too loudly. "What a delight. And Mr. O'Mara. Sir Hubert. Your Highness. Welcome, welcome. Do come and meet everybody."

As he led us into the group of people I thought again that he might have invited us to score points on the social scale. A bit of a social climber, then. One who was not born to a title and perhaps was still not comfortable with it.

"See, Ethel, what did I tell you? There's royalty present," said a decidedly northern-accented voice right behind us. "Now aren't you glad you came?"

"Well, it's not Princess Marina or the Duchess of York, I can tell you that much," replied an equally northern female voice. I looked to see a middle-aged couple eyeing us. She was dressed in what was clearly an expensive gown, but it didn't hang properly on a stout figure. They bore down on us.

"Did I hear our host saying that one of you is royalty?" the man asked.

"This is Her Highness, Princess Zamanska," Sir Hubert said.

"Oh. Foreign royalty." From her expression, clearly this didn't count.

But then Sir Hubert went on. "And Lady Georgiana is the king's cousin."

Two interested gazes were turned to me. "Really? Fancy that. You know our new king, then. What a lovely man he is. He came to tour our factory once," the man said. He held out a meaty hand to me. "Percy Crump. I make motorcars. This is my wife, Ethel."

"He's really giving those foreign cars a run for their money," his wife said. "There is talk of a knighthood, isn't there, Percy?"

"We're not supposed to be mentioning it, old girl." He had turned pink. "But if I'm seen as being in service to my country, then I'm not going to object. I'm pleased to meet you, my lady. And you, Your Highness." He nodded to Zou Zou. "We were coming down to London anyway and I saw this advertised in the newspaper so I thought it would be a treat for the wife—a chance to show off the new frock she got in Paris."

"It looks very stylish," I said politely.

It was her turn to blush. "I told Percy it was an extravagance to spend that much on a dress, but he said that we've got the brass so why not. And now I've got the chance to wear it. But yours looks lovely, Your Highness." She gushed as she indicated Zou Zou's frock, stunning as always in midnight blue.

"Do call me Zou Zou. Everyone does," she said with that charm that melted everyone she met.

Now Mrs. Crump went really pink. "Zou Zou. Fancy that. Well, all right, Your Highness."

Sir Mordred clapped his hands, making us look up. "May I say welcome to my humble abode and to what promises to be an exceptional evening. For those who have not met me yet, I am Mordred Mortimer. This is my son, Edwin, and over here is my daughter, Sylvia, and her husband, Stanley."

I glanced to where he was pointing and saw a couple standing off to one side. They did not appear to be at ease with the situation.

She had a discontented, defiant look on her face, and his eyes were darting around nervously. But they managed a weak smile.

"And may I introduce my neighbors," Sir Mordred went on. "Lord and Lady Mountjoy, Sir Hubert Anstruther and the princess Zamanska, Lady Georgiana and Mr. O'Mara." He paused, then added, "You see I live in a frightfully well-connected area. "

"You've omitted us," Mrs. Bancroft said.

"Oh, my apologies," Sir Mordred replied. "So I have. Colonel and Mrs. Bancroft also live in the neighborhood. Although they were formerly in India. But not the same part as my parents."

"Big place, India," the colonel said.

"I'm expecting my publisher to join us and he'll be bringing some more distinguished people with him. Edwin, go round to the front of the house to wait for them. Go on. Off you go."

Edwin obeyed. We exchanged polite conversation as we sipped champagne. Then we looked up as more guests arrived.

"Oh good. This must be them now," Sir Mordred said. Then he frowned. "I have no idea who this is."

A big man with the ruddy outdoor complexion of a farmer was coming toward us, followed by a petite and shy-looking woman. Sir Mordred stepped forward. "Good evening," he said. "And you must be . . ." He held out a hand.

"Don't you recognize me, old chap?" the man said in a hearty voice. He gave a loud laugh. "Well, I suppose it has been almost forty years, and I don't exactly recognize you either." He clapped Sir Mordred on the shoulder. "It's Tubby, old chap. Tubby Halliday. I know it's been a while since we played on the rugby team together at Harrow. You were a damned useful fly half, I remember."

"Oh, good God. Tubby Halliday," Sir Mordred shook his head in disbelief, making that silver hair sway with a life of its own.

"So you do remember. Jolly good! I wrote to you after I saw the article on you in the *Daily Express*. I said to Mildred, 'It says the chap went to Harrow and he has to be about the same age as me. So it has to be Shrimpy Mortimer. He was in Druries House with me.'"

"Tubby Halliday," Sir Mordred repeated. "Druries House. Well, that takes me back. You're right. I would not have recognized you, apart from the girth."

Tubby patted his impressive paunch and chuckled. "She puts me on a diet from time to time. Doesn't do any good. The quack tells me I have to watch what I eat or the old heart won't like it, but I enjoy my food too much. You only live once, that's what I say." He guffawed again and glanced at his wife, who gave him a disapproving frown. He turned back to Sir Mordred. "I can't say you've got a middle-age spread. You always were a skinny little thing. You've grown taller since, and that hair, old chap. Nothing like that dark mop you used to have. Went gray early, did you? Don't tell me it's dyed?" He laughed again. "I suppose writers have to look the part, don't they?"

When Sir Mordred didn't reply he went on. "When you didn't answer my letter I said to Mildred, 'It must have got lost in the post. They are so dashed inefficient these days,' and we decided to come to this do of yours to see if I'd got it right and you really were the Mortimer who was in my dorm. And by God, you are!"

Sir Mordred nodded, giving what seemed like a forced smile.

"But don't tell me Mordred was your real name. Wasn't it something ordinary like Billy?"

"Robert," Sir Mordred confessed. "Although I was gifted with Shrimpy as soon as I went to school, of course. I found there had been a Mordred in the family, so it made the perfect nom de plume."

"Well, I never." Tubby shook his head. "We only knew you as Shrimpy, didn't we? I can't tell you how glad I am to have met you again. We don't live that far away. Across the border in Hampshire, you know. I farm several hundred acres. Never thought I'd wind up as a farmer, but I inherited the estate and, well, someone has to run it. And I'm the local magistrate, of course. Keeps me busy. Out of Mildred's hair, eh, old thing?" And he put an arm around her slight shoulders.

"Do have some champagne," Sir Mordred said, rather stiffly. "And the food is quite good. We've got a French chef for the occasion."

"Don't know if we're big fans of foreign food," Tubby said. "Good plain English fare is enough for us, eh, Mildred?"

I noticed she never said a word but nodded each time she was addressed. Champagne was handed to them.

"We completely lost touch with you after school," Tubby said as he drained his glass rapidly and looked around for a second one. "Wondered where you were. I heard you went abroad. Was that right? Back to India? You did come from India, didn't you?"

"I did. But actually I did what sons of the junior branch who are not going to inherit anything do. I went into the army right after school and was sent out to South Africa during the Boer War."

"That must have been a lark," Tubby said. "Having those Zulus charging at you with their spears while you mowed them down with your guns."

"They were damned brave," Sir Mordred said sharply. "Quite fearless, actually. Good fighters, and of course there were many more of them, which made it quite an even playing field."

"And what about the Afrikaners? You had to fight them too, did you? That can't have been too hard. A lot of bloody peasants waving their pitchforks at you. Not a trained fighter among them."

"I felt quite badly, if you want to know the truth," Sir Mordred said. "It was their country after all. They were there first."

"But we won, that's the main thing," Tubby said.

"War is never pleasant. It left me feeling quite disillusioned. I had no wish to return to England with my regiment after it was over. I'd had enough of army life."

"Don't tell me you deserted?"

"Oh no. All quite legit. I'd done my seven years by then."

"So where did you go?"

"I stayed on in South Africa for a while," Sir Mordred said. "I rather liked the wide-open spaces. And then I found I'd inherited this title and the estate that went with it, so I returned here."

"Lucky for you. I didn't realize you had a title in the family."

"Neither did I," Sir Mordred said. "It turns out he was a third cousin I'd never met. Quite a surprise when I got the letter from the solicitor, I can tell you."

"And when did you start writing books? Once you became lord of the manor? Mildred loves them, don't you, old thing? The scarier the better."

Mildred nodded again.

"I'd always dreamed of being a writer, toying with writing since I left school," Sir Mordred said. "Actually I'd written poetry before that."

"You sly dog." Tubby gave that big laugh again. "I don't remember you writing poetry at school."

"It's not the sort of thing one broadcasts to other boys, is it?"

"No, I suppose not."

"Were you always fascinated by macabre topics, Sir Mordred?" Zou Zou asked, bringing us into this conversation.

"Not really. I think it was the war, seeing witch doctors in action and the way the chaps there believe in the whole spirit realm. I started to look into it. And then the desert when we were prospecting—the sun, the wind, the sand, and the remoteness of it. It plays with the imagination, you know. I got the idea for my first book on the passage back to England and the rest is history, as they say."

"Made a packet of money at it, I see." Tubby nodded as he looked around the grounds. "Nice spread you've got here. But this wasn't the house you inherited?"

"Good God, no. That's in Northumberland. I have it rented out to a tenant these days. I prefer living closer to London and my publisher."

"Well, now we've hooked up again, we must get together with the other chaps from the rugby team," Tubby said. "You'll come to the next Old Harrovian dinner, won't you? Sitwell-Smythe and Tomlinson would be tickled pink to meet you again. And remember Buffer Benson? Good old Buffer. He's now an MP, of course. Sir Henry Benson. Pompous as hell. But he was asking about you only the last time we met. Happy days at school, eh?"

"Not particularly for me," Sir Mordred said. "I was far from home and my family. I felt a bit lost, to tell the truth."

"You never showed it. You were a good sport in those days. Rugger. Cricket. Midnight feasts."

"Father," Edwin called, making Tubby break off from his happy memories. "Sorry for interrupting, but I think your publisher has arrived."

A group of people had just come around the side of the building. At the front was a balding, serious-looking man with horn-rimmed spectacles and a worried look on his face, and behind him a most glamorous and good-looking couple. I had never been to the theater much, but I thought I recognized them from magazines. And behind them a more ordinary-looking older couple who had a healthy outdoor look to them.

"Mordred, old man. Good to see you," said the first of the group, obviously the publisher.

"Phillip. Good to see you too. I see you've brought a whole charabanc-full with you."

"As requested, old chap. May I present Mr. and Mrs. Laurence Olivier."

The gorgeous dark-haired man came forward. "How do you do?" he said in a voice to match his appearance. "My wife, Jill."

The equally gorgeous woman gave a charming smile and shook Sir Mordred's hand. "How lovely to meet you. We adore your books, don't we, Larry?"

"If I ever get time to read something that's not a script I have to learn," Laurence said. "But I have to admit I'm intrigued about the possibility of playing a vampire, if we film your book."

"You'd be perfect," Sir Mordred said. "Let's talk about it over dinner, but first I must greet these other new arrivals. Please have some champagne, and the canapés are quite delicious." He turned to the publisher as he took another couple by the arm and ushered them forward. "Not more film stars, Phil?"

"No, old boy. But I bring you a couple of celebrities. This is the world-renowned archeologist, Max Mallowan. And his wife is another of my clients. I don't know if you two have ever met. Her name is Agatha Christie. Agatha, come and say hello to a fellow scribbler."

And the simply dressed woman moved toward us. "How do you do?" she said in a deep, rich voice.

Chapter 13

JULY 25

AT BLACKHEART MANOR

All going swimmingly so far, although Sir Mordred seems a little
out of sorts. I rather suspect he didn't expect his publisher to
bring a fellow writer. Her name is Agatha Christie and it seems
that most of the company have read her books. Her husband is
jolly interesting too. He has conducted digs all over
Mesopotamia.

Sir Mordred gave a formal little bow, then shook Mrs. Mallowan's
hand. "I've heard of you, of course. Delighted to meet you. What
is it you write again?"

"She writes crime novels, just like you, old boy," the publisher said.

"Only my murders are not quite as dark and violent," Agatha
Christie replied calmly. "Not a demonic possession in sight. Nor a
tortured serial killer. Or a haunted mansion."

"But you look like far too nice a lady to be writing any sort of crime," Sir Mordred said, attempting to be gallant.

She gave a little smile. "I've always found that the most innocent-looking people are capable of the cleverest crimes, haven't you? That's why our novels are so important. In real life they probably get away with murder most of the time. We have a chance for justice."

"That's exactly what I've been saying," Sir Mordred said, grabbing a passing tray and handing her a glass of champagne. "In real life you can kill with the most ordinary of substances and nobody ever suspects."

"That's why we have to have our clever sleuths," Agatha said. "The quiet ones. The observers."

"I like my detectives to be rather flamboyant," Sir Mordred said. "Especially the one who is a vampire."

"Quite." Agatha nodded pleasantly, but I thought she had put him in his place rather well. He obviously hadn't enjoyed the encounter either. As they moved into the crowd Sir Mordred sidled up to his publisher. "Whatever did you want to bring her for?" he hissed. "Surely one crime writer is enough for this gathering. Are you trying to steal my thunder?"

"Not at all, old chap," the publisher replied. "They happened to be visiting the office and mentioned that they were staying with friends in the next village over from this place. I said I was coming to see you and she expressed interest in your poison garden. So I could hardly say no."

"I would have." Sir Mordred moved away from him. He looked around. "We all seem to be assembled, I see. Why don't we take our tour of the grounds. Edwin, Sylvia? Where are my assistant tour guides?"

His gaze fell upon his daughter, who looked as if she was in the process of creeping back to the house. "Where do you think you're sneaking off to? Come on. Buck up."

"You don't need us, Daddy. Surely you only want one center of attention today?"

Sir Mordred eyed her coldly. "You're supposed to be the hostess here. Look lively and take a group of folk around the kitchen garden." He walked over to her and took her arm. "You're my daughter. I expect you to behave like it," he said in a low voice.

She shrugged him off.

"You hardly notice my existence for the rest of the year," Sylvia said. "You don't ever treat me like a daughter, and now suddenly you want me to pretend I live at this monstrous place and we're one big happy family."

Sir Mordred frowned. "There's gratitude for you. The best schooling. A coming-out party and now this." There was an icy silence. Then he said, "Suit yourself, then. But don't come running to me next time that pathetic husband of yours has another business failure."

"You wouldn't help out last time," she said. "Why should I expect anything different?"

And she broke away from the group, stalking off toward the house.

"Young girls. So temperamental." Sir Mordred turned to give the group an embarrassed smile. "I blame that husband of hers. Not the right type of person. Way too common. I warned her. She'll regret it." He clapped his hands. "Right. Edwin. Lead on. You take some of the group to the kitchen garden first so there won't be too many of us in one spot at a time."

Edwin looked very uncomfortable after the unpleasant scene. I nodded to Darcy. "Come on, Edwin," I said. "You can be our tour guide."

Darcy followed, as did Mr. and Mrs. Mallowan, Zou Zou, Sir Hubert, and his friend the explorer. Those two were in deep conversation and lagged behind all the time, making us wait for them to catch up.

"Do buck up, Hubie darling," Zou Zou said.

So he was now "Hubie darling," was he? She liked to move fast.

I found myself at the front with Edwin.

"She won't hear the last of this," Edwin said as Sir Mordred's group moved off in a different direction. "My father does not take kindly to people who oppose him. Unfortunately he can't cut off her allowance. That was left to her by our mother. She was the rich one."

"You also get an allowance from her, do you?" Darcy asked.

"We were both left a small allowance, but I don't inherit the bulk of the fortune from her until I'm twenty-five. Neither does Sylvia. A stupid condition of her will, influenced, I suspect, by my father. I can't wait. A penniless position is not one I enjoy."

"Your mother was American, I believe," Darcy said.

"She was. The proverbial American heiress come to find herself a title in exchange for a fortune. I don't think there was ever much love involved. In fact I've always wondered . . ." He broke off, staring at his father's back. His father was now opening the gate to the poison garden.

"She died rather suddenly," Edwin said. "It was quite a shock." He glanced back at the group following him. "Right, if you'd all come this way. I'll show you what a currant bush looks like. And an artichoke if you're very good."

He strode on ahead, leaving me wondering about what he had

said. Was he hinting that he suspected his father had something to do with his mother's death? I glanced at Darcy but he seemed not to have noticed, chatting now with the archeologist, Mr. Mallowan.

"I've always wanted to visit Mesopotamia," I heard him say.

"Have you seen much of the world yet?" the older man asked.

"Quite a bit, but not the Middle East. Except we did land in Egypt and the Sudan on our way to Kenya. But that's hardly seeing the country."

"Now you're one up on me," Mr. Mallowan said. "Kenya's a place I'd like to visit."

"Not too many archeological finds to be had there, I'd imagine," Darcy said.

I fell into step with Agatha Christie. "You've traveled with your husband?"

She nodded. "Oh yes. We've had some wonderful trips together. I never feel happier than when we're in the desert, away from everywhere and finding exciting bits of pottery." She glanced down at my feet, and then her own. "I don't know if these shoes are going to hold up to tramping through miles of grounds," she said. "It was hard to know what to wear, wasn't it? Frankly we only came to please Phillip. He felt a bit awkward escorting two famous film stars and we are staying so close by. Do you know the Finlays?"

"I think we've met them," I said.

"They are old friends of Max's. They are dying for us to report back to them," she said. "They've always been curious about Sir Mordred. Silly name, isn't it?" She gave me a small secret grin. "You live nearby too?"

"Yes, but about five miles in the other direction."

"A lovely part of the country, isn't it? Although not as nice as Devon. That's where my heart is, where I grew up."

"I grew up in a bleak part of Scotland and I have no regrets about leaving," I said, laughing.

She moved closer to me. "So have you seen this famous poison garden?"

"Only briefly. Sir Mordred let us peek inside the gate but didn't take us around."

"Fascinating, though." She nodded with satisfaction. "I am rather interested in poisons."

"Well, I suppose you would be if you have to kill off people in your stories."

This made her laugh. "Actually the fascination started before that. I worked as a dispenser at a hospital during the war. I learned a lot about poisons. So many substances that can be helpful or deadly depending how great a dose you give. One had to be so careful. But the knowledge has come in jolly useful in my books, I have to confess."

"Do you enjoy killing people—in your books, I mean?"

She smiled. "I like bumping off the unpleasant ones. But I feel great regret when the nice ones have to die. I suppose I'm rather like my detective, Miss Marple. She's an old lady who lives in a village and solves crimes, if you haven't read any of those stories. She really cares about people, not like some of these callous detectives. That awful Sherlock Holmes."

We picked our way past rows of strawberries, raspberry canes, red and black currants, runner beans, tomatoes, and all manner of vegetables. There were tall bushes, laden with berries, against the walls.

"I must say it all looks rather splendid," Agatha said to me. "He obviously likes to eat well, in spite of his skinny appearance. I understand tonight's meal is to be quite spectacular."

"I think so. I've lent my chef for the evening and he's awfully good. French, you know."

"They always are, my dear." She nodded.

"Right," Edwin interrupted our chat. "You've seen the healthy stuff. Now on to the stuff that will kill you." And he laughed.

We spent a fascinating half hour in the poison garden. Edwin appeared very knowledgeable, identifying each plant, how it was poisonous, and what it did to you. None of them sounded pleasant. But as Sir Mordred had said, I was amazed at how many were plants to be found in any garden.

"We have Virginia creeper climbing up our wall," I commented to Edwin.

"Just don't let your pets or children nibble on the berries," Edwin said.

Oh dear. I hadn't thought about that aspect of parenting—I'd have to worry about keeping my children safe. Golly. I'd never had to be responsible for anyone before. Suddenly a trained nanny sounded like a good idea.

Chapter 14

JULY 25

AT BLACKHEART MANOR

It has all gone so smoothly and wonderfully. I can't believe it. Even
Queenie had no disasters and the dinner was exquisite. Now to
stop Sir Mordred from stealing my chef!

I was so relieved when we finished the tour of the poison garden,
then the healing garden, and were led back toward the house. I suspect those of us with high heels and pointy toes were a little foot-
weary. I certainly was, but I was feeling the heat at this time and it
was still jolly warm at seven o'clock. Quite un-British of it! I had
hoped to escape to a ladies' room at last, but Sir Mordred insisted
on giving us a tour of the house first. We went from one gloomy
room to the next—a library that was cold, damp, and dreary
enough to make anyone decide never to read a book again, a music
room complete with an enormous harp that Sir Mordred confessed

nobody could play, but he'd purchased it with the house. The morning room was halfway pleasant, looking out over the gardens we had just toured and getting the last of the evening sunshine. We were then taken upstairs and shown several bedrooms containing four-poster beds and heavy velvet curtains.

"We have ten of them," Sir Mordred said. "So if anyone does not feel like driving home tonight, you're more than welcome to stay. I can't vouch for breakfast, however, since my elderly chef does not rise early." At this everyone assured him they would be driving home. I don't think I'd have wanted to spend the night there even if I hadn't lived nearby. The bedrooms certainly had that cold feel to them that goes along with a ghost or two.

It seemed that most people were staying with friends in neighboring villages and only Laurence Olivier and his wife were being driven to the train station by Phillip Grossman, the publisher. Last on the tour we were shown a small room at the back of the house that Sir Mordred had turned into a laboratory.

"I've been reading up on my various plants," he said, "and trying out some experiments. I thought it would be good if I found the cure of some disease or other, you know. No luck so far. But it occupies my time." He chuckled.

I was quite relieved when we were finally shown a lavatory and I could freshen up and have a pee. It was clear that this house lacked a woman's touch. Many of the furnishings were old and heavy and needed a good dusting. The lavatory was grim and ancient, with a chain that had to be pulled several times. I wondered how long ago his wife had died. Had she ever lived in this house?

I returned to the group, who were now in the morning room, in spite of it being evening.

"We had to come in here," Sir Mordred was saying. "Best view in the house at this time of day. Quite spectacular, isn't it?"

We agreed that it was. The same young men who were supposedly Edwin's friends had come inside and were now serving us sherry and cheese straws. Edwin came over to me to hand me a glass.

"I think I'll skip it this time," I said. "The champagne and the heat are making me feel a little woozy."

"Why don't you sit down?" he suggested.

"Nobody else is. It would be a little rude."

"Nobody else is pregnant," he said. "Should I get you a glass of water?"

I thanked him and he returned with it.

"Did you enjoy your tour of the most ghastly house in the world?" he asked. "Mind you, our house in Northumberland wasn't much better. And it was colder up there. But Mummy worked wonders with it. Lots of fresh soft furnishings and flowers. She loved flowers."

"Your mother never lived in this house?"

"Yes, she did, for a few months when we first moved in. The house was Father's idea, of course. He bought it without telling her. I think she was happy to move closer to civilization, but she never really had a chance to put her own touch on this place. She died quite suddenly, you know. One moment she was bright and chirpy and then the next they told me she was dead. It was quite a shock to an eight-year-old, I can tell you."

"My husband also lost his mother young," I said. "She died in the great influenza outbreak. So did his two young brothers. Such a tragedy."

"At least she had the excuse of a pandemic," he said. "I've always wondered exactly what killed her. Nobody explains to an eight-year-old."

What a strange thing to say.

His father summoned him to go and check that all was as it should be in the dining room. I sat there, apart from the others, watching the interactions: Mr. and Mrs. Crump so impressed and willing to please, Mrs. Bancroft still complaining . . . "And do you know, they had the nerve to cut across our field. . . . No, I don't read that sort of book. I don't read much, actually. Too busy with my various volunteer activities: the Women's Institute, the Girl Guides, the parish council. They all rely on me, bless them. Ah yes, I devote my life to others."

Mr. and Mrs. Mallowan were the recipients of this monologue. Mr. Mallowan was trying hard not to look bored, but Agatha Christie was looking around, examining the company with a keen gaze. Laurence Olivier and his wife were being sophisticated and witty to our neighbors Lord and Lady Mountjoy. Sir Hubert was off to one side with his explorer chum and an elderly woman I hadn't noticed before. She was dressed in a black silk high-necked dress adorned with a long string of jet beads, and her hair was held up by two tortoiseshell combs. Someone from a bygone era, I thought, and wondered what she was doing here. An elderly female relative?

By now I was feeling quite tired. I would willingly have gone home and not had to face polite conversation at the banquet. But of course I had to be a good sport. At least I was brought up to do my duty. Robert Bruce Rannoch would have been proud of me!

"They should be ready for us by now," Sir Mordred said irritably. "I did say eight o'clock and I hear it chiming." He stalked off, leaving us, only to return a little later looking pleased.

"All is well," he said. "We'll let my butler do the honors or he'll feel neglected."

Right on cue the old butler came in, carrying a gong that looked too large and heavy for him. He beat upon it. Bonnnngggg. The sound reverberated. He waited until it had died down before announcing, "Dinner is served, sir."

We were then directed to line up, in formal fashion, rather like children coming in from playtime at school. This took a bit of maneuvering, as some members of the party had never been subjected to this silly custom before. Sir Mordred took my arm and led Darcy and me to the front of the procession, much to my embarrassment.

"You do outrank us, my dear," Sir Mordred said. "You represent your family."

So of course I couldn't refuse, and we were led down the dark hallway, through the gallery, and into the banquet room. Sir Mordred had been right, in a way. It did look more cheerful with the candlelight playing on crystal and silver, but nothing could stop it from being a gloomy room. The sun had now set and a red glow came in through those narrow windows, distorted by the glass in the tiny panes.

"Your names are in your places," Sir Mordred said. "Please do sit when you find your place."

It was like a game of musical chairs until we were all seated. I was near the top of the table, which was rather flattering. Sir Mordred sat at the top with the actress Jill Esmond beside him. I had her husband, the dashing Laurence Olivier, on one side of me and the archeologist Max Mallowan on the other. Next to him was the old lady whom I now saw was called Miss Ormorod. Darcy was somewhere across from me, as were Zou Zou and Sir Hubert. Agatha and Edwin were a little farther down. Colonel and Mrs. Bancroft and the Crumps were out of sight at the far end. I also noticed Sylvia and her husband, plus a couple of Edwin's friends who had been serving champagne, now were seating themselves at the bottom of the table, presumably to make up numbers. Sir Mordred had hoped for thirty, but I think he had fallen short.

I was about to sit down when I saw the curtain pulled back a few inches on the alcove where the food was to be delivered. To my horror it was Queenie standing there. I scurried around the table and grabbed her. "What are you doing here?" I hissed.

She shrugged. "He told me to come up here, didn't he?"

"He?" (She'd naturally pronounced it "ee.")

"The old bloke. Bad-tempered old sod. Our chef wanted the old bloke to come up here and make sure everything was plated properly, but he said he still wasn't feeling well, that he wasn't anyone's skivvy and he wasn't about to climb stairs. So Pierre said I'd better do it instead and not to screw up or there would be hell to pay."

Oh golly. If there was one thing that could go wrong with a banquet, it was Queenie being let loose near the plates. I pictured gravy being slopped over edges, vegetables dropped on the floor . . . "Queenie," I said in my most severe voice. "I am relying on you not to let the side down. The honor of our house is at stake. Make sure you are a credit to Monsieur Pierre, to Mr. O'Mara, and to me."

She had rarely heard me talk with such severity and stared open-mouthed. Then she shrugged again and said, "Bob's yer uncle, missus. Don't you worry about nothing. You go and have a good old slap-up dinner."

I tried to look composed and at peace as I resumed my seat. Darcy gave me an inquiring look as to why I had vanished behind the curtain, but I didn't want two of us to be eating in a state of perpetual terror. Sir Mordred gave a short speech of welcome. He introduced the guests of honor again, which meant those of us at the top of the table, and said how pleased he was to be celebrating with us. His new book was about to be released and this was a splendid kickoff party. He also thanked Miss Ormorod for coming and hoped that the money would be put to good use for the plight of South African orphans. Miss Ormorod nodded but didn't manage a smile. Sir Mordred raised his glass and suggested a toast. I noticed that our first glass of wine had already been poured in anticipation of our arrival.

"Before we drink the toast I should tell you that I have procured genuine mead to go with our medieval banquet," Sir Mordred said. "It's made by the nuns at a convent in Sussex. Not everybody's cup of tea, I'm sure, but don't worry, as we've some good wines to follow."

We toasted and drank. I only took a sip. It was rather too sweet and I was already feeling a little squeamish. Also I was more than aware that I should go carefully through this long meal.

The crab mousse was served smoothly and efficiently by two footmen who must have been professionals and not just Edwin's friends from Oxford. It was beyond delicious, light, fluffy, and topped with caviar, surrounded by fresh lettuce leaves. I said a prayer of thanks that Queenie had been able to corral the escaping crabs from the table. The cream of asparagus soup came next, followed by a marinated artichoke sitting in a salad of various unidentifiable greens.

"I must say, this is awfully good." These were the first words Laurence Olivier had addressed in my direction. Sir Mordred had kept him engaged in conversation and there was lots of talk of vampires, which didn't seem quite right at a dinner table.

"You should see the dungeons here, old chap," Sir Mordred said. "I didn't show the group today as the footing is not too safe, but they are amazing. One can only wonder what kind of things they did down there. Oh, the tortures they got up to in those days. I had hoped to find the remnants of a rack or an iron maiden."

I turned away, not wishing my dinner to be spiced with methods of torture. Max Mallowan had been chatting with Miss Ormorod. "I've just been telling this lady about our next expedition to the Middle East," he said.

"Quite fascinating," the old lady said. "I myself have never traveled, but my charity does wonderful work abroad, so in a way I feel as if I've been to all these places."

"It must be very nice for you to have Sir Mordred organizing this event for your charity," I said.

She had a strange look on her face. "Oh yes. Very nice," she said primly, and I got the feeling it wasn't very nice at all.

The glasses of mead were whisked away and replaced with wineglasses, filled with a crisp white. Then came the quenelles of sole, stuffed with tiny shrimp and served with a rich sauce. After this a lemon sorbet to clear the palate. A red wine was now poured and the duck was brought in. I had kept glancing at that curtain throughout the meal, waiting for the inevitable swear word or cry of alarm, but none came. My duck sat prettily on its plate with the right amount of orange sauce, tiny new potatoes, and fresh peas.

"This is perfectly divine," Zou Zou said from across the table, echoing my own sentiments. Unfortunately it was also perfectly rich. We had now had canapés, champagne, and a lot of rather rich food. I was beginning to feel that I didn't want to face another mouthful. The duck was cleared away, a dessert wine was served, and then the pudding course was brought out. The server went to place a fruit tart in front of me. It looked very pretty, with a rich pastry, topped with a custardy layer, then mixed berries, and then either a light meringue or a heavy cream. I couldn't tell which. In either case my stomach took one look and said, "No, thank you."

"Oh, I won't have any, if you don't mind," I said. "I have to be so careful what I eat right now."

"Very good, miss." The footman whisked mine away and placed it in front of Max Mallowan instead.

"This looks bloody good," Tubby Halliday said from the other side of Miss Ormorod. "If there's a second one going, you can leave it here, old chap." He leaned forward to address Sir Mordred. "Damned fine meal, Mortimer. Better than you'd get at the Savoy. My compliments to your chef."

"Thank you, Tubby," Sir Mordred said.

"That's where we meet, we old Harrovian chums from the rugby team," Tubby said, his voice echoing down the table. He cleared his wineglass and motioned for a refill. "God, what a rugby team we had our year, didn't we? Thrashed Eton. And Rugby School! And you were doing splendidly until you broke that finger."

"Yes, most unfortunate," Sir Mordred said.

"Nasty break too, if I remember correctly," Tubby went on. "Doesn't it hinder you with your writing at all? Do you use the typewriter?"

"It's all water under the bridge, old chap," Sir Mordred said smoothly. "And I write in longhand anyway. I scribble it down and I have a wonderful little woman who makes sense of it and types it up."

"Thank God for that," the publisher said. "His handwriting is quite illegible."

Tubby Halliday frowned, went to say something more, then

turned his attention to his pudding instead. The cheese board and fruit bowl were offered around. I managed a thin slice of Stilton and an apricot.

"I suppose we should do the correct thing and send the ladies away while we indulge in our port and cigars," Sir Mordred said jovially. "Sylvia, my dear, take the ladies through to the gallery. The coffee should be ready there."

"And what if we want port and cigars?" she asked. I couldn't tell if she was joking.

"Don't be ridiculous. Go on. Off with you."

Lady Mountjoy, always a stickler for good manners, rose from her seat. "Come on, girls. Let's leave them to their nasty habits."

We followed suit. I would have liked to check on Queenie and tell her that she had done well, but one does not chat with servants at a formal dinner party. But I can't tell you how relieved I was that there had been no major mishaps.

I followed the other ladies first to the downstairs cloakroom, where we reapplied our lipstick and powder, and then to the gallery, where one of the young men was waiting to serve coffee. Although the day had been a warm one, this room felt chilly, with a draft coming in, and I wished I'd brought a heavier shawl. I took a place on the sofa next to Agatha and the elderly lady and accepted a coffee.

"I don't think I will, thank you," Miss Ormorod said. "I feel everything has been a little too rich for me. When one lives so simply the rest of the time, such a meal is overwhelming to the stomach."

"Yes, it was a little too much for me too," I said.

"I should never have eaten that tart, but it was delicious," she said. "But a cup of coffee and I won't sleep a wink tonight. I'm staying with my friend Beryl Parsons in the next village, you know. We've been friends since school. I should have liked to invite her to this dinner, but of course at twenty guineas it was way beyond my budget."

"It was a lovely meal, you must admit," Zou Zou said. "And all those people who were leaving when we arrived. He must have raised a tidy sum today."

"He must indeed," Miss Ormorod said. "I rather feel we shall be lucky if . . ." Then she stopped short. "We shall be lucky," she said.

"I've never known my father to do anything for charity before," Sylvia said, overhearing this conversation. "Or to benefit anyone else, for that matter. It was hard enough to get my school fees out of him. I had to agree to invite him to address us on speech day. But he does get nostalgic from time to time about South Africa. I think he truly enjoyed his time out there. He wasn't cut out to be lord of the manor."

"So tell me," Mrs. Bancroft said. "Are there a great number of orphans in South Africa?"

"No more than any other relatively poor country," Sylvia said.

"Poor?" Lady Mountjoy exclaimed. "With all those natural resources? Gold? Diamonds? I thought it was supposed to be prosperous."

"For the white people," Miss Ormorod said quietly.

Lady Mountjoy pursed her lips. That put a damper on the conversation and we were glad when the men joined us. I whispered to Darcy that I would like to go home as soon as seemed decent. Zou Zou picked up on my flagging, in the way that women do.

"My poor dear," she said. "You look as if you're ready to drop. We should not have put you through such an ordeal so near to your time. Hubert, darling, we must take Georgiana home." She went over to our host. "Do excuse us if we beat a retreat, will you? Lady Georgiana looks quite worn-out."

Sir Mordred was most solicitous. He kissed my hand and hoped it hadn't all been too much for me. He escorted us personally to our motorcar. I noticed that Sir Hubert's pal, the explorer, was coming with us.

"I told him he couldn't possibly take a train to London at this ungodly hour," Sir Hubert said. "We can find him a room for the night, can't we?"

"Oh, of course," I said.

So we piled into the car, a little squashed in the back seat, and off we went. I gave a small sigh of relief as we drove out through the gates. The whole evening had gone smoothly. Pierre had produced a stunning meal; Queenie had not let me down. All in all quite satisfying.

$\mathcal{C}hapter$ 15

JULY 26
EYNSLEIGH

It seems I was a trifle premature in my assessment of last night.

I awoke to rain battering on the window and the growl of thunder. So yesterday's clammy heat had been a precursor to a storm. I turned over to Darcy, but he was already up and gone, so it must have been quite late. I realized I had a bit of headache—too much rich food and alcohol. I wondered where my morning tea was. Perhaps Darcy had told Maisie not to wake me. I reached out of bed and tugged on the bell pull. In remarkably short time Maisie appeared with the tray.

"I'm sorry, my lady, but Mr. O'Mara said not to wake you," she said. "He suggested you might want your breakfast in bed, only it will have to be something simple because Queenie is feeling poorly this morning."

"Oh no. What's wrong?"

"I don't know, my lady. I only know she didn't get up to start the breakfast and Mrs. Holbrook had to go looking for her and came down and said we'd just have to make do." She gave me a knowing look.

I could just picture Queenie in that anteroom, tucking in to any good bits that came back from the table. I smiled. "That's all right. We'll let her sleep it off. Just a boiled egg would be very nice, thank you."

The egg arrived. I ate, dressed, and went downstairs to find Zou Zou, Sir Hubert, the explorer, and Granddad all in the morning room.

"I had hoped to show you around the estate," Sir Hubert was saying. "We've a fine herd of a rare Asian deer of which we're very proud. But this beastly weather."

"How lucky it didn't break yesterday," Zou Zou said. "Mordred's spectacle would have been a washout."

"But then we wouldn't have had to tramp for miles through the grounds," I said, joining her on a sofa.

"So you had a good time, did you, my love?" Granddad asked.

"I don't know how to answer that," I said. "It was all jolly interesting—his various gardens, and his son was extremely knowledgeable about the plants."

"He was, wasn't he," Mr. Robson-Clough said. "I asked him some questions and he certainly knew his stuff. A bright young man, I think."

"And yet he plays the duffer to his father. I wonder why," I said. "Claims he was useless at school."

"Probably to annoy the old man," Sir Hubert said. "I think there was little love lost between those two."

"Or the daughter," Zou Zou said. "But I have to agree the husband was a very poor choice, wasn't he? Hardly said a word all evening. No social graces."

"You ask me if I enjoyed it, Granddad," I said. "The food was wonderful. Pierre outdid himself. But I found I was holding my breath all evening, waiting for something to go wrong. Queenie was helping to serve, you know."

"It's strange because I felt a little ill at ease, all the time," Sir Hubert said, his eyes holding mine. "Not a very pleasant house, was it? Certainly not warm and welcoming."

"Absolutely ghastly," Zou Zou exclaimed. "The downstairs loo, darlings. I half expected to see a bat hanging from the ceiling. It was so atrocious that I almost decided to hold it until we got home—or visit the bushes outside. Perhaps it would have enhanced the poison garden." And she gave that delightful laugh.

"I have learned over the years not to disregard feelings of unease," Mr. Robson-Clough said in his slow, careful tone. "Our subconscious picks up signs of danger before we are aware of it. I remember once in the Congo not getting into a dugout canoe. There was something that warned me it might be unstable. So my fellow travelers went off without me." He looked up, frowning. He had remarkably bright eyes for a man of his age. "Turns out there was nothing wrong with the canoe, but they were attacked by locals from the banks and the whole lot of them were slaughtered."

Well, that wasn't the most cheerful tale with which to begin the morning!

"Does anyone know where Darcy is?" I asked.

"I think he went to the study to make some telephone calls," Granddad said. "He was up quite early and wasn't too pleased to find the coffee wasn't ready, I can tell you. A few choice words muttered under his breath."

"Oh dear," I said. "Perhaps I should go and see Queenie. I hope she's not just malingering."

I went up to the servants' floor, breathing heavily as I climbed the second set of stairs. Golly, the nursery would be up here. I hoped I was more agile once this big bump had disappeared.

Queenie was lying on her bed, looking horribly green. There was a bucket beside her bed. I tried not to look at it. "I'm so sorry, missus," she said, "but I feel like a dog's dinner warmed over. I just couldn't get up and come down to make breakfast. The very thought of food makes me want to puke."

"Oh dear. I'm sorry. No, you stay put and we'll manage. Pierre can make us a simple luncheon. Was it something you ate, do you think?"

"Must have been," she said. "I was right as rain as we drove home last night. Pierre was in a good mood because the dinner went well, and we were singing with Phipps in the motorcar. Then I woke up in the middle of the night with god-awful cramps in my stomach and I had to run to the lav and it's been bad ever since."

"Perhaps you overdid it," I suggested tactfully. "Did you help yourself to the leftover food? Food you are not used to and is very rich? I myself felt rather queasy by the end of that meal."

"I suppose it must have been," Queenie said. "I did try a bit of that duck and it wasn't half good. And them tarts. There was a couple left over and I thought it would be a shame to send them back down to the kitchen because I knew there were more down there. Pierre made a few extra in case the pastry got damaged on any of them."

"Those tarts did look awfully rich with that creamy stuff on top. Was it meringue?"

She shook her head as if the thought of it was unbearable. "No, it was some kind of thick sweet cream. Bloody good but . . . I can't even bear to think about it. It don't half turn my stomach."

I gave her a sympathetic smile. "Well, you take it easy today. I'll have Pierre make you some toast and Bovril. That always worked for me when I was a child and didn't feel well."

"You're very good, missus," she said. "I did all right yesterday, didn't I? I didn't drop nothing and I worked that silly lift sending the plates up and down."

"You did splendidly, Queenie," I said. "A real credit to us."

"I try my best, missus," she said. "I really do."

I crept out, leaving her lying with her eyes closed. Poor old Queenie. Still, she had the constitution of an ox, didn't she? I tried not to feel worried. This was so unlike her.

As I came down the stairs the telephone was ringing in the front hall. I heard it picked up, presumably the extension in the study by Darcy, as the foyer was deserted as I came into it. A minute or two later Darcy appeared.

"That was Sir Mordred," he said. "He wanted to know if we're all right. It seems he has a bad case of food poisoning. I told him we all seemed just fine. He asked if we could bring Pierre over to his house so we could find out exactly what was served."

"Very well," I said. "I'm sorry he's feeling ill. And by the way, we are not all just fine. Queenie is lying in her bed looking as if she's at death's door."

"Queenie? She didn't eat the food, did she?"

I had to laugh. "Darcy, this is Queenie we are talking about.

She probably helped herself to some of the leftovers. And she confessed to having two of the tarts."

"Oh dear." He gave a small laugh, then his face grew serious again. "I wonder what it can have been? We came through unscathed and yet we ate the same food, didn't we?"

"In Queenie's case I put it down to overindulging in unfamiliar dishes, but if Sir Mordred is also stricken . . ."

Darcy touched my arm lightly. "We'd better fetch Pierre and head over to Sir Mordred's as quickly as possible. I'm at a loss to know what could have caused this."

PIERRE HAD ONLY just woken up and was quite belligerent when we imparted the news to him.

"They say my food is not good? No, a thousand times no. I will not believe this. Everything I cook is fresh and clean and cooked with great expertise. I will come and I will tell this Sir Mordred that he insults my honor."

"Oh golly, please don't challenge him to a duel, will you?" I asked.

Darcy chuckled.

We reported to the rest of the company what had transpired and that we were taking Pierre over to Blackheart Manor.

"What a cheek," Zou Zou said. "Implying it was Pierre's cooking. The man obviously drank too much last night. He was knocking it back all evening, wasn't he?"

"It's hard to understand what it could have been," I said. "All of us are okay and we ate exactly the same things all evening."

Mr. Robson-Clough cleared his throat. "I have to admit I woke in the night not feeling too chipper," he said. "Stomach cramps and a trip to the . . ." He cleared his throat rather than using the dreaded word in front of ladies. "But then I have an iron constitution. I've eaten rat and snake, even roasted crickets, so if I was at all inconvenienced, then it could have been worse for others."

"Was there anything you ate that we didn't?" Sir Hubert asked him. "A different canapé maybe?"

The explorer shook his head. "Smoked salmon on toast, those little round pastry balls . . . nothing there that could cause a problem."

"I ate a good selection and my stomach is really delicate at the moment," I said. "As Mr. Robson-Clough says, those canapés were all quite innocuous. So how are you feeling now? Is there anything we can get you?"

The explorer chuckled. "Right as rain, young lady, but thank you for asking. I've had to set out on a twenty-mile trek after a night of gippy tummy. My body knows it needs to heal itself quickly or else!"

"We'd better get over there right away," Darcy said, taking my hand. "We need to clear Pierre's good name, don't we?"

"Absolutely. We'll be back to report soon."

Famous last words.

Chapter 16

JULY 26

AT BLACKHEART MANOR

Oh golly. This looks worse than I feared. Poor Pierre. I hope he's not in deep trouble.

We braved the downpour as Darcy drove back to Blackheart Manor. We were not going to make Phipps face conditions like this, as he tended to be a nervous driver and the lanes were awfully narrow. I sat beside Darcy while Pierre hunched in the back seat, glowering.

"Why does this man wish to speak to me? I have done my very best for him. I have created a masterpiece for him and now he insults me."

"I'm sure there is a good explanation, Pierre," I said. "Maybe Sir Mordred has a delicate stomach and he overindulged. I'm sure that's what Queenie did."

Blackheart Manor was living up to its name today as we drove in through the canopy of trees, which seemed to reach out menacing arms over our heads, swaying and grasping in the wind. Just as we came out of the tunnel of trees there was a flash of lightning over the house followed by a great crash of thunder. Blackheart Manor was highlighted, dark and menacing against a black sky. I inched closer to Darcy. I'm not very good with storms.

We were met at the front door by Edwin, holding a huge umbrella, and were whisked inside.

"Good of you to come," he said. "What a beastly day. Please be warned. My father is in a foul mood. And the roof is leaking again too. So all in all not too jolly. If I had a motorcar I'd be somewhere miles away from here."

"Is your father in his bedroom?" I asked.

"No, he's had a fire lit in the morning room, which is small enough to actually be warmed by a fire."

The aged butler appeared in that mysterious way that butlers have. "Should I serve coffee in the morning room, sir?" he asked.

"I don't think you'd better serve anything at the moment, Ogden," Edwin said. "Not with my father's stomach in such a delicate condition."

He followed him down the long, narrow hallway, which was even darker and gloomier than usual in this light. Edwin knocked, then opened the door to the morning room. As we stepped inside there was another flash of lightning, followed by a clap of thunder. I started nervously. I think Pierre did too. Darcy, not being scared of little things like thunderstorms, stepped confidently into the room.

"I'm sorry to hear you are under the weather, old man," he said to Sir Mordred.

The man was lying on one of the sofas, wrapped in an eider-down with a cold compress on his face. He took this off and gave us a cold stare.

"You've brought the malefactor with you, I see." He attempted to sit up. "So what have you got to say for yourself, young man?"

Pierre drew himself up proudly. "I say that my food—it ees the freshest and finest in the land."

"And yet here I am, near to death's door, having eaten a meal cooked by you."

"Have you seen a doctor yet?" I asked.

"He is supposedly on his way," Sir Mordred said. "I gather trees have been brought down in this storm. But what good can a doctor do? A load of quacks, all of them. He'll prod me and then tell me I ate something that didn't agree with me. He'll tell me to stick to crackers and tonic water. Then he'll charge me a guinea for the trouble."

"Sir Mordred," I said. "The strange thing is that we all ate the same food. Our party is all fine." As I said this I remembered that the explorer had had an unpleasant experience in the night but now had recovered. And then there was Queenie. "I ate the food and I am in a rather delicate condition at the moment. So how do you explain your current state?"

"Something he served was off, obviously."

"But let's go through the menu," I said. "The crab was very fresh, as I saw the crabs running around my kitchen only a few hours before dinner. The caviar?" I turned to Pierre.

"Came from the finest supplier in London and was kept on ice." He tossed out the words in French as a challenge. I had to translate. "The fish were sent up from a fisherman on the coast who caught them yesterday morning. Also the shrimp. The duck were supplied by you and cooked in your kitchen, but I examined them carefully and they were fine birds. Apart from that the vegetables and fruit came from your garden and the cream from our local farmer. There was nothing that could have spoiled before being served. As you know, your kitchen is quite cool." He paused, considering. "Maybe one of those canapés that were not prepared by me? Prepared by your chef, eh? They were out in hot sun. It is just possible . . ."

I duly translated.

"I have spoken with Mr. Henman," Sir Mordred said. "He assures me that the canapés were only brought up from the kitchen the moment before they were needed and were made of the freshest ingredients."

"There you are, then." Pierre spread his hands in a dramatic shrug. "There is no explanation except that perhaps you do not tolerate one of the foods served? There are people who cannot eat shellfish, who cannot eat cream . . ."

"I have a wonderfully strong constitution," Sir Mordred said. "I have no such problems."

"I wish we could be of more help," Darcy said, "but it does appear that the chef is blameless in this." He paused, looked at me for confirmation. "So if there's nothing more we can do, we should perhaps take Pierre back to our house so that he can prepare our lunch."

There was the sound of a telephone ringing at the other end of the house. We broke off talking, and a moment of tense silence followed as the rain lashed the windows and a fierce draft came down the chimney, sending sparks whirling up from the fire. Footsteps could be heard coming toward us. Edwin entered, looking somber.

"That was Miss Ormorod, Father," he said. "She was also taken ill during the night."

Sir Mordred looked furious. "There you are! What did I tell you? Something that bloody Frenchman served us was just not right. Isn't part of the crab supposed to be poisonous? I know there are parts you have to discard when you dress it. Never done it myself."

Pierre had not understood this and I translated. He waved his arms dramatically. "Do you not think I know how to dress a crab?" he replied in French. "Me, I have dressed hundreds of crabs. I know the good meat. And the good brown crab butter. I know these. I am a trained chef."

I duly translated. Sir Mordred did not look convinced. "If it wasn't the crab, then what was it? Something has made me and my guests unpleasantly sick." He attempted to sit up again and waved a finger at Edwin. "Go and telephone the rest of the guests. Let's see if anyone else has been stricken."

We waited, still standing, as we had not been invited to sit. I glanced nervously at Darcy, then at Pierre, who was still looking defiant. An uneasy thought was going through my head. Pierre had boasted to me about being a communist. He had taken this job because he wanted to further his standing as a chef, but what if he secretly despised our kind of people and was out to get us? He had had complete access to the gardens, after all. Could he have sneaked into the poison garden when he was supposed to be picking fresh fruits and vegetables and added something lethal to one of the dishes?

I stole a glance in his direction. He still looked defiant and a little scared. Would there not have been an air of triumph if he had scored a point for the communists against the idle rich?

At last we heard feet coming back toward us. Edwin came in.

"Not good news, I'm afraid," he said. "Mr. Mallowan was also ill during the night but is feeling considerably better this morning. Mrs. Bancroft, that obnoxious lady, was sick in the night and is still horribly weak. At death's door, as she described it. She said she knew no good would come from employing a foreign chef." He paused, trying not to grin. "I couldn't get hold of your film actors. Mr. Grossman said he'd be in touch with them, but he himself was fine. Lord and Lady Mountjoy were in good health and thanked me for the lovely dinner. I've no idea where to locate Mr. and Mrs. Crump. And nobody answered when I called Mr. and Mrs. Halliday, so they must be out and about. He's a farmer, isn't he? I expect he's milking something."

"So there you are, then," Sir Mordred said, pointing a finger at Pierre. "Two more people stricken during the night. Luckily they have both recovered. But I'm going to look into this, trust me. I presume there was some food left over from last night's banquet? I shall take it to my laboratory and see if any of it was tainted." He paused, considering this. "Or maybe doctored? Didn't this man confess to being a communist? Well then, now we have our answer, don't we? He bears a grudge. He has a mission to do away with us. Why else did he take the job? He wants to eradicate the aristocrats of the world."

Pierre had not understood this rapid tirade and I thought it wiser not to translate for him at this moment.

"Oh, I say," Darcy said. "Let's not leap to conclusions and judge a chap because he's foreign."

"Well, we shall see, shan't we?" Sir Mordred sat up fully and threw off the eiderdown. "He did not reckon with my having a laboratory in my house. I have never tried testing food before, but I'll give it a good shot. Edwin. Help me to stand up. We'll go down to the kitchen and take a closer look." He gave a dramatic groan as Edwin helped him to his feet. "He forgets that I have created one of the cleverest detectives in literature. A small crime like this would seem nothing to him."

And he set off across the morning room.

Chapter 17

Things are not looking good for Pierre. The one thing I can't understand is how some people became ill and others did not. I do hope we can clear this up quickly. I really like Pierre. And I adore his food! I'd hate to lose him and go back to Queenie.

Sir Mordred looked even whiter and paler than ever by the time we descended to the kitchen.

"Fetch me a chair, Edwin," he said. Darcy pulled one out before Edwin could reach it. Sir Mordred plumped onto it and wiped the sweat from his brow with his handkerchief.

"Right, young man," he said. "Bring me whatever was left from last night."

"If you wish," Pierre said. "You will find no wrong."

He spotted the terrified kitchen maid trying to hide in a corner.

"You, girl. *Cherchez* crabs," he said, his arms miming words he didn't know. "Bring all foods from the menu. Your master wishes to taste them again."

He stomped off to retrieve some dishes for himself.

Edwin was standing behind his father and gave me a worried look.

"Should you really be doing this?" I asked Sir Mordred. "You're awfully weak. It's not good for you to exert yourself too much."

"We have to strike while the iron is hot, young lady," he said. "By tomorrow the food would all be disposed of."

I considered this. "If Pierre had done something to contaminate the food deliberately, do you really think he'd leave the evidence lying around to be examined? He'd have had plenty of chance to dispose of it last night and we'd have been left with no proof."

I saw a shadow of doubt cross his face. "Well, maybe I did go too far. I'm feeling so god-awful right now that my temper is not the best."

"It's not the best at the best of times, Father," Edwin said dryly. "You get upset when anything doesn't go your way. It's your nature."

"True, I suppose," Sir Mordred said, "but we have to get to the bottom of this. I have a reputation to live up to. I cannot let the word get out that people become sick at my parties."

"It might be rather good for your reputation, Father," Edwin commented. He had perched himself on one edge of the kitchen table and looked almost as if he was enjoying this. "If you can work out what poisoned everybody, you can tell the tale when you give your next speeches."

"This is not amusing, boy," Sir Mordred said. "I don't think you realize how sick I was during the night. Spilling my guts. If I had had a weaker constitution it might have been the end of me. And that old woman, Miss Ormorod. She might well have succumbed. She still might. And then what, eh? A murder case on our hands. Police investigating?"

Pierre returned carrying a couple of tureens with their lids on. The kitchen maid followed, carrying more bowls. Pierre set his down on the table in front of Sir Mordred a little too forcefully. "Voilà," he said. "My dishes. Crab mousse. Duck. Soup. Fish. And the dessert."

Sir Mordred took the bowl containing the crab mousse. He sniffed it, tasted it, then passed it to us. We had to agree we could see nothing wrong with it. He then asked for small ramekins and placed some of the mousse in one. "I shall attempt to test for unknown substances," he said. "I have equipment in my laboratory upstairs that should do the job."

"But that makes no sense," I blurted out before realizing this was a little impolite. "We all ate some of this mousse and yet most of us were not affected."

"Nevertheless, I shall do my best," Sir Mordred said. He then proceeded to take small samples of the soup, the quenelles of fish, and the shrimp sauce and then asked to see the duck.

"Since most of the portions of duck did not sicken anybody, you're unlikely to find one that did," Edwin commented, still perched on the table.

"That only leaves the pudding," Sir Mordred said. "Do we still have one of those tarts?"

"Naturally," Pierre said. "I always make more in case there is damage to the crust during serving. They have to look perfect."

He pushed a couple of fruit tarts onto the table. They still looked jolly appetizing to me, and I realized that I would have eaten one last night if it hadn't been for the rich hat of cream.

"And the cream," Sir Mordred said.

A bowl of cream was put in front of him. We all took a tentative taste. Delicious. But he scooped some into the ramekin to be tested.

"I admit I am perplexed," he said. "All seems to be as it should. And yet . . . four people were taken violently ill. We all ate the same food. It makes no sense." As he spoke he was staring at the tarts. Suddenly he leaned forward, dug his fingers into the tart, and held up something. "What is this?" he demanded.

It looked like a small black berry. Sir Mordred examined it, held it up to his nose, and sniffed. "You know what it is?" he said. "It's an elderberry. He served us tarts with elderberries in them. No wonder we were so ill."

"But surely elderberries are edible?" Darcy asked. "We always had elderberry wine at home."

"They are perfectly edible," Sir Mordred said, looking triumphant now, "if you cook them first. If you serve them raw they contain a toxin that will give you a nasty upset stomach."

"Golly," I said.

"I see now this was all a horrible accident," Sir Mordred said. "I told the chef to help himself from our kitchen garden. There is a large elderberry bush against the wall. Mr. Henman makes a really good elderflower cordial. So this man is French. Perhaps he is not familiar with elderberries. He adds them to the mix and . . ."

If Queenie had been here she would have said "Bob's yer uncle."

"What does this man say now?" Pierre had not followed along.

I explained. Pierre gave an explosive "No! This is not true. I do not use these strange black berries in my tarte. I use the strawberries, the raspberries, the dark ones . . ."

"Loganberries," I said for him.

"And the *cassis*?" He turned to me to translate.

"Currants."

"Yes. These things I use. But not small ugly black berries. No, no." He glared at us. "Somebody has done this to me, to make me look bad. And I know who it must be. It is the old man, the chef of this house. He does not want me here. He wishes to destroy my reputation."

"Very well," Sir Mordred said. "Where is Mr. Henman? Let's see what he has to say for himself." He looked around the kitchen.

"Please, sir, I think he went out to talk to the gardener," the kitchen maid said, her eyes still wide with terror in case she was in any way to be blamed for this.

"Then, go and fetch him immediately," Sir Mordred said. "Tell him the master wishes to speak with him."

She ran off in the direction of the scullery and presumably the back door. We waited. Sir Mordred examined the three tarts that were left and found two more elderberries in one of them. He waved them in triumph. At that point Mr. Henman came in, red-faced as if he had been hurrying.

"Sorry, sir. I was out talking to the gardener. I was asking when the marrows might be ripe. I know you love a stuffed marrow, don't you?" He paused, eyed the three of us suspiciously, and then demanded, "What was it you wanted?"

"Mr. Henman," Sir Mordred said, holding up one of the berries, "what would you say this was?"

Mr. Henman took it, sniffed, and prodded. "An elderberry, sir."

"An elderberry. Quite right. And where was it found? In one of the tarts that this French chef prepared for last night's dinner. Elderberries that have so far caused four people to be ill."

Mr. Henman glared at Pierre. "There you are, then. What did

I say? I told you you were making a mistake hiring a foreigner to cook your fancy meal. He repays you by trying to poison you all."

"Pierre swears he did not pick any elderberries," Sir Mordred said. "But somebody did. Somebody inserted these berries into the mixture with the intent to cause harm. It had to have been done when nobody would notice. Which makes me wonder, Henman"— dramatic pause—"whether you decided to get a little revenge, show this Frenchman, make him look like a fool?"

Mr. Henman's face turned an interesting shade of puce. "You think I would stoop so low? I am mortified. I would never do something like that. Besides, that girl he brought with him, the large and uncouth one, she was the person who finished the tarts and sent them up in the dumbwaiter. I suggest you ask her."

Sir Mordred turned to stare at me. "Yes, where is this girl? Why was she not brought here today?"

"The answer to that is that she is lying in bed groaning with the same complaint as you. She was horribly sick in the night. She admitted to eating leftovers, including one of the tarts."

"Oh." Sir Mordred considered this. "I thought you said none of your party was ill when I spoke to you. But your cook would hardly have been likely to have poisoned herself, would she?"

"My thoughts exactly," Darcy said. "She is not the brightest person. I don't think it would ever enter her head to use a particular sort of berry to make anyone ill."

"Then we are back to square one, it seems," Sir Mordred said as he stood to leave the kitchen. "Unless one of them is lying."

The elderly butler appeared at the door, wheezing after the exertion of coming downstairs. "If you please, Sir Mordred, the doctor has arrived to examine you."

Sir Mordred turned back to us. "We shall continue this inquiry until I get to the bottom of it," he said. "Edwin. Assist me up the stairs and to my bedchamber. I don't think we should keep you any longer, Mr. O'Mara, Lady Georgiana. I am sorry for disturbing your morning, but at least we have found the culprit in terms of what sickened us. Now all we need to find is who sickened us, and why."

With those words he leaned on Edwin and slowly ascended the stairs back to the foyer.

The doctor was standing just inside the front door. I recognized him immediately as our own physician, Dr. Farnsworth. I would have greeted him but I didn't have the chance. He was looking rather put out and went straight up to Sir Mordred.

"Oh, there you are, Mortimer," he said. "From what you said on the telephone I expected to find you at death's door, but here you are walking around."

"I assure you I have been at death's door," Sir Mordred said. "I spent a most unpleasant night enduring cramps and diarrhea."

"A touch of food poisoning, was it?" the doctor asked. "Or simply overdoing it? I know you like to indulge."

"Overdoing it?" I thought for a moment that Sir Mordred was going to hit him. "My dear man, I'll have you know that we have been poisoned. Not just me but several of my guests. What is more, I have discovered the substance that poisoned us. The pudding course last night was a tart topped with various berries. Among the more normal ones like strawberries and raspberries were some elderberries."

"Elderberries? You mean raw?" The doctor frowned. "That was a damned silly thing to do. They are toxic unless cooked. What was your cook thinking?"

"Both my chefs have denied any knowledge of them. If they are telling the truth then someone added them with malicious intent."

"Extraordinary," the doctor said. "Do you have any ideas on the subject? A servant with a grudge?"

"My servants all worship me," Sir Mordred said. "I pay extremely well. My cook has been with me for years. Apart from him the butler is an old retainer who is close to retiring. There are a couple of maids and that's it. The only other people in the house were the guests, and I don't see how any of them had a chance to visit the kitchen before the food was served."

"The food was brought up to that little anteroom," I pointed out.

The doctor seemed to focus on us for the first time. He gave me a smile of recognition. "Lady Georgiana. I'm surprised to see you here. Shouldn't you be at home resting for the great event?"

"Darcy and I were guests last night," I said. "And it was our chef who cooked the meal. We brought him back to be questioned this morning and he is quite adamant that he did not use any elderberries."

"How very peculiar," the doctor said. "But you yourself were not stricken last night?"

I shook my head. "I was not." And suddenly I remembered. "But I didn't eat one of the tarts. In fact the tart meant for me was placed in front of the person beside me."

"And did that person have a bad reaction?"

"Yes. He was one of those who were ill. But he's quite recovered this morning."

"Then consider yourself fortunate, young lady. A bad upset at this stage could have brought on early labor."

I swallowed back the word "golly."

The doctor paused, considering. "Although I'd have to say that you'd have to eat quite a lot of elderberries to do serious damage. A few cramps and diarrhea from a berry or two is what I'd expect.

Were there many of these berries in the tarts? If so, why weren't they noticed when the tarts were served? I'd certainly notice a berry I didn't expect to see."

"There was only the occasional elderberry in the tarts we just examined," Sir Mordred said.

"Then a mild upset would be the most that should be expected. I'm surprised that one or two caused any problem at all."

"Of course there could have been more in the tarts that people actually ate," Sir Mordred pointed out. "Some people ate the pudding and were perfectly fine. It seems so horribly random."

"Someone playing a malicious prank by the sound of it," the doctor said.

My thoughts went immediately to Edwin and his pals from Oxford. I could just see a group of young men getting together and giggling about putting something wicked in the food to upset the stodgy old people who had paid a fortune for the banquet. I went to say something, then thought better of it. No sense in putting Edwin further into his father's bad books until I'd had a chance to talk to him.

"Well, now that I'm here, I suppose I'd better examine you," Dr. Farnsworth said. "Do you want to do it down here or shall we go up to your bedroom?"

"Oh, upstairs, I think," Sir Mordred said. "I'd want a thorough examination. Just in case there is any lingering damage to my system."

I thought I saw the doctor give the twitch of a smile and suspected that Sir Mordred was a bit of a hypochondriac. "Very well," he said.

"I bid you good day, Lady Georgiana, Mr. O'Mara. And I'm glad that you have come through this little episode unscathed."

Just as they headed for the stairs the telephone rang again. Sir Mordred looked around for a servant, then went over to answer it himself. I saw a look of horror gradually creeping over his face. "Oh, I see. Yes, of course. But that's absolutely terrible."

He put down the receiver slowly, then turned to us with a stunned look on his face. "That was the county hospital," he said. "Tubby Halliday was admitted in the middle of the night. He's just died."

$\mathcal{C}$hapter 18

Things have suddenly become much more serious. This is no longer
a prank.

There was a moment of absolute silence apart from the sonorous ticktock of the grandfather clock in the gallery.

"Did they say what he died of?" the doctor asked.

Sir Mordred shook his head. He looked even paler, if that were possible. "This is terrible," he said. "I invite people to be guests at my home and one of them dies. Who could have done this to me?"

"I noticed he did like to indulge, didn't he?" Edwin said. "He was knocking back the booze all evening, and shoveling in the food."

"And didn't he mention having some kind of heart problem?"

Darcy suggested. "He said something about his quack always telling him that his lifestyle was bad for his heart."

"It may have been the combination of the two, then," the doctor said. "Too much alcohol can affect the heart and then the strain of a gastric upset was just too much." He looked up abruptly. "Was he a large man? Carrying a good deal of weight?"

"He was always known as Tubby at school," Sir Mordred said. "And he hadn't become noticeably slimmer over the years."

"Well, there you are, then. I can always tell when my patients are an accident waiting to happen. Heart problems, excess weight, alcohol, plus the toxic berries." He shook his head. "We'll have to wait until we know more. Let's just hope that this doesn't lead to any sort of inquiry, Mortimer, or it could be unpleasant for you."

"For me? What in God's name did I have to do with this? I entertained. My only failing could have been that perhaps I was too generous with the booze. But I had no idea someone would maliciously put poisonous berries into the desserts."

As they spoke I was trying to process an alarming thought that had surfaced in my brain. I remembered refusing the tart. Had the waiter put mine in front of the next person, Mr. Mallowan, and then did his go to Miss Ormorod, both of whom had become ill? But Mr. Halliday was next to her and he had said he'd have the extra tart. If that extra one, meant for Miss Ormorod, had contained more berries, then he'd have had a double dose.

I corrected myself with this train of thought. I'd used the words "meant for." But that was rubbish. Surely the tarts were sent up in the dumbwaiter on trays, in no particular order. So it was just bad luck that Mr. Mallowan, Miss Ormorod, and presumably Mr. Halliday got tarts that contained the poisonous berries. It had to be random, because if there was an order, then someone had intended to poison me!

"What's wrong, Georgiana?" Darcy asked, seeing my troubled look.

"I was remembering that I refused my tart last night. I'd had too much rich food and was feeling slightly nauseous. So Mr. Mallowan got mine, and Miss Ormorod got his, and Mr. Halliday said he'd have the extra one. So he must have had a double dose of the berries."

"Well, that might explain things," Sir Mordred said.

But the doctor shook his head. "In my experience it would take an awful lot of elderberries to kill somebody," he said. "I've treated children who've feasted on them and had violent gastric upsets, but they didn't die. I'd say this man's heart plus the amount of alcohol would be the more likely culprit."

"Poor fellow," Sir Mordred said.

"I'm sorry about your school friend, Father," Edwin said. "What a beastly thing to happen, especially after you had just met up again."

Sir Mordred turned to his son. "The trouble is, Edwin, that he never was my friend. Why do you think I didn't answer his letter when it came a few weeks ago? If you want to know, he was always a bully; so were those other chaps he mentioned. When I arrived at Harrow I was a skinny little runt. Hence the nickname Shrimpy. I had arrived straight from India with no idea of how things were done in England. And those boys loved to pick on me. I was an easy target." He looked from one of us to the next, wanting affirmation. "Oh, they were very cunning about it," he went on. "They'd hide one of my gym shoes. I'd get a beating for losing my shoe. Then it would miraculously reappear. It was only later when I grew a bit and turned into a useful rugby player that they sort of accepted me as one of them. But I'd never have described any of them as bosom friends. Which is why I never looked them up when I returned to England."

There was another awkward pause.

"Well, we should be getting along," Darcy said, "if you don't think we can be of any more use here."

"No, absolutely not," Sir Mordred said. "Thank you for coming."

"And you don't mind if we retrieve our chef, Sir Mordred?" Darcy asked.

"I suppose the chap professes his innocence," Sir Mordred said testily. "I still want to get to the bottom of this, but not now. Not today." He turned to his doctor. "Perhaps you'd be good enough to listen to my heart, Doctor. I don't want to find I'm about to keel over like that poor fool Halliday. Edwin, I suppose we'd better write a letter of condolence to the wife."

"Sylvia can do that," Edwin said. "Women always seem to know the right thing to say on such occasions."

"Where is the dratted girl? Don't tell me they are still in bed at this hour. Lazy female. That good-for-nothing husband of hers is worse than she is. Always holding out his hand for something. Never done an honest day's work in his life. I was brought up to . . ." He stopped, shaking his head. "Ah well. She's married to him, so it's her bed to lie on. Edwin, see these good folk out. Doctor, you can help me up the stairs."

As he made for the stairs someone else was coming down. Sylvia appeared, dressed in riding breeches and an open-necked shirt. She was wearing red lipstick and looked glamorous and fresh.

"Hello, what's going on?" she asked. "Have I missed something? I hope I'm not too late for breakfast."

"Anyone who rises at this infernally late hour does not deserve breakfast," Sir Mordred said coldly.

"I like that," she said, tossing her head angrily. "I hardly slept a wink last night with that awful row going on. The windows rattled like crazy in the storm and the draft blew down the chimney and then the thunder kept us awake. Poor Stanley is lying in bed with one of his headaches. He always gets them in stormy weather. He's so delicate, you know. But I'm now extremely hungry."

"As it happens you are extremely lucky that you are still hale and hearty," Sir Mordred said dryly.

"What's that supposed to mean?" She had reached the bottom step and noticed that the doctor was among us. "Oh hello, Doctor," she said. "Don't tell me someone is ill?"

"I was taken ill, Sylvia." Sir Mordred waved his hands dramatically. "Your father was poisoned last night. So were several of our guests."

"Oh gosh," she said. The veneer of sophistication gone, she now looked rather young and scared. "Poisoned, you say? Food poisoning, you mean? But we all ate the same things."

"It seems that someone had a little joke at our expense, Sylvia," Sir Mordred said. "Someone inserted some elderberries into the berry tartlets. Raw elderberries that give one a gastric upset."

"How beastly." She looked from one face to the next. "Did you find out who?"

"Not yet, but I intend to." Sir Mordred gave her a long, hard stare. Then he said, "Come on, Doctor. Let's not waste any more of your valuable time or you'll be billing me double." He gave a brittle laugh and started up the stairs.

"And I'm off to get breakfast," Sylvia said. "Let's hope it's not poisoned."

"I'll show you out." Edwin looked embarrassed as he addressed us. We followed him to the front door. The rain had now subsided and patches of blue were appearing among the clouds.

"God, what an awful business," he said as we stood on the porch. "The old chap is clearly shaken by it. I'm sorry you had to go through this." He held out his hand. "Thank you for coming so promptly, Lady Georgiana. And you, Mr. O'Mara. Then he nodded to Pierre. "I'm glad you escaped this strange business, old chap."

"Why he thinks I am old?" Pierre asked as we returned to our motorcar.

"The same as *mon vieux*," Darcy said. "Just a figure of speech."

We drove away with me sitting in the front seat beside Darcy and Pierre again in the back. "What on earth do you make of that?" Darcy asked me.

"I still think it must have been some kind of prank," I said. "After all, Edwin did have his Oxford friends there for the evening, and they helped serve, didn't they? How easy to stick an elderberry or two into some of the tarts, knowing what the result would be."

"But you didn't bring this theory up to Edwin?"

"It didn't seem the right moment," I said. "He is not on good terms with his father. I didn't want to suggest something like this until I'd had a chance to talk to him alone. And now that the prank has gone so horribly wrong, he wouldn't be willing to admit to it, would he?"

"And it seems you dodged a bullet, didn't you? Turning down your tart?"

"I did. It made me feel quite queer when I realized." I looked across at him. "Those tarts with the poisonous berries in them had to have been quite random, didn't they? Because otherwise somebody was trying to poison me."

"But that's absurd," Darcy snapped. "Who would wish to harm you? For that matter who would wish to harm anybody at that dinner? Most of us were strangers to each other. No, it absolutely had to have been a spiteful random act. And now somebody has died. I don't think we should let whoever did it get away with it. You and I should look into it, Georgie."

Chapter 19

JULY 26

BACK AT EYNSLEIGH

I don't know what to think. Who would poison people with no real
motive?

I felt secretly glad that Darcy had suggested we should look into it
together. That meant that he had come to value my investigative
skills. He also hadn't said that I should stay home and take it easy
because of the impending birth of our child. I liked being treated
as an equal. At the same time I didn't see how we could find out
who might have done this.

"Don't you think the police will now be involved?" I asked.
"Mr. Halliday's death will have to be labeled as suspicious, won't it?

"Possibly," Darcy said. "If he died of a heart attack, for example,
they are not likely to examine the contents of his stomach." He
turned back to Pierre, who had been sitting silently in the back seat.

"Pierre, I don't know how much you understood," he said, switching to French (which was not as fluent as mine), "but one of the guests last night became sick and has died. This makes it very serious."

"You think that I have something to do with a man's death?" Pierre demanded. "You say that my food killed a man?" He waved his hands dramatically, almost rising from his seat. "But this is terrible news for me. If word gets out it will ruin my career. It will haunt me. Everywhere I go they will point at me and say, 'This is the chef whose food killed a man.'"

"Calm yourself. Of course it wasn't your food," I said quickly. "We now know that somebody put those elderberries into some of the tarts. This man ate two of them, so he got a double dose. But let us start with you. Tell us exactly how those tarts were prepared."

"I made the *pâte sucrée* shells in the morning," Pierre said. "I left them on the table to cool. I went out to the garden and I picked the berries, as I have told you. I brought them in, gave them to the kitchen maid to wash and hull, then they were left in the colander until the time to assemble the tarts in the afternoon. I made the *crème pâtissière* to place inside the tarts and I completed one of them with a pleasing arrangement of berries. Then I showed this to Queenie and told her to complete the rest to look the same."

"Did she do a good job?"

"She did, for once."

"And nobody helped her? Mr. Henman didn't help her?"

"That man claimed he was feeling ill. He stayed far away from me all day. He only came in to prepare his appetizers, groaning and complaining, then he went again. He was no help at all."

"So who was in the kitchen, Pierre?" Darcy asked.

"Only me, Queenie, and the girl. She was not much use either. She is untrained with no idea how to do things."

"You were there all day?" I asked. "Did anybody else come in at any time?"

"I told you that the old man came and went a few times. But he did not come near us."

"And the berries in the colander—where were they?"

"On the counter, by the sink."

"Near an open window?"

"Quite near." He gave me a worried look. "You don't think somebody reached in from the outside and added those bad berries?"

"It's possible," I said. "If nobody else came into the kitchen, then it's hard to see how else they were added."

"But surely this girl Queenie is not so stupid that she does not notice strange berries in the mixture?"

"Maybe she sees them but thinks that they are what you selected and doesn't like to question you."

"*Mon dieu*, but that is terrible," he said. "Surely one of us would have seen a person come to the window and reach inside. That person would have had to lean in a long way. And are the windows not quite high up? A person would have had to stand on something."

"They could have watched and waited for a moment when you were all busy. Perhaps you called Queenie and the kitchen maid over to show them something and at that moment all eyes were on you."

"Yes," he agreed. "You are right. That could be possible. But no. I examined the tarts when Queenie had completed them and before I added the cream on top. I would surely have noticed the strange berries."

"Possibly not. If there were only one or two per tart, perhaps they were hidden. And you would not have noticed an odd one or two."

He reached forward and touched my shoulder, something that is forbidden for a servant. "You must help me, my lady. You must find out who did this terrible act, or my career will be in ruins."

If it hadn't been so serious I might have laughed at his dramatic delivery. But it was serious and I could see that he was right.

We arrived home. Holly and Jolly came bounding to meet us, acting as if we had been away for long months and every second without us had been a torment. Pierre, not the greatest dog lover, nimbly avoided them and headed straight down to the kitchen without another word. I could understand that. He'd had an emotionally draining morning. I stared after him, absent-mindedly patting Holly's blond head. I suppose everything he had said was true, wasn't it? He seemed angry at being accused, distraught that someone doctored his tarts, but how did I know that he wasn't a superb actor? Maybe his communist sympathies had risen to the fore and he had decided to play a trick on members of the aristocracy. Or worse still, to bump off a few of us.

I frowned, still staring at the door now closed behind Pierre. But surely he wouldn't have wanted to harm me, would he? He had seemed to genuinely like me. But then I remembered all those members of the aristocracy who had been willingly sent to the guillotine during the Revolution. There must have been some nice people among them, some kind landlords, but their heads came off with the rest.

"What's wrong?" Darcy asked, forcing down Jolly as he jumped up excitedly. "Down, Jolly. Sit. Oh, you are hopeless!"

"Wrong?" I snapped out the word, my nerves now close to the breaking point. "Oh nothing, apart from my chef having been accused of poisoning people, a man having died of presumably eating a tart I might have eaten. Apart from that it's been quite a delightful day so far."

He put an arm around my shoulders. The dogs, now horribly jealous of such closeness that did not include them, tried to nose their way between us. "I'm sorry. That was a silly thing to say, wasn't it? Of course it's been an upsetting morning. Why don't you go and lie down for a while? I'll have a cup of coffee sent up to you, or would you rather have tea?"

"I don't feel like lying down, Darcy. I'm too wound up for that. I agree with you. Someone has to get to the bottom of this and we have to start with our own members of staff. They are the prime suspects at the moment, after all."

"Hardly the prime suspects. Pierre is most adamant that this had nothing to do with him."

"But how do we know, Darcy? He might be a brilliant actor. He does have motive, after all. He is a communist."

"Rather in name only, I suspect. It sounds good to espouse that sort of thing. In real life I don't see him heading off to Russia to join the starving peasants, do you?"

"I suppose not."

"Then let's agree that Pierre was in the wrong place at the wrong time yesterday. Someone must have had a better reason for creating havoc and we should try to find it."

I nodded.

"I should have another word with Queenie," I said. "Let's see if she can throw any light on what might have happened."

"Good idea," he said, "although that girl is so dense that a potential murderer could have climbed in through the window, stuck every tart through with poisonous berries, and then gone out without her batting an eyelid."

"She can be surprisingly astute at times," I said. "Anyway, let's hear what she has to say."

"When you use the word 'let's' I hope that doesn't mean that you want me to come up to a female's sickroom. I might be the dashing head of the household, but I have a delicate stomach for such matters."

I laughed. "I can see I'm going to have to train you in the changing of nappies," I said.

He leaned closer to me. "I'm going to say one word of advice to you. Nanny."

"And how exactly can we afford one?" I asked. "We're not exactly rolling in money."

"Perhaps we'll have to compromise. You mentioned that Maisie was good at looking after her young brothers and sisters. Maybe it will have to be a nursemaid, not a trained nanny."

"I think I'd like that better," I said. "A trained nanny can be rather terrifying. I've known nannies who won't let the parents near their own children. I was lucky that my nanny was kind and gentle. Was yours?"

"We never had a proper nanny," Darcy confessed. "My mother looked after us. She was a thoroughly modern woman who believed in raising her own children. We did have a maid who helped out, but mostly I remember my mother reading to us, playing with us, singing us to sleep."

"You must have really missed her," I said.

I saw tears well up in his eyes. "The worst moment of my life was when the headmaster called me into his study and told me my mother had died of the flu. Not just my mother either. My two little brothers. All at the same time. My sisters and I only escaped because we were away at school. And my father never forgave me. As if it should have been me who died and not her."

"That's all water under the bridge now, surely," I said. "You have a good relationship with your father."

"Yes, finally it's better." He had been staring past me, across the foyer, but then he looked at me. I saw the pain in his eyes and reached out to touch him.

"We should invite him over when the baby arrives," I said. "He should meet his grandchild."

"Of course." He stroked my shoulder again. "Are you sure you don't want to rest?"

"No. Quite the opposite. I need to be doing something."

"Then go and have your talk with Queenie and then we'll take the dogs for a walk. We can talk through what we know so far."

"Good idea." I headed up the stairs.

Chapter 20

JULY 26

EYNSLEIGH

I have to admit I feel completely in the dark about this. How would we ever get anyone to confess? If someone was playing a silly random prank, then they would never confess to it now that a man had died.

Queenie was lying on her bed giving a good impersonation of La Dame aux Camélias, about to expire from consumption. She turned to give me a mournful gaze as I came in and managed to utter the words "Whatcha, miss" (forgetting I was now a missus).

"Are you feeling any better?" I asked gently, hovering in the doorway because the room did not smell too savory.

"I still feel ruddy awful if you want to know, missus," she said.

I felt a tremor of alarm. Another of the guests had eaten more than one of the tarts and had now died.

"I think we should call the doctor, Queenie," I said. "Just to make sure."

"Don't worry about me, missus," she said. "I'm sure I'll be right as rain soon."

"I'll have Pierre make some barley water for you," I said, "and maybe some beef broth?"

"I don't fancy nothing," she said. "I don't think I will ever want to eat again."

This really was alarming.

"I am calling the doctor," I said. "But I wondered if you feel strong enough to answer a few questions."

She gave me a scared look. "What sort of questions? I only ate what was left over; you know I didn't pinch nothing I shouldn't have. Honest."

"I know that, Queenie. But a terrible thing has happened. Some of the guests have also become sick after the meal. Not only guests but also Sir Mordred himself. It seems that someone put poisonous berries into the berry tarts."

"Poisonous berries?" She tried to sit up. "It wasn't me, missus. Honest to God it wasn't."

"I know that, Queenie. You'd hardly have eaten the tarts you tried to poison, would you?"

"You're bloody well right. I wouldn't, would I?"

"At least you should sip some water." I came in, closed the door behind me, and went over to open the window. "Let's get some good fresh air in here, shall we? I see it's stopped raining, which is good."

She didn't bother to reply to this. I perched on the end of her bed. "If you can think back to yesterday, maybe you can shed some light on this. Someone deliberately put elderberries into the berry tarts."

"Elderberries? They're all right, ain't they? I know I've had elderberry wine. It was quite nice."

"Yes, but you have to cook them first. When they are eaten raw they give you stomach upsets like the one you've just had."

I saw her frowning, trying to digest this news. "Someone put them berries in the tarts, you say?" She thought about this. "How did they do that? When could they have done that? It don't make sense."

"I agree, so we have to get to the bottom of who might have done such a nasty thing. Let's go through the entire day. Pierre says he went and picked the berries himself."

"That's right." She nodded, showing a little more enthusiasm now. "And then he gave them to that girl to clean up and hull them." She turned to look at me. "I tell you, missus, she's thick as a plank, that one. My old dad used to say I was daft. If he saw her, I don't know what he'd say. I had to show her three times how to hull the strawberries and even then she made a mess of it and I had to take over before Chef saw and blew his top."

"You went through the berries?"

"Well, I did when I had to put them on the pastry shells. Chef showed me how they should look and I had to copy his design." She managed a weak smile. "He told me I'd done a good job. How about that, eh? I told you he'd come around to liking me."

I ignored that last remark. "So you noticed what sort of berries they were?"

"Yeah. All the normal type you'd put on a fruit tart."

"You didn't notice any small black berries among them, then? They'd have looked like small black currants."

She paused to think about this. "There were the big ones what look like blackberries. But no little black ones. I'd have noticed, I'm sure."

"What happened to the tarts when you had finished putting the berries on?"

"Chef made the glaze and then later he came and topped them with the crème."

"And after the tarts were finished, what happened to them?"

"They were put on trays, ready to send up to the dining room."

"Just left out in the kitchen, then?"

She nodded, not sure where this was going.

"Think, Queenie. Did anybody come into the kitchen at any stage of the day that you can remember?"

"Only the old bloke, the chef from the house, and that girl Mavis. She was there most of the time. The old bloke was right pissed off at us, you could tell. So he stayed well away most of the time. And when he did come to finish his canapés he stayed down the other end of the kitchen."

"You didn't notice him come near your fruit tarts?"

"He did. He passed by when I was finishing up putting the berries on and he muttered, 'Foreign rubbish.'"

"Do you think he might have had time to put the elderberries in among the mix?"

She looked horrified. "He wouldn't have done that, would he? What? Make his own employer ill? It would be more than his job was worth."

She was quite right there. If he had wanted to show up Pierre, he'd have arranged it so that Sir Mordred did not get one of the offending tarts.

"Anyway," she went on, "like I said, he stayed well away from us and then the trays were put on the side table near the lift and he'd have had no call to go near them."

"So nobody else came into the kitchen? No footmen? Servants?"

"I don't think he has no proper servants, not like us, missus," she said. "There's the old butler and he came in for a cup of tea at teatime. And there's a maid. But that's about it."

Outside the window a pigeon started cooing loudly. I wasn't quite sure where to go next with my line of questioning.

"This might seem a bit embarrassing," I said, "but you didn't see Pierre add anything to the tarts, did you?"

"Add anything?" She sounded confused.

"I meant any of those elderberries at the last minute. You didn't see him putting anything more on the tarts?"

"Our chef?" She looked horrified. "He wouldn't do a thing like that. He's a decent bloke. A smashing bloke, actually. All he put on was the crème, and I saw him do that. Then he said they'd turned out well and he was pleased. And then they went on the trays ready to be sent up."

"And when were they sent up?"

She thought about this. "The cold stuff went up in advance. Before the people came into the dining room. I was told to go up into that little room at the same time to get the plates out of the lift and arrange them on the tables in order. That was the crab mousse and the artichokes. The salads came later, I think because Chef was making them at the last minute."

"So you were up there in that little room all the time from the moment the food came up?"

"That's right. We put the trays into the lift. It has little shelves so you can stack a lot of food in at once, and then Chef told me to go up and unload them. He said I had to stay up there and take the food out and then load in the dirties. And he told me not to mess up and drop anything or it would be you and the master I was letting down. So I was extra careful."

"And how did it work from then on? There were two servers. They weren't footmen belonging to the house?"

"Oh no, miss. One of them spoke quite posh. They treated it like a bit of a lark. But they were good and quick."

"Was there a particular order that the plates were in?"

"An order?" She wasn't quite sure about this.

"Yes, I mean were you told you had to put out the plates in a particular order for the servers to take them?"

"Oh yes, missus. I had to put the crab nearest the door, then the artichokes."

"But not arrange the plates in any way?"

"I don't understand."

"You just took the plates off the tray and put them down willy-nilly on the tables."

"Yeah. I suppose so."

"So there was never a particular plate that was destined for a particular person?"

Again she frowned, shaking her head. "I wasn't never told." She thought about this. "If you want to know, it was bloody hard work, keeping up with that ruddy lift. Plates came up, piping hot, some of them. Nearly burned me fingers. I think I gave a little yell once. I hope they didn't hear me. I had to get them out, then fill the lift with the dirties, and then the next lot came up."

"So I presume the tarts came up at the end of the meal. That would have been the one time you didn't have a chance to keep an eye on them while you were working upstairs."

"That's right," she said. Then she attempted to sit up. "'Ere. Hang on a minute. That's not bloody right. They came up with the cold stuff at the beginning. I had to put them out on the table on the other side, out of the way."

"So they were up with you throughout the whole meal?"

"Yeah. They were." She had that defensive look now, as if she might be blamed for something.

I tried to phrase the next question carefully. "Queenie, apart from the servers, did anyone come into your little room?"

"Only the funny bloke, Sir Whatsit, the one what owns the house. He just popped in before the meal and asked if everything was ready and his butler could call in the guests." She paused, then smiled. "He looked around, said we'd done a splendid job and everything looked very nice."

So that was that, then. I was no nearer to a solution than when I started. I knew that Queenie wasn't always the most observant girl in the world and if she'd seized a moment to grab a bite or two of leftover food she might not have noticed someone popping into the anteroom, but it would have taken more than a moment to stick random elderberries into tarts. Even she would have noticed.

I gave her hand a little pat. "Thank you. You've been very helpful and I'm sorry you're not feeling well. Just be grateful that you're starting to recover. One poor man was rushed to hospital and has since died."

"Blimey," she said. "My mum always did say I had the luck of the devil."

I left her then. From what she had said there was no time during the preparation of those tarts when they could have been sabotaged. It made no sense at all.

Chapter 21

JULY 26
EYNSLEIGH

Things seem to be going from bad to worse. I wish I'd never agreed to let Pierre cook that blasted dinner.

The sound of lively conversation was coming from the morning room. I entered to see Darcy now sitting with Sir Hubert, Zou Zou, Mr. Robson-Clough and my grandfather. The tray of coffee and biscuits was on the low table. They broke off, looking up expectantly as I entered.

"Well?" Darcy asked. "How is Queenie? Is she any better?"

"She's not any worse," I said. "She says she never wants to eat again, which shows how serious it is, knowing Queenie, but at least she's no longer vomiting."

"Could she shed any light on exactly what happened?" Sir Hubert asked.

"Not at all. It's quite perplexing. She says nobody came into the kitchen, apart from Pierre, Sir Mordred's chef, and the kitchen maid. Queenie was the one who put the berries on the tarts, and she says there were no little black berries among them. She was sure she would have noticed. And the tarts came up in the dumbwaiter to the little serving room, and she was there to receive them and put them out on the tables."

"I'm afraid we have to consider that one of them was the culprit," Sir Hubert said. "We know very little about the new French chef, after all. The French are known for a deep-seated hatred of the English. What did his references say?"

I felt my face turning red. "He didn't come with references. I met him in Paris when he was acting as a waiter at a café I used to visit."

"A waiter in a café?"

"But he told me he was a trained chef who couldn't find a job in Paris. So I thought it might be a good idea to give him a try. One step up from Queenie, anyway."

"My dear girl." Sir Hubert gave me a chastising frown. Then he corrected himself. "As it happens he's turned out to be a fine cook, but in future always check their references. People can tell you anything you want to hear. You might find yourself hiring an escaped murderer."

"Oh, I don't think Pierre is an escaped anything," I said, hastily pouring myself a coffee so he didn't see my red face. "He was very visible and chatty at the café and everyone there liked him." As I said this I was thinking that another person at that café had been friendly and likable and yet had been a murderer. But that had been different. I have come to think that any one of us is capable of killing if we are backed into a corner with no way out. Pierre had no such motive for wanting to kill any of us. And if he had really been intent on killing, he had a whole poison garden at his disposal. He could have dispatched the whole lot of us easily enough. Instead we were only dealing with a few elderberries, known to create an upset stomach but not to kill.

As I sat down with my coffee I sensed Sir Hubert watching me, probably thinking along the same lines. "All the same," he said, "I think I'll get in touch with the French Sûreté and find out if they might have anything on him. He might have been part of some communist agitation group, sent over here to do harm."

"He seemed so horrified to be accused," I said. "And on the way home he was close to tears. He said it would ruin his reputation and blight his career."

"I've met murderers who were great actors," Granddad commented as he put his coffee cup down on the table beside his chair. "They'd look you right in the eye and swear they were innocent. Swear on their mother's grave."

"Of course, you were once in the police force, weren't you?" Zou Zou flashed him her dazzling smile. As with all men, this had an instant effect. Granddad flushed pink. "You must have dealt with some fascinating characters in your time, Albert."

"Well," Granddad said, looking embarrassed but pleased, "I suppose I have met a few, although most crimes in real life are quite simple and sordid. Someone bashes someone else over the head when they've been drinking, or when they want to get their hands on the money. It don't take a genius to figure them out." He paused, enjoying the attention. "Although I will say this: I've noticed most murderers give themselves away at one point. When they think they've tricked you and you're not watching them, you'll spot it on their faces. They'll give a little smile or an excited look that they've fooled you."

"I've noticed that too," I said.

"You should not be having anything to do with murders, my girl," Granddad said. "You get yourself involved when you should stay well away."

"Oh, I don't get myself involved deliberately," I said. "I just seem to be in the wrong place at the wrong time. I don't ask for trouble, I promise you."

I noticed the explorer looking at me with interest. I just hoped he wouldn't start questioning me about murderers I had known.

"It seems as if you had a narrow escape this time, my poor darling," Zou Zou said. "Darcy tells me you might have eaten one of the tarts that caused the sickness."

"I know. Thank heavens I was already feeling a bit sick and I passed mine along to my neighbor."

"So were the people who became ill all sitting next to each other?" my grandfather asked.

I hesitated, picturing the table. "My tart went to my neighbor, Mr. Mallowan. His went to an old lady, Miss Ormorod. And hers, I suppose, was the extra tart that Mr. Halliday ate. It was he who died."

"So it was just one batch of tarts that were tainted." Granddad pressed the point. "All sitting next to each other."

"No, that's not correct, because Sir Mordred became ill and he was sitting at the top of the table, and also Mrs. Bancroft, the colonel's wife. And she was over on the other side of the table, quite far away."

"And I was next to Mrs. Bancroft," the explorer reminded us. "I also became ill."

"Oh, of course," I said, realizing with embarrassment that he was the kind of man one tended to overlook. "I'm so glad you're feeling better."

"As I said, cast-iron stomach, my dear. In the sort of life I've led, you either recover quickly or you're finished. In my case I can't say it was that bad. It could have been put down to too much rich food. I stick to a simple diet usually. There were an awful lot of cream sauces, and crab, and all those different wines. Enough to upset most stomachs."

"That mead at the beginning of the meal. Too sweet, wasn't it? Quite wrong for the palate," Zou Zou said. "I couldn't drink mine."

"I didn't like it much," I agreed. "And I was certainly feeling a bit queasy by the end of the meal, which is why I decided against the dessert."

"So was there a particular order those tarts were served in?" Granddad asked.

"As a matter of fact I was served first, because I was the ranking lady. I think the other footman served Sir Mordred at the same time, but Mrs. Bancroft and Mr. Robson-Clough wouldn't have been given theirs until much later." I paused. "Besides, Queenie insists that there was no particular order in which she took the tarts out of the dumbwaiter and laid them on the table."

"So the whole thing had to have been quite random," Sir Hubert said. "How strange. One almost has to think it was some kind of malicious prank. If the object had been to cause real harm, there was a whole poison garden at their disposal."

"That's exactly what I thought," I said.

"If it was a prank, then by whom? That's the question," Zou Zou said. "And how did they manage it? If nobody could have got anywhere near those tarts except for the kitchen workers . . ."

We lapsed into silence.

"I don't see how it could have been our French chef who did it," Darcy said, staring out of the window as he spoke. "I mean, he was right. It has damaged his reputation. If he wants another job, the rumor will be that he served food that made people sick. And if he had really wanted to poison people, as Hubert says, he had a garden full of lethal plants."

"And if he'd done that, he'd have hightailed it out as quickly as possible back to France, don't you think?" Zou Zou asked.

My head was spinning. We were going around in circles and getting nowhere.

"My own money would be on Sir Mordred's chef, if we had to pick one of them," I said. "He was seriously put out that a new chef had been brought in to cook the meal. He'd have been delighted to make Pierre look bad. But there's only one thing against that. His own employer was served one of the tarts. You'd have thought he'd make sure he didn't kill off his own master."

"Unless the object was, as you said, to make them sick—to make it look like food poisoning," Darcy said. "Sir Mordred's doctor did say it would be unheard of to kill someone with elderberries. He said children eat them all the time and get tummy aches."

"But Mr. Halliday has died," I reminded them.

"We don't know what caused his death yet," Darcy answered. "We do know he had a heart problem and he was overweight. So it's possible his death had nothing to do with eating elderberries. It could have been a fatal heart attack, brought on by overindulgence and too much alcohol, and the excitement of the evening meeting up with an old school chum."

"Although Sir Mordred said they weren't exactly chums at school, didn't he?"

"Absence makes the heart grow fonder," Granddad said with a chuckle.

"And Sir Mordred is rather famous these days," Zou Zou added. "It's remarkable how people are drawn to connect themselves to fame."

"I've noticed that myself," Sir Hubert said. "If I come back from an expedition and there is an article on me in a newspaper, I can guarantee that some buffer at my club will miraculously decide that we're bosom friends when I've hardly said two words to him."

"So what will happen now?" Mr. Robson-Clough asked. "Does Sir Mordred intend to take this further?"

"He was very angry," I said. "At one point he was going to test all the various items we had eaten at dinner in his laboratory. But that was before he discovered the berries in the leftover tarts."

"I think that proves how random the whole thing was," the explorer said, reaching forward to help himself to a second cup of coffee. "Why waste tarts that were laced with the berries when some people at dinner obviously ate tarts without them."

"If he wants to get to the bottom of this, he should insist the police question all the helpers," Granddad said. "Sometimes it takes a man in uniform to make someone break down and confess. Your chef. The old chef who you say has a chip on his shoulder. And what about the kitchen maid? Nobody's mentioned her, but she was there all the time."

"Queenie described her as thick as a plank, and coming from Queenie that has to be pretty dire." I had to smile.

"Sometimes they're not as dumb as they make out," Granddad said. "She could have some kind of personal grievance. Perhaps Sir Mordred was unkind to her. Perhaps he made advances . . ."

"Or it could have been that an act like that gave her a small feeling of power," Zou Zou said. "You know those at the bottom of the heap often feel powerless. That would explain the randomness of the whole thing. She just knew she was going to make some people feel ill. It didn't matter which people."

"That seems the most likely suggestion so far," Sir Hubert said. "Good thinking, my dear."

They exchanged a long look. Oh golly. It was getting serious. I toyed with the idea of the kitchen maid sneaking berries into tarts. It didn't seem likely to me.

"She'd be the type who would break down easily enough under questioning," Darcy said. "Maybe it might be a good idea to bring in the police. Especially now there has been a death."

"It's not up to us," Sir Hubert said. "I think we should leave well alone. It's up to Sir Mordred what he chooses to do."

"If he is going to do anything, he should act quickly," I said. "Most people were only down for the weekend. We should find out if any of the guests saw anything we didn't." I waved a finger as a thought just struck me. "The two men who were servers. We haven't added them to the equation. I definitely think we should check them out. After all, they handled the food, didn't they? One of them might have had a chance to drop the odd elderberry into the tarts as he carried them out."

"Were they not Sir Mordred's house servants?" Zou Zou asked. "They were most attractive young men. I noticed." Of course she would.

"I have a feeling they were his son Edwin's friends, who are fellow students at Oxford. It was his friends who were handing around the canapés, and I believe two of them also served at dinner. Queenie commented that one of them sounded posh."

"Now, one might suspect that students would do that kind of

thing for a lark," the explorer said. "I got up to a lot of silly pranks when I was up at Cambridge."

"I wonder if they are still staying at the house," I said. "We should question them before they go."

"We should not do anything," Sir Hubert said firmly, with the emphasis on the first word. "Especially not you, my dear. You are in a delicate condition and should be conserving your strength for the big day. Don't you agree, Darcy?"

Darcy's eyes caught mine. "I've never yet managed to get my wife to do what she should be doing," he said with a grin.

$\mathcal{C}hapter$ 22

JULY 26

BACK AT BLACKHEART MANOR

**After no suspects and no motive, now it seems there might be too
   many!**

We finished our coffee. Sir Hubert offered to show Mr. Robson-
Clough around the grounds. The morning's storm had now passed
and white puffy clouds were racing in from the west. Zou Zou
declined to accompany them.

"I suppose I should be getting back to London," she said, toying
idly with the scarf she was wearing.

"Do you really have to go?" Sir Hubert asked. "We all enjoy
having you here."

"Sweet of you, dear man, but there are things to be done, you
know. I can't ignore all my other friends, and my little plane starts

to sulk if I don't fly it for a while. And there's my racing stable. I haven't visited my lovely horses in ages . . ."

I understood exactly what she was saying. She was now worried that things might be getting serious with Sir Hubert and she was remembering that she was fond of Darcy's father, who managed her racing stable. She was keeping her options open. Wise woman. I rather suspected she enjoyed being adored by all, not tied to one man. I think I gave a small sigh of relief. I did still have Sir Hubert pegged for my mother one day, if only I could drag her out of Germany.

"But you'll be back," Sir Hubert said.

"Of course I will, silly boy." She reached across and patted his hand. "But I'm the type who likes to be doing things. I'm not good at lounging around." She got up, came over to me, and kissed my cheek. "Bye-bye, my darling. I'll be down again as soon as the baby arrives. You need your rest and space at the moment—time to build your nest."

"Build her nest?" Darcy chuckled. "She's not a duck, you know."

"All animals like to prepare for the birth in their own way," Zou Zou said, giving him a reproving frown. "Will you ask your adorable chauffeur to run me to the station?"

"We'll be happy to do it, won't we, Darcy?" I said before anyone else could answer.

He gave me a questioning look and then said, "Of course we will."

"I'll go up and get my things together," Zou Zou said. "I am all packed, thanks to your lovely little maid. Down in a minute."

"And we'll take that tour of the grounds, I suppose," Sir Hubert said. "Well, good-bye, dear Zou Zou. Don't leave it too long."

"If I did that, you'd be off racing up another bloody mountain," she said. She came over to him, cradled his cheek with her hand, then gave him a gentle kiss, her hand lingering for quite a while. He actually blushed. It was very sweet.

"I suppose you're right," he said. "Like you, I'm not very good at staying put and pottering around. Freddie here has been telling me about Nuristan. Now, there's a place I've never tackled. And such interesting people."

"Nuristan is the one place I've been where I truly believed the people would happily kill me," the explorer commented. "They do not welcome outsiders."

"Then you are absolutely not going there, Hubert," Zou Zou said. "I forbid it. In future you go to nice civilized mountains like the Alps where you can come down and have a fondue and a schnapps."

Darcy and I were chuckling as they left the room.

"So what was that about?" he asked me when we were alone with just my grandfather.

"What?"

"Insisting on driving Zou Zou."

"I thought you and I should go back to Blackheart Manor and have a chat with Edwin and those servers before they all disappear."

"We can hardly go and accuse them of poisoning everybody," Darcy said.

"Just a gentle chat," I said. "Just to feel out the lay of the land."

"No harm in that, I suppose," he agreed. "And I do feel we owe it to Pierre to clear his name. We did get him into this, after all. And he did cook an outstanding dinner."

"You want to be careful, ducks," my grandfather said. "Just remember that someone at that house could be dangerous."

As we waited for Zou Zou in the front hall, Darcy drew close to me. "We have overlooked the fact that one of the guests could be responsible."

"I don't see how." I frowned, considering this. "We were all together having sherry until we were summoned in to dinner, weren't we? And we were all strangers to each other. None of us would have had a reason to harm anyone else."

Darcy nodded. "You're right, but don't we have to ask ourselves what all those people were doing at the dinner?"

"What do you mean?"

"I mean what brought them all? Such an odd bunch. We had the Crumps, rich but common, who clearly came because they wanted to mingle with the aristocracy, and because they could afford it. We have local people like the Mountjoys and the Bancrofts, who were curious to see the house and grounds. We have Mordred's publisher and the actors who were keen to get parts in an upcoming film. The writer and her husband came because he's her publisher too. And we had that poor Halliday chap who just wanted to reconnect with an old schoolmate."

"And the old lady. Don't forget her," I reminded him.

"Oh yes. One tends to overlook her. Why was she there again?"

"I gather she represented the charity to which Sir Mordred was donating the money. South African orphans."

"His time in South Africa must have affected him, then."

"He did say something about that. He felt that the English army had been brutal to the Dutch settlers."

"So he does have a heart after all. I would have thought hosting a fundraising event and donating to orphans seemed quite out of character. He shows no warmth to his own children. He has created this strange otherworldly persona for himself and yet he worries about orphans in a far-off country."

"Perhaps he had to do something as a soldier that has weighed on his conscience ever since. He might have had to kill civilians, parents, and realized that orphaned children had been left behind."

"That is, of course, possible," Darcy said. He looked up as Zou Zou came down the stairs, followed by the dutiful Phipps and my maid, Maisie, their arms both full of suitcases and hatboxes. Zou Zou never traveled light.

"Here I am, darlings. Ready to be borne away from this delightful spot. I shall leave a portion of my heart here, you know."

"You are welcome back whenever you feel like it," I said, accepting the kiss she planted on my cheek.

"I know, and I do love it here. It's just that I'm not good at doing nothing. I should never have been born an aristocrat. I'd have been much better as a doctor or even a shopkeeper."

"You could have been a queen," Darcy pointed out as we headed to the waiting car. "Then you would have had to rule."

"Darling, no, thank you." She shook her head in horror. "I can assure you I've no desire to rule anybody. My poor husband tried to rule our little corner of Poland and what happened to him? Hacked to pieces by angry peasants with communist fervor."

Darcy helped me into the front seat—no easy feat with my current bulk—and we started off.

"Hasn't it been a strange couple of days?" Zou Zou said, leaning forward to chat as we drove away. "That hideously creepy house and the strange dinner and people going down like flies. Do you think there could be a curse on it? He did say it was haunted, didn't he?"

"One has to assume it was an ordinary human person who decided for some reason to upset the apple cart," Darcy said.

"I presume that's what you intend to find out after you've

dropped me off." Zou Zou was always astute. "Otherwise Phipps would have done perfectly well, in spite of the fact that he's not the best driver in the world."

"You are too smart for your own good, Zou Zou." Darcy grinned.

As we unloaded her belongings to a porter at the station, she kissed us both. "Now, you will keep me apprised of everything that happens, won't you? About this strange elderberry matter, I mean. And also the moment you get a twinge of labor pains you're to telephone me. Shall you be having the baby at home? I never asked."

"No, I'm booked into a private nursing home in Haywards Heath," I said. "It's supposed to be very good. My doctor said it's better to play it safe with the first baby."

"Good idea. I hope it's the sort of place where they will pamper you. New mothers deserve to be pampered and not lift a finger for two weeks."

"Oh, I do look forward to being pampered," I said.

"One would think your normal life was working in the fields at sunrise the way you talk," Darcy said as Zou Zou followed her porter onto the platform.

"I know we do live a most privileged life," I said, "but it will be a comfort to be surrounded by nurses who know what they are doing and can teach me how to look after the baby."

We set off for Blackheart Manor. The sky once again threatened the promise of rain. The front gates were open but there were no other vehicles parked outside the house when we arrived. We had to ring the doorbell, and it was finally answered by Ogden, the aged butler.

"I'm afraid the master is indisposed, my lady," he said. "He will not be receiving visitors today."

"It was actually Mr. Edwin we came to see," I said. "Is he available?"

"I believe Master Edwin has gone out," he said.

"Do you happen to know where, or when he might return?" Darcy asked.

"I think he was going to visit his friends, who are staying nearby," the butler said. "You might have noticed there were several young men in attendance yesterday. They were classmates of Master Edwin from his Oxford college."

"They didn't stay here, then?" I asked.

The old butler shook his head. "Sir Mordred is not fond of houseguests. He doesn't usually enjoy entertaining. Last night's banquet was quite a departure from his normal routine."

"Would you happen to know where the young men might be staying?"

He hesitated with that unwillingness butlers have about divulging any information that concerns their family. "Is it an urgent matter, my lady? I am sure Master Edwin will be returning later today."

"It is rather urgent, actually." I wasn't about to tell the butler that we were delving into the mystery of the poisoned tarts. He would not have approved of our interfering in family matters.

"Well, in that case, I believe I heard one of the young men mention that they were staying at the White Hart pub in the next village. Quite a pleasant place, for a public house, in fact I used to visit it myself back in the days when I could get out more."

We thanked him and left. Poor old Ogden, I thought. Servants have to rely on their own feet or at most a bicycle if they want to go anywhere on their days off. And I'm sure it was years since he could ride a bicycle.

$Chapter$ 23

STILL JULY 26

AT THE WHITE HART IN THE VILLAGE OF DITCHLING

Things only seem to get more complicated. Oh dear. I wish I didn't
have these suspicions.

The White Hart was the perfect sort of country pub. I remember
driving past it and thinking that it looked inviting. It was a low,
whitewashed building with baskets of geraniums outside the windows and a lawn beside it that sloped to a stream in which swans
were swimming. As we pulled up I spotted a group of young men
sitting at a picnic table under a willow tree, a pitcher of beer between them.

"Now, be very careful what you say, Georgie," Darcy said as he
helped me from the motorcar. "We don't want to sound as if we're
accusing anyone."

"I understand."

He took my arm as we crossed the grass toward them. One of them was in the middle of a tale and they laughed raucously, breaking off suddenly as they noticed us. First confusion and then recognition. Edwin had been sitting on the far side. He got up and came toward us.

"Lady Georgiana. Mr. O'Mara. What a pleasant surprise. At least I hope it's a pleasant surprise. I've had enough bad news for one day."

"We went to see your father," Darcy said, "but the butler told us he was indisposed and not up to seeing visitors. I hope he hasn't taken a turn for the worse."

Edwin suppressed a smile. "Quite the opposite. The doctor told him that he was right as rain. That he'd eaten something that didn't agree with him and should only eat and drink bland foods for the rest of the day." He paused, now allowing the grin. "My father thrives on drama. He wanted to be told he was at death's door, so he's gone to bed in a huff."

"I'm glad he has recovered," I said. "Was there any more news about the poor chap who died?"

"Not a thing yet," Edwin said. "And I gather your lot are all okay?"

"Most of us came through unscathed," I said. "But you remember Mr. Robson-Clough, the explorer, who was part of our group? He was sick during the night. And our undercook, Queenie, was quite ill. It seems she helped herself to leftover tarts."

"Well, at least that should prove that the cooks were not responsible for what happened, doesn't it?" Edwin said.

"That's what we think," Darcy said.

We noticed the students at the table looking at us with interest.

"Would you introduce us to your friends?" Darcy said, reverting to formality.

"Of course. Chaps, this is Mr. O'Mara and his wife. They were guests last night."

"Of course. We remember," one of them said. He was a serious-looking chap with glasses and a worried expression. He nodded at me. "You didn't want your pudding course."

"Oh, you were the one who served me," I said, realizing with some embarrassment that one does not notice the servers. "I was jolly lucky as it turned out. I believe you gave my tart to the man next to me and he was ill during the night."

"Blimey." He glanced across at Edwin. "I felt quite sick myself this morning when Edwin came over and said a lot of people had been taken ill and it looked as if someone had poisoned the tarts. I mean, Henry and I served those bally tarts. We felt awful."

"It wasn't your fault," Edwin said.

"It certainly wasn't my fault," the other young man, a slim languid-looking type said. "I wouldn't know an elderberry from an apple. I'm strictly a man-about-town."

"Just because you live in Chelsea doesn't make you a man-about-town," another of them said. "You have to earn that epithet." And laughter broke out again, easing the mood.

"So you are all Edwin's friends from Oxford?" Darcy asked. "I'm a Baliol man myself. I read PPE."

A lively interaction followed about the merits of professors and memories of exams and Oxford pubs, leaving me feeling left out and inadequate, as always happened when schools and universities were discussed. My education had been mainly with a governess and left a lot to be desired. Finishing school in Switzerland had taught me how to be presented at court and how to snag a rich husband, but not much more. Oh, and Belinda had taught me how to sneak out at night and how to smoke.

"So how did Edwin manage to rope you in for yesterday's do?" I asked, feeling a trifle impatient as the banter went on.

"Always willing to help out a chum in distress," the chap who had served me said.

"Go on, Smithers. You came because my father offered to pay you," Edwin said.

Smithers laughed. "That too. Funds are rather tight and I have a chance to join a party on a yacht in August if I can find the fare to Cannes."

"You did jolly well," I said, giving him the encouraging smile that I have found works well. "I hardly noticed you at all."

More laughter.

"Well, Smithers is rather forgettable," one of them commented.

"No, seriously. I didn't mean that. I meant that you handled it quite professionally."

"He's had experience. That's why I called on him," Edwin said. "He and Henry."

Smithers gave an embarrassed grin. "Unlike some of you chaps, I was not born with a silver spoon in my mouth. My parents are both teachers. I'm at Oxford on a scholarship. So I've worked at various things during vacations, including as a waiter at a posh club."

"And I act," Henry said. "I had to play a waiter in a farce. I got rather good at juggling plates."

"And the rest of us just came along for a lark," one of the other men said. "Actually we've been dying to see this famous Blackheart Manor after Mortimer's description of it."

"Was there something you needed from me?" Edwin must have realized that we had been chatting for a while.

"We thought your father might need help in getting to the bottom of last night's incident," Darcy said. "We've both had a little experience in investigating, so we thought we'd start with you chaps. As outsiders and servers you'd presumably have noticed a lot."

Their faces were now earnest.

"I can't say we noticed anything, did we, chaps?" Smithers said. "We discussed it earlier when Edwin came over and told us. I mean, Henry and I handed out those tarts."

"You two had to go in and out of the serving room," I said. "You didn't see anyone else go in at any time?"

"Only the serving girl who was there," Henry said. "Big beefy girl. Tried to flirt with both of us."

"And nobody told you which order to serve those tarts?"

Smithers frowned. "I was told to serve you first, as you were the first ranking lady. And Henry was told to serve Edwin's dad."

"But you just took tarts from the table in any order?"

Smithers frowned. "Yes. I picked up four plates from the table, came out with them, offered one to you, then to the next chap, an old lady, and the big fat man said he'd have two." He paused, his mouth open. "Oh crikey. He wasn't the one who died, was he?"

"He was," Darcy said.

"How awful. I feel terrible."

"It wasn't your fault, old chap," another of the men said. "How could you have known?"

"What I don't understand is why," a red-haired boy whose face was covered in freckles spoke up. "I mean what was the purpose? If you wanted to actually harm somebody, you could never arrange for that person to get one of the tainted puddings."

"Darcy and I wondered if it started out as a prank," I said, realizing I was taking a risk.

I saw this register in their faces.

"So that's why you came here," Edwin said. "You thought that maybe one or more of my friends might have decided to lace the tarts with elderberries."

"It was one of the only things that made sense," Darcy said. "Give a few people an upset stomach. Isn't it the sort of thing college students might do?"

"It seems a bit mean-spirited," the redhead said. "We're not above pranks. I've been known to knock off a policeman's helmet or play the odd trick, but putting something poisonous in food—that's different. As we now know, eating two of those tarts has proved fatal for one bloke."

"We don't know if it was the tarts that killed him," Darcy said. "His death could have been quite coincidental. He did eat and drink an awful lot and he said something about the doctor warning him about his heart."

"In any case, none of us would have considered a prank like that," the redhead insisted.

"I'm sorry to have troubled you," Darcy said. "Enjoy the sunshine. And give my regards to Oxford."

"I'll walk you back to your car," Edwin said.

We set off across the lawn, Edwin walking between us. At first we walked in awkward silence, hearing the banter of his friends dying away. I remembered what Darcy had said about treading carefully, but I decided to go ahead anyway.

"Edwin, you don't think any of your friends really did plan this as a little prank, do you? Of course they'd not want to admit to it now, after someone has died, but . . ." I left the end of the sentence open and turned to look at him.

He glanced back at the table. The young men were laughing again.

"I don't see how," he said. "I mean, they were involved with setting up the tables and handing around canapés before we went inside. They wouldn't have had a chance to pick any elderberries. And to think they might have come with elderberries in their pockets—that goes too far, surely. They couldn't possibly have known that we would have had those fruit tarts on the menu."

That, of course, was true. They would have had no idea what was being served. The only people to know in advance were Sir Mordred, Edwin, Pierre, and myself. And the rest of the kitchen staff once they were being prepared.

"Besides," Edwin said, "why would anybody want to make other people sick? None of them even knew my family or any of the guests. It could have been a lot of frail and elderly people who would have been seriously ill."

"The old lady Miss Ormorod was among those who were taken ill," I said. "I hope she's recovered by now. Perhaps you should telephone her when you get home."

As we reached our motorcar I held out my hand to say good-bye and I saw something on Edwin's face. A thought. A realization. "There is one thing I hadn't considered before," he said.

"Henry's father is an author. Not a very successful one. Like me he is kept horribly short of cash and has had to take all sorts of odd jobs to pay his way. Could it be possible that he was jealous of my father and his success? He would have had a better chance than anybody at interfering with those tarts, wouldn't he?"

"And he served your father first," Darcy said.

"But he didn't serve any of us on my side of the table." I looked up at Darcy. "How could he have had a chance to put berries into our tarts without his companion or Queenie noticing?"

"It's quite perplexing." Edwin sighed. "My father is still furious.

The moment he feels better he's going up to his laboratory to make sure none of the other items were poisoned. And he's still convinced it was your chef who did it."

"I'd say it was more likely that it was his chef," I said. "He's an older man, obviously felt slighted. Replaced by a foreigner, maybe worried that he'd be replaced permanently and he'd be out in the cold. You know how busy kitchens are before a big meal. It might not have been too hard to have walked past the table and casually inserted a few berries here and there, knowing that Pierre would get the blame."

"You could be right," Edwin said. "But how does one prove it or get a person to confess? He won't have left fingerprints on a berry tart."

"Maybe the kitchen maid might have noticed but not realized it," I said. "Apparently she didn't do too much work but stood around, according to Queenie."

"I'll try and have a word with her, then," Edwin said. "Although I don't think I'm cut out to be a sleuth. I have the sort of face that gives what I'm thinking away."

Darcy opened the car door for me and helped me in.

"Do let us know if there are any developments, won't you?" he said to Edwin. "And give our best wishes to your father. Thank him for a splendid time last night."

Edwin gave a sad little smile. "I feel rather sorry for the poor chap," he said. "I never thought I'd say that. I normally have as many tender feelings toward him as he has toward me. But this has spoiled his big moment. All those people visiting his estate during the day and fawning over him, wanting their photographs taken with him, and then his big elegant banquet at night. And now this happens. If it gets into the newspapers it's publicity of the worst sort."

Darcy closed my door and came around to the driver's side. We set off.

"One thing we haven't considered," he said, staring straight ahead as we navigated the little lane, "is Edwin himself. He has shown he has little love for his father. He's not made welcome at home. He's kept short of money, when his mother has apparently left him a fortune. He would have had an opportunity to pick elderberries and put them into some of the tarts. As long as other people fell ill, as well as his father."

"The only argument against that is that the tarts were apparently served in a random order," I said.

Darcy glanced at me with an excited look on his face. "He was in it with his friends. He could have persuaded his father to hire them, to let Henry and Smithers serve the food, and indicated which tart they should take first."

"But what was his motive? Did he want to kill his father and get his hands on his inheritance, or did he simply want to punish his father and make him suffer? Because if it was the former, why use elderberries when he had a whole poison garden at his disposal?"

"I can't answer that one," Darcy said.

"And another worrying thought," I said. "You just surmised that he indicated which tarts the boys should serve first. I was the one whom Smithers served first. That means he actually wanted to harm me."

$\mathscr{C}$hapter 24

JULY 26

BACK AT EYNSLEIGH AND THEN AT BLACKHEART MANOR

I wish we had never attended that horrid banquet. I am supposed to
   be resting and thinking good thoughts before the baby arrives,
   but here I am a mass of worry! Surely nothing more can go
   wrong?

We arrived home to find a late cold luncheon had been left out for
us. I didn't feel like eating much. My stomach was still in knots
from the stresses of the day and the nagging thought that somebody
might have tried to poison me. I couldn't think of any reason for
this. I knew nobody at the dinner. And if anyone there was an anti-
royalist, there were thirty-four people closer to the throne than me.
As this thought passed through my mind I remembered that Pierre
was an anti-royalist. But then he could poison me in my own household any day he felt like it. Not a comforting thought!

While I was spreading piccalilli on my ham Mrs. Holbrook came in.

"A letter arrived for you by the midday post, my lady." She handed it to me. I looked at the crest on the envelope. The Rannoch crest of crossed claymores and a stag rampant. "Oh, it's from my brother. How nice."

I opened it and started to read. Darcy saw my face.

"Not bad news, is it?"

"The worst," I said. "It couldn't be any worse than this. It's from Fig, not Binky. Listen."

And I started to read:

My dear Sister-in-law,

We send you fond greetings from Scotland where the weather has been bracing for the time of year. You have been much in our thoughts at this time as you await the arrival of your child. The birth of a first baby is a life-changing experience, Georgiana, to say nothing of the importance of another member in the line of succession to the throne, albeit only thirty-sixth.

We discussed it and felt that it was a time when families should show solidarity and stick together. You'll need an experienced mother beside you at your hour of need—your own mother being sadly lacking in maternal skills. With that in mind we have decided to make the sacrifice and come down south in time for the birth, which we gather should now be getting close.

By the time you receive this letter we shall be on the train, coming south. Binky has an appointment with his foot specialist in Harley Street so we shall be staying at Claridge's for a couple of nights (no sense in opening up the London house for such a brief visit) and then we'll head straight down to Eynsleigh.

We shall not be bringing the children as they benefit so much from the fresh air and outdoor activities in Scotland. Podge is riding his pony so well now and Addy is also showing interest in learning to ride. We'll have to acquire a second pony if we can stretch the budget.

So it will be just Binky and myself. I realize he will be absolutely useless when it comes to babies but he and Darcy can have a good old chin-wag together while I provide you with the support you need. Expect us in a few days. We'll telephone from London for you to send the motorcar.

Fondly, your loving sister-in-law, Hilda, Duchess of Rannoch

I gave Darcy a despairing look. "Golly. Not Fig. It will be awful, Darcy. What are we going to do?"

"Send them a telegram and tell them not to come."

"From what she says they are already on the train."

"Then telephone Claridge's tomorrow. Tell her it isn't convenient. You're so weak and frail that you couldn't handle extra visitors at this time. Say the doctor has forbidden you to get excited and her visit would excite you too much. Say we all have the measles."

I shook my head. "It would be no use. She wouldn't listen. You know Fig. Once she's made up her mind she won't give up. Oh, Darcy, how awful. When I'm lying there giving birth the last thing I want is Fig telling me how much more it's going to hurt in an hour or so and how much agony she was in for days."

Darcy had to laugh. "I'm sorry, old thing," he said. "I know it's not funny. At least you will be in the nursing home for the actual birth and we can have them forbid visitors."

"Maybe I can check in a few days early," I said. "I'll claim to have twinges of labor pains and need to be under medical supervision."

"What, and leave me alone here to entertain her?"

"You'd have to be at the nursing home to hold my hand."

"You're right. We'd leave Hubert and your grandfather to entertain her."

"Poor things. What have they ever done to offend you? But we could summon Zou Zou down again. If anyone can keep Fig in her place it's Zou Zou. After all, she knows that a princess trumps a mere duchess, and a worldly, stunningly beautiful princess at that."

"Poor Zou Zou," Darcy said. "But don't worry. We'll manage somehow. It is a big house, after all."

I looked down at my plate of half-eaten lunch and decided that I wasn't hungry anymore. The rest of the day passed in a cloud of gloom. A day ago I had felt lively and excited, looking forward to a banquet and then the arrival of my baby. Now my chef was a suspect in doctoring fruit tarts and my dreaded sister-in-law, she who could never say a kind or positive word, was arriving to make my life miserable. I tried to think of a good reason that they should not come. Darcy's suggestion of measles seemed ever more promising. But then she'd be concerned that measles would affect the baby and probably send down specialists from Harley Street to take care of me.

Dinner was a quiet affair. Sir Hubert was clearly already missing Zou Zou. The explorer tried keeping the conversation lively with recounts of his exploits. Since most of these involved something dangerous and disgusting like having to eat grasshoppers or someone having a toe cut off, they did not serve to lighten the mood. When I told Granddad about Fig I saw his expression change.

"I should go home, then, ducks," he said.

"Why?"

"That sister-in-law of yours wouldn't want me here. She always acts as if I'm stepping out of line, don't know my place and I should be back in the servants' quarters."

"But you're my grandfather and this is my house," I said. "If she's rude to you, I'll speak up." I took his hand. "I want you here, Granddad. I want you to see your great-grandchild. Please don't go."

His expression softened. "Well, for you, my love, I'd put up with a lot. And I won't mind if that explorer friend of Sir Hubert's is staying on. He's an interesting cove, isn't he? Lots of good stories. And he seems interested in my stories too. Not that I've had any earth-shattering crimes to solve, but I have had my fair share of excitement at the Met."

"Well, there you are, then," I said. "You two old gentlemen can amuse each other and stay well clear of Fig."

I went to bed trying to shake off the feeling of impending doom and did not sleep well. It was a hot and sticky night and I found it hard to get comfortable in the first place. I lay there, aware of every little night noise—the hoot of an owl, the bark of a fox—and prayed for daylight to come. At first light I got up, dressed, and took the dogs out for an early walk. They thought this was a splendid idea, bounding over the dewy grass, chasing rabbits, and generally having a great time. I watched them with envy, thinking how nice it would be to be a dog, with only thoughts of food and fun, none of the worries of our lives. But I came back in a much better mood and requested a large breakfast.

Darcy and Sir Hubert joined me at the breakfast table. Darcy examined the morning post. "I should go up to London sometime this week," he said. He saw my warning frown. "But of course I'd want to be here when your brother and his wife arrive."

"I wonder if they've made any progress on who put the wrong berries in the tarts," Sir Hubert said. "I doubt it. I suppose we'll just have to put it aside as a practical joke that went wrong."

He had barely finished speaking when I heard the front doorbell ring. We sat, waiting expectantly. Nothing happened.

"Maybe a delivery," Sir Hubert said. "Brought to the front door by mistake."

We went back to spreading marmalade on toast. Then there were footsteps coming toward the dining room. Mrs. Holbrook entered, an expression of alarm on her face. "Sorry to trouble you, sir, my lady," she said, "but a policeman is here. He's come to take Pierre. I thought you should know."

"What the devil . . ." Darcy and Sir Hubert had both risen to their feet. Darcy was already heading to the door with Sir Hubert in hot pursuit. I got up and followed too. There was a commotion in the front hall. Pierre was in handcuffs, being led out by a young bobby. An older policeman was standing nearby.

"What is the meaning of this?" Sir Hubert demanded.

"Sorry to inconvenience you, sir, but we have orders to arrest this man on suspicion of murder," the older one said.

"Murder?" I said. "A few elderberries? The doctor said it would take an awful lot of them to make someone seriously ill. Surely the chap that died had a weak heart."

The police constable looked embarrassed and cleared his throat. "We were not given any details of the case. Only told to bring in this French chappie. And there is also a request that you accompany us to Sir Mordred's house, where the inspector wishes to question all those present that night."

"Very well," Sir Hubert said. "We will most certainly come. We want to ensure that our employee is treated properly, since his knowledge of the English language is limited." He looked back to where our housekeeper lingered by the stairs. "Mrs. Holbrook, have Phipps bring the motorcar around. Darcy, you can drive. We will follow you, Officer."

A short time later we were following a police motorcar through the leafy lanes. Fortunately he wasn't ringing the bell or driving more than twenty-five miles an hour.

"I'm sure this will all be sorted out," Sir Hubert said, giving my hand a pat. "Clearly that Mortimer chap has seized upon Pierre because he's foreign, but there would be no way to prove any wrongdoing unless someone actually saw him putting poisonous berries into the tarts."

"I wouldn't put it past Sir Mordred's elderly chef to claim that he saw something," I said. "He was clearly put out by having Pierre in his kitchen."

"And the realization that he might be given the boot in favor of Pierre," Darcy said.

"They must have found out something more, to make the police spring into action like this," Sir Hubert said. "Yesterday it was all vague and supposition. Perhaps they have now done an autopsy on the chap who died and it has revealed something other than a heart attack."

"Oh golly." I felt sick.

There were several motorcars outside Blackheart Manor and another police constable standing at the door. It struck me that we hadn't asked who had died. We'd assumed we were talking about

Mr. Halliday, but what if it was Sir Mordred himself? What if his son . . . I switched off those thoughts. They were too horrible to contemplate.

As we got out of the motorcar Pierre was being extricated from the police vehicle, still protesting loudly in French. I heard the words "stupid English" and "French ambassador."

The policeman at the door stopped us from following them.

"Sir Hubert Anstruther," he said in the calm, authoritarian voice that aristocrats use in case of emergency. "That is my chef you have arrested and I want to make sure he has a fair hearing. This is Lady Georgiana Rannoch and her husband, Mr. O'Mara. They were also present at the banquet."

"Oh, right you are, sir." The policeman gave a half salute. "Go on in, then, sir. The inspector is in the big room off to the left."

We entered the gloom of the front hall. The suit of armor with the axe stood there, menacing as ever, although it hadn't moved. Off to our left we heard voices, then Pierre's voice, raised in protest. Before we could enter, Sir Mordred's daughter and her husband came down the stairs.

"What on earth is going on now?" she demanded. "Is there never to be a minute's peace in this house? We really need to go home, Stanley darling. This tension isn't good for your health, or my nerves, for that matter."

"But I thought . . ." he began. "Well, all right. I suppose . . ." He didn't finish that sentence either. I hadn't heard him speak before. His voice had a definite working-class tinge to it. No wonder Sir Mordred, with his ultraposh accent, had objected to the match.

The policeman who had been standing at the door stepped forward. "I'm sorry, madame, but nobody is to leave. Inspector's orders."

"How dare you!" Sylvia, in contrast to her husband, now

sounded at her most upper-class. I've found that my class of person does revert to poshness when we are dealing with annoying authority. "Do you know who I am? This is my father's house. I can come and go as I please."

"Not right now you can't, missus," he said. "This is now a murder investigation."

"Murder? But I thought . . . I know people became ill, but murder? Are you sure? Who was murdered?"

"I'm afraid I'm not privy to details, missus. I was just told nobody was to leave."

"At least we can go for a walk in the grounds, I presume," she said, glaring at the policeman now. "We're not likely to run away and leave all our belongings here."

"You'd better stay put for the moment," the constable said, his jaw firmly set, although he looked a little uncomfortable. "The inspector will want to question you."

"About what?"

"He'd have to tell you himself, madame. I'm just doing my job and guarding the entrance."

"Really, this is too much," Sylvia said. "Treated like prisoners in our own house. Bossed around by uppity policemen. Come on, Stanley. Let's go back upstairs. They can send someone to find us if they need us."

I watched her stomp back upstairs, every step displaying her indignation. Sylvia had an axe to grind, I thought. She and her husband were living in poverty because she couldn't get her hands on her inheritance until she was twenty-five, and her father despised her husband and wasn't willing to help her. Maybe she wanted to get some revenge in a petty way, such as making people ill at his dinner party.

"You should go in now, if you don't mind." The policeman interrupted my train of thought. We entered the gallery through open double doors. In spite of the sunny day the long oak-paneled room still felt chilly and decidedly gloomy. Various people were sitting on scattered sofas and chairs. Pierre, still held by a police constable, was standing in front of a youngish man nattily dressed in a blazer and flannels. He looked as if he could have come straight from a cricket club or even an entertainment on the pier somewhere. Certainly not like your average policeman.

"I am not understanding," Pierre was saying, waving his hands in dramatic fashion. "Not speaking good the Eeenglish."

I hurried forward. "Let me translate for him," I said.

"And you are?" the man gave me a cold stare. I suspect it was meant to be intimidating.

"Lady Georgiana O'Mara," I said. "This man is our chef. We lent him to Sir Mordred for the occasion of the banquet." I heard my own voice and realized I was doing exactly what Sylvia had done—reverting to extreme poshness.

"Right," the man said. "I am Inspector Sturgeon, newly transferred to this area from Scotland Yard, where I have undergone the most up-to-date training in detection methods. So I hope to have the matter swiftly sorted out if you'll all cooperate."

I examined him. He was standing a few feet from me, not much taller than I was and slight in build. His fairish hair was parted in the middle and slicked down. His face pale and colorless. He had bulging eyes and a bristling fair mustache. Sturgeon was a fish, wasn't it? He did have a fishlike quality to his stare, but the mustache made him look more like a walrus.

"This is Sir Hubert Anstruther, who owns Eynsleigh, the house where we now live about five miles from here," I said, gesturing to him, "and my husband, the honorable Darcy O'Mara."

"You were all present at the banquet?"

"Yes. We were."

The inspector looked around the room. "So are all your guests now here, Sir Mordred?"

I followed the inspector's gaze and saw the Mountjoys on one sofa, Colonel and Mrs. Bancroft, both looking extremely annoyed, and on another sofa Edwin and Sir Mordred."

"No, at least half of them are still missing," Sir Mordred said in his clipped tones. "I believe we were just over twenty at final count, weren't we, Edwin?"

"Princess Zamanska was my guest," Sir Hubert said. "She has gone home but I can report that she was with me the whole time, as was the world-renowned explorer Mr. Robson-Clough."

"My publisher brought a party of people with him, all of them most distinguished," Sir Mordred said. "A writer, an archeologist, a couple of film stars. Then there was an industrialist from the north of England—quite out of his depth in society like this, I fear. They will probably have gone back up north. I can give you contact information for all of them, although I doubt that any of them would have been interested in killing a local farmer, having never met him before."

"None of us had met him before," Mrs. Bancroft said. "That's the point."

"Wasting everyone's time, that's what you're doing." Colonel Bancroft spat out the words. "Exceeding your authority. You do realize, young man, that most of us are on friendly terms with the chief constable of this county, don't you?"

"I'm sorry if I'm inconveniencing you," Inspector Sturgeon said, "but I want to sort this thing out as quickly as possible and it makes sense to bring everyone back to the scene of the crime so that your memory might be triggered to something you noticed. I've found that people don't realize they may have seen something of importance, until they have to re-create the experience. It might be something quite trivial, like a person handing another person a dish in a strange way."

"If it was indeed this chef who was responsible for adding poisoned berries, then none of us would have witnessed it," Lord Mountjoy said quietly from the sofa. "He remained in the kitchen, I presume. Chefs usually do."

Pierre let out another outburst in French. He seemed to have understood something of what had been said.

"My chef says that he personally picked all the berries freshly from the kitchen garden and there were no elderberries among them. He says nobody was near the tarts except for my assistant cook, who was actually assigned to put the berries on them."

"Then why is this assistant cook not here too?" the inspector asked. "He or she should be questioned."

"She is our assistant cook, at Eynsleigh," I said. "And at this moment she is lying in bed, having been very ill as a result of eating one of the tarts. So she is hardly likely to have poisoned herself, is she?"

"I suppose not." The inspector was frowning. "Have you spoken with her about what she might have observed?"

"I have," I said. "And she can throw no light on this at all, except that nobody from the outside came into the kitchen all day."

"So there we have it," the inspector said. "It all comes back to you, monsieur." (He pronounced it as written—"mon-sewer.") "Sir Mordred mentioned to me that you are a communist. That you despise the upper classes, so why take a job at their house to start with?"

I translated.

Pierre gave a Gallic shrug and rattled off a reply.

"He says he might be a communist at heart but he is also proud of his chosen profession. He had been unable to find a job as a chef in Paris and when I offered him a position at Eynsleigh it seemed like a chance to add to his résumé and make a name for himself in society. He was sure I would have connections that could help him. He says his political leanings have nothing to do with his cooking."

There was a long pause. Then the inspector strolled nonchalantly over to the fireplace and rested an arm on the mantelpiece. If he had had a pipe or a cigarette in a long holder he would have fitted well into a drawing room comedy. "You met this man in Paris?" he asked.

"I did. I met him with friends at a café there. He was well liked by them and I needed a chef so I offered him a position. He has proved to be an excellent cook. We are well satisfied."

Another long pause. "I've dealt with communists before," the inspector said. "And I've found they are all passionate about the cause. They all want the destruction of our way of life, equality for the masses and down with the rich. So I think this man seized his chance to further the communist ideals. He'd come here and one by one he'd bump off members of the upper classes. When he was asked to cook for this banquet it was handed to him on a plate, so to speak." He started pacing the room. "I see it all now. He's a communist. You are all rich. So it doesn't matter which one of you he kills."

"I keel nobody!" Pierre gave me a desperate glance. "I am chef, not keeler."

"Excuse me, Inspector," I interrupted. "But are we sure we are dealing with murder? We have established that somebody put elderberries into the tarts that were served, but the doctor tells us you'd have to eat an awful lot of elderberries to do real damage and there only seemed to be one or two in the tarts we examined."

The inspector turned those bulging eyes onto me.

"The man who died was carrying a good deal of weight and ate and drank a lot," I went on. "Is it not possible that too much alcohol and rich food caused a heart attack?"

"For your information, young lady," he said, "the cause of death was not elderberries. The autopsy found atropine in his system, enough to cause tachycardia, coma and death."

"Atropine?" Sir Hubert asked.

"Atropine. Belladonna. Tropane alkaloids, sir. We think he was fed deadly nightshade."

"Good God!" came from the colonel.

At that moment the door opened and Mr. Mallowan and his wife entered.

Chapter 25

JULY 27

AT BLACKHEART MANOR

Oh no. The inspector is convinced he can pin it on Pierre. Gosh,
I hope he didn't do it. I really like him. And he's a wonderful
cook.

"Sorry we're late," Mr. Mallowan said. "We received a phone call
from Phillip Grossman telling us the police were now investigating
what appeared to be a murder and wanted to speak with all of us.
He's on his way down from London. Agatha wasn't sure I was well
enough to travel, but I thought it was important to be here if we're
now dealing with something serious." He crossed the room and
held out his hand to the inspector. "Max Mallowan," he said. "My
wife, Agatha. You may know her as the writer Agatha Christie."

From the change in the inspector's face he had clearly heard of her. Maybe he read her books. Maybe his new methods were based on Hercule Poirot's detection.

"You were also guests, I take it?" he asked. "And you also became ill after the banquet?"

"Quite unpleasantly so," Mr. Mallowan said. "Am I to understand it was elderberries? I'm surprised. I'm sure I tried a few when I was a child without dire consequences."

"I'm afraid it now appears it was more serious than a few elderberries, Mr. Mallowan," the inspector said. "Do take a seat. We've just started to piece things together."

"More serious than elderberries?" Agatha asked, her sharp gaze fixed on the inspector as she sat. "We were fed something more lethal in those tarts?"

"Deadly nightshade, it would appear," the inspector said.

"So we are dealing with murder, then," she said. She gave a serious little nod.

There was a moment's absolute quiet in the room as everyone digested this.

"You think we ate tarts with deadly nightshade berries in them?" Agatha asked. Then she shook her head. "No, that couldn't be right. Max's symptoms were not at all those of atropine poisoning."

"You'd know the difference, would you?" the inspector said with a smirk in his voice.

"Oh yes." Agatha regarded him coolly. "I used to work in a hospital laboratory during the war. I've dispensed atropine many times. I am quite aware of its properties and its side effects. No, Max had a classic upset stomach. There was none of the confusion, the delirium or hallucinations."

Sir Mordred had risen to his feet. "It's just dawned on me. Deadly nightshade, atropine, did you say? That's another kettle of fish altogether. The elderberries might be considered a prank, but just one or two berries containing belladonna could well be fatal." He paused, put a hand to his brow in dramatic fashion. "I wonder if there was a deadly nightshade berry in my tart, then? I certainly felt most queer that night."

"I take it your poison garden does contain deadly nightshade, Sir Mordred?" Inspector Sturgeon asked.

"Of course it does. One of the most noxious of plants. But—"

He was not allowed to continue. "Aha!" The inspector waved a hand at him, as if proving a point. "I thought as much. And I am told that the berry of the deadly nightshade has a pleasant and sweet taste to it. So how easy to slip a couple of berries into a berry tart. Nobody would notice, would they?"

"What a dastardly thing to do," Colonel Bancroft said.

"I agree," Lady Mountjoy said. "Who would do such a thing?"

"Quite right, Lady Mountjoy. So the question is, then," Inspector Sturgeon said, bringing out the words with great emphasis, "who would have wanted to harm guests at your table? And more importantly, why? If this man professes his innocence, then who else could it be?"

I considered mentioning the elderly chef but instead I said, "I presume your men will question the rest of the kitchen staff, Inspector."

"Most definitely," he said. "There were other people in the kitchen, then, besides this man and his assistant from your house?"

"Sir Mordred's own chef was there, as was his kitchen maid."

Inspector Sturgeon pulled a notebook from his pocket. "Chef. Kitchen maid," he said. "Go and get statements from them right away, Johnson."

"Very good, sir." I noticed then that another plainclothes policeman was standing over by the far wall. An older, unassuming chap, the sort that gets passed over for promotion.

"And have this man taken downstairs to the kitchen too," he said. "I shall want to go through with him where he was minute by minute and what the others saw."

"Come along, then, you." Johnson took Pierre by the arm.

"Where are they taking me?" Pierre asked in French.

"Only down to the kitchen so you can show them what you did as you prepared for the banquet," I said. "Don't worry. I'll come down to translate for you when the inspector is ready to speak to you."

Pierre flashed me a frightened glance. I think it was that more than anything that made me decide he was not the killer. Murderers, in my experience, tend to be more cocky and defiant. He looked genuinely terrified. We sat in silence as they crossed the room and their footsteps died away.

Inspector Sturgeon now stood, surveying us. "Now, let's recap where we've got so far. The guests arrived. They were served canapés on the terrace. None of them went into the house. Correct?"

"Correct," Sir Mordred said.

"Then you offered them a tour of the grounds, including the poison garden. Did they all come?"

Sir Mordred looked to Edwin for confirmation.

"I believe so," Edwin said. "You'd have to check with my friends who were handing out the canapés. They'd know if anyone stayed behind."

"And where would I find these friends?"

"They were staying at the White Hart in Ditchling for the event," Edwin said, "but they will have gone home by now. I can give you their addresses."

"And why did nobody question them before they went?" The inspector glared at the policeman still standing at the door.

"We didn't know it was a crime scene, sir," the policeman said. "Nobody contacted us before this morning."

"I can't see where this is leading," Sir Mordred said. "The young men who helped out were my son's friends from Oxford. From the best of families."

"I was not insinuating that they were responsible for the crime but that they might have witnessed something important."

"I did question them yesterday," I said. "But I don't think any of them saw anything out of the ordinary."

The inspector frowned at me. "You spoke to them? Questioned them? For what reason?"

"Inspector, my chef was accused of poisoning people. I wanted to help in any way I could, and since these students had handed around the food it made sense to speak with them."

"I do wish you amateurs would leave the questioning to the professionals," the inspector said in a petulant tone. "You only do more harm than good. You might have tipped off a murderer that we were on to him, and thus given him time to make up a good alibi."

"I'm sorry, but at that time we thought that the elderberries might have been a prank, and who more likely to pull such a stunt than a group of university students?"

He nodded. "You do have something there," he admitted grudgingly. "So did you actually find out anything of worth?"

"I did establish that the tarts were served in a random order."

"Which would again indicate that the perpetrator did not care who he killed," the inspector said. "That all points back to your communist chef, Lady Georgiana. We'll see whether he changes his tune when I get him alone down at the police station and I use the latest police methods of psychology on him. I find they usually break down and confess in the end."

Oh golly, I thought.

"I hope you'll allow an interpreter in the room, Inspector," I said. "I will willingly offer my services if you don't wish to bring in a professional."

"Gracious of you," he said offhandedly. "But let's just get back to the matter in hand, shall we? If Lady Georgiana thinks her chef is innocent, then who else could it be?"

"We can rule out any of my guests," Sir Mordred said indignantly. "They were all the most respectable of people. Most of them did not even know each other."

Inspector Sturgeon frowned. "May one ask why you had assembled such a varied bunch who didn't know each other? Is that normal when aristocrats give dinner parties?"

Sir Mordred gave a patronizing smile. "I had an open house for the public, Inspector. For charity, you know. Everyone has been dying to see the place where I live and write my novels, so it seemed like a good idea. And then a few weeks ago I had dinner with these charming people"—he gestured in our direction—"and their chef cooked such a magnificent meal that I had a brilliant idea. We'd finish the day with a banquet, medieval-style, in the banquet room. All the trimmings. And charge a pretty penny—again for my charity. So I put out an advertisement and various people answered."

"They paid to come? They were not actually guests, per se?" The inspector sounded close to a sneer now. "It was a moneymaking business, was it?"

"For my charity, Inspector. The whole thing was done for my charity. South African orphans."

I looked around the room and a thought struck me: half of the people had been guests of Sir Mordred or his publisher. He wouldn't have made as much money as he hoped. Did that matter? I looked across the room and caught Agatha Christie frowning as she stared at Sir Mordred. Maybe she was thinking along the same lines.

"And you say most of these people were strangers? Not known to you?"

"I'd say it was about half and half, wouldn't you, Edwin?"

"Most of them had had some connection with my father." Edwin addressed the inspector directly. "He had met some of them before, at a dinner party given by Lady Georgiana. I believe it was only the actors, the Mallowans, and the couple from the North who were complete strangers to us. And one could hardly imagine any of those coming with murder in their hearts."

"The man who has died, Mr. Halliday, wasn't he a complete stranger?"

"He was," Sir Mordred said. "That is to say, I had not seen him for the past thirty-plus years. He was in my house at school and even then he wasn't a particular friend. He came to the dinner because he lived nearby. He had seen an article on me in the *Times*, mentioning that I had been to Harrow. He wanted to check whether I was the same Mortimer who was in his house."

"And were you?"

"I was."

"An old school chum, then. But you'd lost touch over the years?"

"We were never great friends. One doesn't keep in touch."

"Then why look you up now?"

Sir Mordred grinned. "When you are famous, as I am, you find that all sorts of people suddenly remember being your bosom friend. But to give the old boy his due, perhaps he had reached an age when nostalgia makes us want to reconnect with our pasts."

"Were you pleased to see him? To reconnect with your past?" Inspector Sturgeon asked.

"God no!" Sir Mordred said emphatically. "I had a miserable time at school. Couldn't wait to leave and certainly not anxious to meet up with fellow Harrovians. I hardly spoke to the man. We exchanged a few pleasantries about school life in the way that one does."

"Did he appear to know anybody else at the party?"

Sir Mordred appealed to us, then shook his head. "I don't believe so."

"His wife was with him," Darcy pointed out. "Has anybody spoken to her?"

"Only briefly," the inspector said. "The poor woman is still in a state of shock."

I looked around the room and caught Agatha Christie staring intently at the inspector. Was she thinking, as I was, that a dinner party among strangers would be a good way to get rid of an unwanted husband?

Chapter 26

I'm very concerned for Pierre, as I think the inspector is discounting
the rest of us. But what a stroke of luck to have Agatha Christie
here. It seems we might have several suspects . . .

"Right." Inspector Sturgeon now walked over to the window and
turned to face us, his face now in shadow. "Let's get the order of the
evening clear. The guests arrive. They eat canapés. Drink champagne." His face showed what he thought of this. "They go on a
tour of the grounds, including the poison garden, in two separate
groups. So in fact everyone in this room would have had the opportunity to pick a deadly nightshade berry. You linger behind the rest
of the group, pretend to be examining a plant, and when nobody is
watching you grab a couple of berries."

"I don't think so, Inspector," Sir Mordred said. "I was leading my group and Edwin was leading his. We kept turning back to explain things. It would have been extremely risky to try to pick a berry."

"Murderers enjoy taking risks, in my experience," the inspector said, "but I am not for a moment hinting that one of you did pick the poison berry. I'm just clarifying for myself the way things went so that I'm absolutely sure nobody else but the chef could have pulled this off."

He looked around at us, rather pleased with himself now. "Only one man had time and opportunity to pick berries when nobody was watching, and that was Mon-sewer Pierre."

"Or anybody else who worked in the kitchen here, I presume," I added.

"Yes, but . . ." He didn't finish the sentence, dismissing it. "So to sum up—we have a group of people who have almost no connections pay to come to a dinner party at which several fall ill and one dies. Unless there is a madman among you, that can only mean one thing—someone in that kitchen placed poison berries in the tarts, not caring who ate them. Am I right?"

"It does appear that way," Sir Mordred said.

I felt sick. I knew I had to do something to help Pierre, but I wasn't sure what.

"Let's go on and work our way through the rest of the evening," Inspector Sturgeon said.

"You came back from your tour of the grounds."

"Then Sir Mordred gave us a tour of the house," Lord Mountjoy said.

"I take it that tour did not include the kitchen?"

"It did not," Sir Mordred said hastily. "I knew they'd be frightfully busy so we left them to get on with it. I showed them the ground-floor rooms and a couple of interesting bedrooms—really to pass the time until the dinner was ready. Then we had sherry in the morning room, because it has the best view of the grounds and the setting sun. Then we were summoned to dinner . . ."

"You were all together until then?" the inspector interrupted.

"Yes, I believe so." Sir Mordred frowned. "I believe various ladies went to freshen up, as they put it. And some of the men also answered the call of nature."

"So anyone would have had the opportunity to dash down to the kitchen and place a few berries in the tarts?"

"Hardly," Sir Mordred said. "It's quite a long walk from the morning room, and besides, the kitchen staff state categorically that nobody entered." He looked around impatiently. "Come on, old chap. You really are wasting everyone's time. These are important people you're dealing with. To insinuate that they dashed down to the kitchen and shoved a deadly nightshade berry into a tart is a little far-fetched, even for me as a novelist."

"Just getting everything straight in my own mind, sir," Inspector Sturgeon said placidly. "Now to proceed. Everyone is back from having freshened up and you go in to dinner. All at once?"

"We processed in, in formal manner," Sir Mordred said. "Led by Lady Georgiana and her husband, of course."

"Why of course?"

"Because she is the highest ranking of us all, related to the royal family."

Inspector Sturgeon actually went red. "You're royalty, miss?"

I didn't have the nerve to correct him and point out that I should be addressed as "my lady." "The king is my cousin," I said.

I have to say I rather enjoyed the look on his face.

"I see. Right. So you led the procession into the dining room. And were there assigned places at the table?"

"There were," I said. "Sir Mordred and his film actor guests at the top of the table and I was at the right-hand side next to Laurence Olivier."

"Nice for you, I'd imagine. He's rather dashing, isn't he?"

"He's very good-looking," I replied. "So is my husband." I caught Darcy's eye for a brief second and we exchanged a grin.

He paused. "So you took your places and then?"

"The crab mousse was served and we drank a toast in mead," Sir Mordred said, sounding bored and impatient now.

"Mead?"

"Medieval drink made from honey. I felt it appropriate since we were in a medieval banqueting room. I don't think anyone liked the stuff, looking back on it. It was rather sickly." He gave an expressive shudder. "But it was a gesture to get us into the right mood, that's all."

"And then various courses were served?"

Sir Mordred recited them, one by one, finally coming to the tarts.

"Lady Georgiana, you said that the servers were sure the tarts were carried out in no particular order?"

"That's what they said. They picked them up from the table in the serving room and carried them out."

"But nobody was sick until after the meal?"

"Oh, well after we all got home, Inspector," Max Mallowan said. "I awoke in the middle of the night with stomach pains. I expect the others did too."

"I certainly did," Sir Mordred said. "Absolutely ghastly. Thought I might expire any moment, to tell the truth."

"Who else became ill? Apart from you and Mr. Halliday?"

Sir Mordred frowned. "Let me see."

"I certainly did," Mrs. Bancroft said. "Horrible experience."

"And my explorer friend, Mr. Robson-Clough," Sir Hubert said.

"Oh, and the old lady Miss Ormorod," Edwin said as if this had suddenly occurred to him. "We heard she was taken ill too, didn't we?"

"Miss Ormorod." Sir Mordred gave a dismissive chuckle. "One tends to forget about her, doesn't one? Not the most prepossessing of people."

"And who was this Miss Ormorod?" Inspector Sturgeon asked.

"She's a representative of a charity that handles orphans in South Africa. Colorless, boring. Does good works, you know the type of spinster, don't you? I thought it only polite to invite her to the banquet. I never thought for a moment she'd come. Not her sort of thing, what?"

The inspector looked annoyed now, as if he too was getting impatient. "So we come to the pudding course. Those berry tarts, right? They were handed around. Who got the first one?"

"I did," I said. "But I declined."

"You declined? Really?" He gave me a long, suspicious look.

"Yes. As you may notice, I'm expecting a baby soon and frankly the rich food was too much for me. I couldn't face a tart with cream piled high on it."

"So what happened to your tart?"

"I believe it was given to the person next to me, who was Mr. Mallowan, but Mr. Halliday said he'd have two, so it could have gone to him."

"And they both became ill and one of them died," Inspector Sturgeon said. "This does change things, doesn't it? I hadn't realized who you were before, Lady Georgiana. So is it not possible that someone—most likely your own chef—wanted to do away with a member of the royal family?"

Chapter 27

JULY 27

STILL AT BLACKHEART MANOR

"Can we get this over with, do you think, Inspector?" Lady Mount-joy asked with an exasperated sigh. "I'm sure you've established that we're all quite decent, sane people with no desire to poison anyone, and Lord Mountjoy and I are hosting the local tennis club this evening. I need to make sure everything is in order."

"All in good time, Lady Mountjoy," Inspector Sturgeon said. "I need to be shown the kitchens and talk to the staff there. Then I'd like to take a look at this poison garden of yours, Sir Mor-dred. I'd like to see how easy it might be to pick an occasional berry without being noticed."

"Very well." Sir Mordred's voice sounded even more clipped and superior than usual. "Although I do sympathize with these people. You really are wasting our time. I'm sure I can guarantee that nobody came here with murderous intentions, certainly not against a chubby and incredibly boring local farmer."

"I can certainly speak for my guests who are not here," Sir Hubert said. "Princess Zamanska is a well-known society hostess and she did not leave my side all evening. My explorer friend is also world-renowned, as am I, I might add modestly." He permitted a little smile. "None of us had met this Mr. Halliday before. Nor did we interact with him during the evening. We were on the other side of the table, too far for conversation."

"Excuse me, Inspector." Agatha Christie spoke up. She had a deep, cultured voice. "But the conversation now seems to be insinuating that Mr. Halliday was the intended victim here, but I thought we had already proved that to be impossible—unless one of the servers planned the whole thing, placed the offending berries in Halliday's tart, and then served him."

"But that wasn't right," I replied, "because by refusing my tart, the others got mixed up. If anyone had wanted to serve Mr. Halliday with a particular plate, they'd have given it to him first, or put it aside. I don't remember my server being at all put out by my refusal and thus mixing up the order."

"Yes, that is a pretty puzzle, isn't it?" Agatha exchanged a glance with me. "It makes one wonder who was the intended victim."

"I thought we'd established that," Colonel Bancroft said angrily. "That bloody Frenchman—pardon my language, ladies—didn't care who he poisoned. Anyone at the table would do. For God's sake, Inspector, go down and question him. Get the truth out of him. These foreigners expect our law to be too lenient and civil. Put the fear of God into him."

"I intend to do just that, Colonel," Inspector Sturgeon said. "But I have to do my job thoroughly and methodically, and that includes establishing a clear timeline and eliminating all other suspects." He looked across at Edwin. "We shall want the addresses of all the servers and will, of course, follow up with them if we get no confession out of the French chappie. And I think we should at least interview the old woman who became ill. Leave no stone unturned, eh?" He started to move toward the double doors, then turned back. "Right, Sir Mordred. Ready to take me down to the Black Hole of Calcutta?" He laughed at his own joke. Nobody else did.

"Inspector, if you are going down to the kitchen to interview Pierre, do you want me to come and interpret?"

"I think not, Lady Georgiana. We don't want to risk you putting words into the gentleman's mouth that he didn't actually say, to help his cause. I have a bit of the old parley-vous myself, and I expect Sir Mordred can assist when necessary."

"Me? Absolutely hopeless," Sir Mordred said. "I never was much good at school, and all those years in South Africa have wiped all but the most rudimentary French from my head. It really might be wise to bring Lady Georgiana to assist."

I rose from my seat, assisted a little by Darcy. "Very well, I shall be happy to translate," I said, "although I resent the implication that I would lie to help my chef. I want justice as much as you do, Inspector." I tried to look at him as my great-grandmother might have looked at a subject. But I hadn't taken more than a couple of steps forward when the policeman who had been standing guard at the front door appeared.

"Begging your pardon, sir," he said, "but the young lady wants to know when they are permitted to leave, as they are anxious to get home."

"Young lady?" Inspector Sturgeon turned to Sir Mordred for confirmation.

"Your daughter, sir. And her husband."

The inspector spun back to stare at Sir Mordred. "You didn't mention a daughter."

"Oh, I'm sorry. Didn't I?" Sir Mordred gave a bored little shrug. "No reason to, really. She's married the most frightful chap, against my wishes, and comes down here as often as she dares to get my free food and booze. But I'm not surprised they want to leave in a hurry. There was always something dodgy about that husband of hers. I've noticed the odd object missing after they've been here. You'll probably find he's got half my silver in his suitcase."

"You are joking, I hope, sir." Inspector Sturgeon was frowning.

"Only partly. The man has always been remarkably reticent about his background. Claims he went to Manchester University but can't seem to get a decent job. Also claims he's a poet. I told Sylvia at the time she was making a mistake, but she was headstrong like her mother and wouldn't listen. Thank God she can't get her hands on her fortune yet."

"This daughter and her husband—were they also at the banquet? Mingling with the guests?"

"Oh yes. Anything for free food." Sir Mordred gave a brittle laugh.

"And they toured the grounds with everyone?"

"No, they didn't," Edwin said. "Father asked her to give guests a tour and she refused. Then he told me to instead while she flounced off."

"So she and her husband were alone for some considerable time?" the inspector asked.

Before anyone could answer this, the subject of the conversation herself stalked into the room. "Daddy, will you please tell these obnoxious little men that I am free to go? Stanley is not feeling at all well and we want to go home."

Inspector Sturgeon took a predatory step toward her. "You are Sir Mordred's daughter, I presume."

"Quick deduction on your part, since I called my father 'Daddy.'" She gave him a look of utter disdain. "And you are?"

If she had had a lorgnette she would have peered through it.

"Inspector Sturgeon of the Haywards Heath police," he said. "Here investigating a murder that took place during the banquet your father hosted. At which you were present, I gather?"

"Oh yes," she said. "Father insisted we join the merry throng since not enough people were stupid enough to cough up twenty guineas for the privilege of dining with him. He told us we needed to mingle with the guests and make up numbers at table. We obliged."

"As if that husband of yours would turn down a free meal, especially one with crab and duck," Sir Mordred said.

"That's unkind and unfair," Sylvia said. "It's not Stanley's fault that he can't get a suitable job right now. The world is still in a depression, you know. And poetry doesn't make a fortune, unlike the drivel you write."

Inspector Sturgeon stepped between them before it could turn into a shouting match. "Then let me ask you a few questions, young lady. Please. Take a seat."

She glanced back at the door, her gaze now uneasy. "Is this really necessary? I'm certainly not going to poison people I'd never met."

"Of course not. But you may have observed something," the inspector said calmly. "I was just telling this group of people that sometimes you notice something but don't realize the significance at the time."

"Very well." Sylvia sank into an armchair with a dramatic sigh. She crossed her legs, revealing an expanse of silk stocking.

"So you are Sir Mordred's daughter, now married?"

"I thought I'd made that clear when I used the words 'my husband,'" she said. "Yes, I'm married. My husband is an intellectual man, a writer. A genius actually."

"But he doesn't write things that make money?"

"Not at the moment," she said.

"You don't live with your father here?"

"No, we have a flat in Putney," she said. "A small and rather depressing little flat, which is all we can afford."

"So if you don't mind my asking, how do you live?"

"I have an allowance from my mother's money. I am due to come into a large sum when I turn twenty-five, but at the moment all I receive is a small monthly sum, just enough to keep body and soul together."

"I see. You feel your father could be more generous?"

"I don't understand what that has to do with a stranger dying after a dinner party. Aren't you just groping around in the dark, wasting everybody's time? If someone was poisoned, one should obviously suspect the person who cooked the food. None of us went anywhere near the kitchen. So may we leave or not?"

"Just a little while longer, if you please," the inspector said. "Your father and I are going down to the kitchen to talk with the staff there. Then I shall want to see this poison garden for myself."

I had sat down again when Sylvia made her entrance. Now I attempted to stand. "Do you want me to come?"

"I think not at the moment, Lady Georgiana," the inspector said. "It will be more in terms of visiting the scene of the crime for myself and speaking with those who might have witnessed something. The real questioning of the chef will come later."

His lips twitched as if he was pleased about this thought.

Chapter 28

I'm really worried for Pierre now, but I don't see what I can do to help.

The moment the inspector had gone the company let out a collective sigh of relief.

"Really, this is too much," Mrs. Bancroft said. "Clearly the man has no idea what he's doing. Lord Mountjoy, you have considerable influence in this county. Can't you telephone somebody on our behalf?"

"I suppose we must cooperate, Mrs. Bancroft," Lord Mountjoy said, "if it is going to help us get to the truth. After all, a murder is a murder, and whoever did it must be apprehended."

"But it's as clear as the nose on my face that it's the damned cook," Colonel Bancroft said. "Blasted Frenchman. Why would he come over here if not to inflict damage? They got rid of their own aristocracy, now he wants to do the same to us."

"Given the random nature of the distribution of the tarts, one has to think that the miscreant did not care who became ill, or even who might die," Lady Mountjoy said. "Do you think he only put deadly nightshade berries into one tart—a sort of Russian roulette?"

"Don't!" Sylvia said. "It sounds too, too horrible for words. Not caring who you might kill? You are describing a madman."

"Or madwoman," Mrs. Bancroft said.

We sat in silence for what seemed a long while.

Sylvia got up and paced around. "I hope they don't start questioning Stanley," she said. "He has such a delicate constitution and does not take well to bullying. He might say anything just to be left alone. I should go and find him before it's too late."

She was on her way out of the room when we heard voices echoing in the hallway. Inspector Sturgeon entered with Sergeant Johnson.

"Well, this makes the matter more complex," the inspector said. "We've just found out that the tarts were sent up to a small holding area off the banquet room before the start of the meal. That means they were available for anyone who wanted to sneak in and deposit the offending berries."

"But we were all together before the meal, Inspector," Colonel Bancroft said. "Traipsing for hours through the damned garden. Then we came straight in for sherry at the other end of the house."

"All except for Stanley and me," Sylvia said. "We did not join in the garden safari. But you can ask our butler. He saw us going up to our room, where we stayed until we heard voices."

"We haven't questioned this butler yet, have we, Johnson?" Inspector Sturgeon said.

"No, sir. I didn't even know there was a butler."

"He's very old and decrepit," Sylvia said. "And so deaf he'd hardly understand you."

"That chef was old too, wasn't he?" Sturgeon said. "Are there no young servants to be had these days?"

"They came with the house, Inspector. My father was too soft-hearted to throw them out."

"But the old cook hinted he was worried that Sir Mordred wanted to replace him with the French chef," Johnson said. "Quite a good motive for revenge, wouldn't you say, sir?"

"We'll bring him in for more questioning too," Inspector Sturgeon said. "But my money is still on the Frenchman. Did you notice how defensive he was when I tried to question him?"

"I don't think your French was quite up to the task, sir," Johnson said with the barest hint of a smile. "It was more he couldn't understand you."

"Hmph."

"Inspector, may I ask what is happening now to our chef?" I said.

"We are making arrangements to have him taken down to the local police station, where I will be able to question him at my leisure. And don't worry, your ladyship, I've had my men put in a request for a local French teacher from the grammar school to come and interpret. He'll get a fair hearing, I guarantee you." Inspector Sturgeon turned to us. "If you'll all come with me, I've asked Sir Mordred to show us the poison garden."

There were mutterings and complaining as we stood up to follow. I fell into the back of the procession, having taken longer than some to stand up. As we left the house and walked out into the warm sunshine Agatha Christie fell into step beside me.

"I can tell you think that your chef is innocent," she said.

"I do believe so," I replied. "The pure shock and terror on his face made me think that he can't believe what's happening to him. I've found on the whole that murderers are quite smug about what they've done—if murder was intended, that is."

"Oh yes. I'd say it was definitely intended," she replied. She gave me a long, hard stare. "So you've encountered murder before now?"

"I have. Too many times," I said. "I seem to be in the wrong place at the wrong time."

"Or the right place, if you helped to solve it." She gave me a little nod. "So what are your thoughts about this one?"

We lingered as the others went on ahead of us across the terrace.

"What confuses me is the random nature of this," I said, looking at those shrewd, intelligent eyes. "I've never encountered a murder with no motive before. I could understand the elderberries as just a spiteful prank. And in this case one might suspect either of Sir Mordred's children. They both clearly have a grudge against him and feel he's keeping them short of money, so they might have wanted to spoil his big dinner party by hinting that the food was tainted. But I'd find it hard to believe that they'd want to kill someone."

"I agree," she said. "But I can't help wondering about the order of the tarts. If someone thought Sir Mordred was going to be served first . . ." She paused, a questioning smile on her face. "Might it have been possible to put the harmful substance in the tart that would have been selected first from the table?"

I stared at her in horror. "To kill him, you mean?"

She nodded. "If one of his children hated him enough . . ."

"Golly. I was served at the same time as Sir Mordred. You mean

that the tart that was given to me—the one I refused—was the one
that contained the deadly nightshade, and it wound up with Mr.
Halliday?"

"It's possible, isn't it?"

I watched the people heading into the poison garden. "It is just
possible, I suppose. I can't tell you exactly who got my tart after I
refused it. I thought it had gone to your husband, but I suppose
your husband might have already been served right after I refused
mine so Mr. Halliday claimed the extra tart. But whoever planned
it was taking an enormous risk."

Agatha paused. "One has to wonder why the daughter is so
keen to leave in a hurry. And her husband, described as delicate?
Maybe he was the one who wanted to pay back Sir Mordred for not
providing for them? Or at least Sylvia fears that he is."

"Golly, you may be right." Sylvia was just disappearing into the
poison garden with the rest. "I confess it did strike me that she was
awfully keen to leave."

"You're on friendly terms with the son, aren't you?"

"Edwin? We've chatted a few times. I found him a nice boy."

"Not capable of killing his father?"

I stopped dead in my tracks. "It's funny you should say that.
When we were talking once, I think he hinted that he suspected his
father had killed his mother. He said one minute she was a picture
of health and then the next . . . Then he added 'of course I was only
eight years old.'"

"His mother was the wealthy one, was she?"

"The classic rich American heiress, come to Europe to snag a
title, so I'm told. She's left both her children a fortune in trust until
they turn twenty-five."

"A trust the father administers until then?"

"So it would seem."

She sighed. "I think we might have found our motive. Money has driven so many people to do unspeakable things."

"So what do we do—share this with the police?"

She shook her head. "Not at the moment, I think. That inspector isn't the sort who takes kindly to interference. Thinks quite highly of himself. No, let him question your cook and hopefully decide he didn't do it. If and when he's searching for other suspects we can make suggestions. In the meantime, perhaps you could have a word with your friend Edwin. He's young and innocent enough to give himself away if he really did do it."

"All right. I'll try to find an opportunity."

We quickened our pace to catch up with the others.

"And other suspects?" Agatha asked. "If not them, who?"

"Do you have any ideas yourself?" I asked. "What would your brilliant detectives think?"

She chuckled. "Unfortunately I do not possess Mr. Poirot's little gray cells, nor his outsize ego, I might say. In real life I have noticed that crimes are never as clever or dramatic as in fiction. Usually it's a hit over the head by someone who is angry or greedy or afraid. Fear is a big motivator, I've noticed."

"The only ones with means as well as motive, apart from Sir Mordred's children, are the servers, I think. They could have placed those berries at any moment without being noticed."

"Did I hear correctly that those serving boys were Edwin's friends?" Agatha asked.

"Yes. Fellow Oxford students."

"Close friends? Extremely close friends?"

I stared at her for a second. "Oh, I get what you are saying. One of them might have acted on Edwin's behalf."

"Precisely."

"And would have had every opportunity to do so." Then I shook my head. "But if the object was to kill Sir Mordred he would have made sure that Sir Mordred was served first, so there could be no mix-up."

Agatha Christie sighed. "It doesn't add up, does it?"

"My money was on Sir Mordred's elderly chef until murder was involved. A few elderberries causing upset stomachs would have made Pierre look bad and have prevented Sir Mordred from wanting to hire him. But surely he wouldn't have risked killing someone."

We had caught up with the rest of the group. Sir Mordred was naming each plant as we passed.

"And here is the deadly nightshade," he said. Then he looked up in surprise and triumph. "And what do we see? I see flowers on it, but as yet no berries. I think we can safely say that the deadly nightshade berries did not come from this garden, Inspector."

Chapter 29

We stared at each other in silence, digesting this latest piece of information. Sir Mordred cleared his throat. "It seems obvious to me, Inspector, that this was a deliberate act against me and my family. Somebody was well aware of the fact that I had a poison garden and for some unknown reason wanted to make mischief."

"Elderberries could be classed as mischief, Sir Mordred," Colonel Bancroft said. "Deadly nightshade is malevolence in the extreme."

"I have to agree with you, Colonel," Inspector Sturgeon said. "Unless the perpetrator was particularly stupid or ignorant he must have known that deadly nightshade berries could kill."

"You keep saying 'he,' Inspector," Agatha Christie said dryly, "but I must point out that poisoning is a favored method of the weaker sex."

"And which member of the weaker sex had you in mind, Mrs. Mallowan?" Sir Mordred asked, sounding almost amused. "The ladies at table were all highly respectable like yourself."

"Not exactly," Agatha said. "First of all there was Mrs. Crump. I'm not suggesting for a minute that she was not highly respectable or might have wanted to cause harm, but we know nothing about her. We do not know whether she is mentally unstable. We do not know if she bears a grudge against the upper classes. One has to ask oneself why the Crumps traveled all this way to attend a banquet with strangers."

"You have a point there," Inspector Sturgeon said. "Johnson, get her details when we're back in the house and have the local police interview them at their home."

"And the victim's wife," Agatha said. "I did notice she found her husband rather tiresome, the way he talked over her and never let her express an opinion for herself. If you wanted to get rid of an annoying husband, what better way to do it than in a room full of strangers."

"Except again she wasn't sitting near enough to her husband to put a berry in his tart," I pointed out, "and she didn't know which plate he'd be given."

"And I suppose we should consider," Agatha Christie went on, "there is this Miss Ormorod, whom everybody seems to forget about. What is known about her?"

"Nothing much." Sir Mordred shook his head. "She is in charge of a charity that supports orphans in various countries. She wrote to me about the open house and banquet, obviously hoping to secure the donation for her own charity. I believe my secretary wrote back that we had made arrangements in South Africa for the funds to go directly there. I was quite surprised when the woman showed up at our dinner."

Inspector Sturgeon nodded. "Elderly spinster, could be a bit batty."

"But again even if you are a bit batty, as you put it," Agatha said, "you don't go around killing strangers. In my experience I have never come across a murderer without what he or she considers to be a good motive. Did this Miss Ormorod know Mr. Halliday? That would be something to find out."

"Except that she also became ill," I reminded her.

We had begun to head back to the house. "We're going round in circles, Inspector," Sir Mordred said. "We have someone who had both means and motive and we're fishing in the dark to come up with someone better. Take the damned fellow away, lock him up, put the fear of God into him, and see if you can make him confess. End of story."

"Hold on a minute," Darcy said. "We are British, you know. Due process of law and all that."

The inspector ignored him. "You may well be right, Sir Mordred," he said. "That's just what I intend to do. I assume it's easy enough to find deadly nightshade growing in a hedgerow."

"Perfectly easy," Sir Mordred said in his clipped tones. "In one of my books I had a child feed deadly nightshade berries to her little friends. Her parents claimed it was unknowingly but the little tyke knew just what she was doing. They had been cruel to her. Excluded her from their play."

"How horrid," Mrs. Bancroft said. "That's why I don't read your books."

"I take it you don't need us anymore, Inspector?" Sir Hubert said. "I feel we should be getting home. I still have a guest at Eynsleigh and it is rather rude to ignore him."

"Oh yes. Your guest the explorer," Inspector Sturgeon said. "He was also at the dinner. Did he, by chance, know Mr. Halliday?"

Sir Hubert laughed. "My dear man, Robson-Clough is world-renowned for his bravery and daring. He's been president of the Royal Geographic Society. He's crossed deserts and battled tribesmen. He's not going to bother himself with a local farmer."

"All the same, I think we'll have Johnson here come and question him, and your cook, Lady Georgiana. The one who also became ill. Just for the record, you understand."

"Fishing in the dark," the colonel muttered again, "when it's plain as the nose on my face."

We went up the steps, one by one, into the house. I hung back deliberately so that I drew level with Edwin.

"I've been thinking about your friends again, Edwin," I said. "The ones who were servers. Is it possible that one of them might have had a reason to spoil a dinner party? A grudge we don't know about?"

Edwin stared at me, then shook his head. "That's ridiculous, Lady Georgiana. They're all decent chaps. All a bit hard up, like me, which is why they jumped at the chance to make a few bob."

"You said Henry's father was an unsuccessful writer. Might there have been hard feelings there?"

Edwin considered this. "Hard feelings, maybe, but Henry? I'm sorry, Lady Georgiana, Henry wouldn't hurt a fly. He's the one who faints at the sight of blood."

I hesitated before I went on. "I can't help thinking that someone wanted to discredit your father. Or worse—to do him harm.

He did say he was very ill that night. Is it possible that he ate deadly nightshade berries but not quite enough to kill him?"

Edwin stopped still and stared at me. "You think this was a deliberate attempt against my father?"

"He was one of those who became ill. Perhaps he has a strong constitution and survived because of it."

"But who might want to kill my father?" he asked. "Nobody there even knew him."

"Your sister did. Her husband did." I paused. "You did."

"Lady Georgiana, are you suggesting that my sister or I would want to bump off our father?"

"You would inherit a lot of money, wouldn't you?"

"Money we're going to get anyway in a few years. Sylvia is twenty-two. She hasn't long to wait."

"And her delicate husband, Stanley? Is he prepared to wait?"

"Stanley wouldn't have the gumption."

"And what about you, Edwin?" I could hardly believe I had dared to say it. "There is clearly no love lost between your father and you. And you even hinted to me that he killed your mother."

Edwin had turned bright red. "Oh . . . I mean . . . not really. I mean as a child I did wonder, but that's ridiculous. I'm quite an ethical chap, Georgiana. If I was going to kill my father, I'd have plenty of opportunity alone in the house with him. Push him down the cellar stairs and make it look like an accident? Child's play. But I'd never have risked putting other people in harm's way. That would not be right."

"I'm sorry I suggested it," I said. "I just had to make sure in my own mind."

He gave me a long, hard stare. "You know, I think you should leave the investigating to the professionals. If there is a clever killer on the loose, he might be coming for you next."

Was that a veiled threat?

STORM CLOUDS WERE gathering as we drove home. The air was muggy and my dress stuck to my back as I leaned against the car seat. I had been reluctant to leave Pierre when I watched him driven off, but the inspector made it clear he was to be questioned at the police station and we were not welcome.

"I hate to leave Pierre in their clutches," I said.

"I'm sure he'll be given a fair hearing," Sir Hubert said. "After all, we British are not barbarians."

"All the same, I have been taken to a police station and locked in a cell in a foreign country, and the experience was not pleasant."

"When on earth was this?" Sir Hubert sounded astonished.

I could hardly say "more than once." "In Paris recently. When a woman died at Chanel's fashion show. I was the last one to be seen with her, so naturally they assumed . . ." I left it there. "I was soon released." I also didn't add that I was only released because Mrs. Simpson alerted the British ambassador on my behalf. Pierre had no such strings to pull, and I didn't want him bullied into a confession when perhaps he did not understand.

"There's not much more we can do at the moment," Darcy said. "We'll check on him in a little while."

"Should he not have our solicitor present? We don't want him to be coerced into saying the wrong thing."

"Good point," Sir Hubert said. "I'll telephone old Haversham as soon as we get home and see what he can do."

This placated me a little. "I don't think much of that inspector and his modern methods," I said.

"All that time and we're none the wiser," Sir Hubert said.

"We know it was more than a prank, that's for sure," Darcy said. "We also know whoever put deadly nightshade berries into a tart, or tarts, came with them to the banquet and did not pick them from the garden. That indicates planning and intent, not a spur-of-the-moment thing to do."

"It's absolutely incomprehensible to me that anyone would want to kill at random like that," Sir Hubert said. "Unless it was our communist chef. One has to accept that he is the most likely candidate."

"But we weren't all aristocrats. He could have killed Queenie, or the Crumps." Darcy turned back to me. "You're awfully quiet, Georgie. Do you have some theories of your own?"

"Actually no. I'm as confused as you are," I said. "And my head is throbbing. There's another thunderstorm brewing, isn't there?"

"Have a cup of tea and a good lie-down when we get home," Darcy said. "I wonder if Queenie's well enough to resume her duties. If they keep Pierre, who is going to do the cooking?"

"I expect Mrs. Holbrook can brew a cup of tea," Sir Hubert said. "After that, I'm not sure. We may be reduced to eating at the pub." He laughed. "At least that will send old Robson-Clough packing. He does enjoy his food, doesn't he? For one who claims he has lived on grasshoppers."

"I thought he was your great friend," Darcy said, turning to him with a grin.

"In small doses. He does drone on a lot."

We were in a better mood by the time we drove up to the house.

The first raindrops were spattering on the windscreen and Darcy hurried me inside.

"I'll get on to the solicitor right away," Sir Hubert said. "Before they can decide to knock off for the night." He headed for his study.

Darcy and I were making our way down the hall when I paused. Voices were coming from the drawing room.

"Oh God. Not company," Darcy muttered. He headed down the hallway. I followed him.

"Here they are at last," said a woman's voice as we entered. "Surprise, Georgie dear."

And Fig stood up from the armchair where she had been sitting and came toward me, open armed.

$\mathcal{C}$hapter 30

JULY 27

BACK AT EYNSLEIGH

Not only is my chef arrested for murder, but now I have Fig to deal
    with. How shall I ever get through the next days until the baby
    arrives? Do hurry up, little O'Mara.

"Fig?" I stammered out the word and had to stop myself from adding, "What on earth are you doing here?"

"We came earlier than expected," she said, turning to scowl at
Binky. "It turns out that Binky got it wrong yet again. Typical of
him, of course. He messed up the date for his foot doctor's appointment. It should have been last month. June, not July. And now the
wretched man has gone on holiday to the South of France for a
month. I'm not surprised he can afford to travel at the prices he
charges us."

Binky had also risen to his feet. "How are you, dear Georgie?"

He came forward and kissed me. "Looking absolutely spiffing, I'd say, isn't she, Fig? Positively blooming."

"Thank you," I said. "Actually I'm feeling a bit worn-out at the moment. We've had a lot going on."

"Well, don't worry, your dear ones are here now to take over everything," Fig said. "You can put your feet up until the baby arrives. How long is it now?"

I was tempted to say three days, but alas, I'm not good at lying. "At least another week, although the doctor did say it could come early."

"There you are, Binky. Exactly what I said," Fig exclaimed, waving her arms in dramatic fashion. "Binky wanted to stay on in London as planned but I said we should get down to the country right away. You never know with first babies, I told him. They can be unpredictable and Georgie will want us there. Besides," she added, "it didn't make sense to pay for an expensive hotel when one didn't need to be in the city."

"And the weather was beastly hot and sticky," Binky said. "London does not handle heat waves well, does it?" He seemed to become aware of Darcy. "What ho, old chap. Ready for the demands of fatherhood?"

"As ready as I'll ever be," Darcy said.

"That's the ticket. Leave it all to the women. That's what I do."

"I take it you've hired a good nanny," Fig said. "Always wise to have one in place ahead of time so that she knows the ropes."

She looked up as Sir Hubert entered. "Oh, you're Georgie's godfather. Lovely to see you," she said.

Sir Hubert gave her a startled glance.

"You remember my brother and sister-in-law, don't you?" I said to him. "Binky and Fig Rannoch?"

"How do you do, sir?" Binky rose and extended his hand. "Good to see you again. Fine house this. Most agreeable."

Sir Hubert glanced around. "Have you seen my explorer friend? I take it he hasn't left?"

"There was an odd-looking chap here when we first arrived, and another old man I seem to remember was your grandfather, Georgiana. They have both gone for a walk around the grounds. Not what I'd do when a thunderstorm was brewing."

"I think I'll go and find them," Sir Hubert said. "I might as well take the dogs. They can probably do with a good walk."

"Those awful brutes are your dogs? They jumped all over me when we arrived. Muddy paws on my silk dress."

"I'm sorry, Fig," Darcy said. "They are only puppies and we're in the process of training them."

"I don't know how Georgiana is going to manage training dogs as well as taking care of a baby, since you are so rarely at home, Darcy. What a thoughtless time to get puppies."

"Oh, but they are great fun. They have lovely natures," I said. "I enjoy my walks with them every day."

The grandfather clock in the corner struck four.

"Ah. Teatime." Fig stopped her tirade and looked up expectantly. "I seem to remember that large girl in your kitchen was quite good when it came to cakes. What was her name? Something outlandish, I remember."

"Ah." I glanced at Darcy. "I'm not sure what we can rustle up for tea today, Fig. Queenie has been quite ill and she won't have been baking for the past few days."

"Oh dear. How disappointing. Anyway, a cup of tea will be most welcome. Do ring for it, Georgie."

I could hardly say that a cup of tea might not even be possible at the moment.

"I'll go and find Mrs. Holbrook," I said. "I don't think the bells are working properly."

I hurried down to the kitchen area and found Mrs. Holbrook sitting at the table. She jumped up guiltily as I came in. "Oh, my lady. I'm sorry I didn't notice the bell. Was there something you needed?"

"We have visitors, Mrs. Holbrook. You've seen them, I hope."

"I have. And I've just sent Sally up to make up the pink bedroom if that's all right with you. That's probably the one that's suitable for a duke, seeing that the explorer man is still in the blue bedroom."

"That will be fine. But they are asking for tea."

"Oh dear." The worried look came back to her face.

"I gather Queenie hasn't shown her face yet."

"She has not. Maisie's taken her up some barley water and broth but she says Queenie isn't interested in food, which you must agree is unlike her."

"Quite unlike." I tried not to smile. "I promised I'd call the doctor and ask him to take a look at her. I should do that right now. Poor Queenie. But in the meantime . . ."

"Is the chef not returned yet? I'm sure he'd whip up some cakes if you asked him."

"I don't know when Chef is returning, Mrs. Holbrook. He's been accused of a horrible crime and the police have taken him for questioning."

"Surely not? He seems like such a pleasant young man. Demanding when it comes to his kitchen, I'll say that for him. He likes everything just so. But he cooks like a dream, doesn't he? And nothing's too hard for him."

"I agree, but some people became ill after the dinner party at Sir Mordred's and the suspicion has fallen upon Pierre."

"Poor boy. You make sure you stick up for him, my lady."

"Oh, don't worry. I intend to," I said. "But in the meantime . . ."

"I'll put the kettle on now and see what cakes we've got in the larder," she said. "But as for dinner tonight . . . I'm not sure about that, my lady. I've cooked for myself, when I was retired, but I've never had to cook for gentry."

"Anything will do, Mrs. Holbrook. I'll explain to them."

She nodded, a worried frown still on her face. I left her to prepare the tea, and as I was coming out into the hall I heard voices and saw my grandfather, returning with Sir Hubert, the explorer, and the dogs. These bounded up to me, tails wagging furiously.

"We've had a nice walk," my grandfather said. "I've learned fascinating things from your friend, Sir Hubert. You won't believe what they do on some of the islands in Indonesia."

"We could do with some tea," Sir Hubert said. "Is there any hope, do you think?"

"I've just spoken to Mrs. Holbrook and she's brewing some now," I said. "But Queenie's not up and around yet, and frankly Mrs. H is worried about what to do next. She's never been a cook in her life, you know."

"Why don't I go down and see what I can do to help?" Granddad said. "I may not be much of a chef, but I can do good, plain cooking and I can give her a hand."

"Oh no, Albert. That wouldn't be right," Sir Hubert said. "You are a guest of the house."

My grandfather chuckled. "There are times, I've found, when the rules have to be bent. And if you want your supper tonight, then I'd say someone has to give that woman a hand. And since none of you know the first thing about cooking, it had better be me."

He headed through the baize door toward the kitchen.

"A most interesting man, your grandfather," Mr. Robson-Clough said. "The tales he's told me—fascinating."

"I should go up and check on Queenie," I said. "See if she needs a doctor. It really is not like her to be off her food for so long."

But I was only halfway up the first flight of stairs when there was a knock at the front door. Sir Hubert went to open it before Mrs. Holbrook or Phipps could get there.

"You'd better come in," I heard him say.

I looked down in time to see a police constable come in, followed by the sergeant, Johnson.

"If you don't mind, sir," Johnson said, in his pleasant country accent, "I've been told to have a chat with your guest, the explorer, and with your cook too."

"Very well," Sir Hubert said. "This is Mr. Robson-Clough. You can speak to him in the library. Lady Georgiana has just gone up to see how the assistant cook is faring. She has been rather ill, one gathers."

"Sorry to disturb her, sir, but Inspector's orders."

I hurried up the last of the two flights. Queenie sat up hurriedly as I came in.

"How are you feeling?" I asked.

"I'm on the mend, thanks, missus. I reckon I should be up and good to go tomorrow if I can keep down some food tonight."

"That is good news, Queenie. I was worried for you."

"So was I. I thought I might have had me chips. Pushing up daisies, you know."

"I'll see about sending you up a boiled egg and some soldiers. That always works well for me when I've been ill," I said. "But I'm afraid you have a visitor. The police want to question you about what happened in the kitchen that day."

"'Ere—they don't think I was the one what put them berries in the tarts, do they?"

"No, I'm sure not. But they do think it was Pierre. And we have to help him, don't we?"

"Pierre? That's bloody stupid, ain't it? You let me tell them. I put the berries on them tarts and they was all nice and proper berries from the garden."

"That's right. You tell them," I said. "Do you think you could come downstairs or shall I bring the policeman up here?"

"If you don't mind, I'm still a bit woozy when I stand up," she said. "But give me a minute to brush me hair and make meself look respectable."

I went down to report this. As I came into the library I heard Johnson say, "Well, sorry to have troubled you, sir, but we had to interview everybody, including those who became ill."

I related that Queenie was up in her room, still too weak to come downstairs, and led him up. We were both a little out of breath by the time we reached the servants' floor. I stayed in the doorway while Johnson questioned her. She was clearly getting back to her old self and answered each question belligerently. No, nobody had come into the kitchen or touched the tarts. She had put the berries on herself and nobody else had been near them. What's more she had been up in the serving room when the tarts were sent up on the dumbwaiter and she'd been there all the time. So she was blowed if she knew how anyone could have poisoned them. She also responded equally forcefully when questioned about Pierre. He was happy in his new job. Why would he want to blow his chances by doing something stupid?

I was quite proud of her by the time Sergeant Johnson left. She had certainly helped Pierre's cause.

"Do you have any idea when they intend to release my chef, Sergeant?" I asked as I escorted him down again. "I don't like to think of him at the police station on his own in a foreign country."

"The inspector is keen on keeping him overnight, I'm afraid, my lady," he said. "Hoping it will soften him up, you know."

"But that's illegal, surely? Has he been actually charged with murder?"

"Not that I know of, my lady. But the inspector says he doesn't have time to question him before morning, and seeing as he's French he'd be a flight risk."

"Then you tell your inspector that I'll be round there first thing in the morning with my solicitor, and please tell Pierre he's not to say anything until he has his lawyer representing him. We've telephoned our solicitor, but just in case . . ."

"I'll tell him, my lady." He gave me a reassuring nod. I just wished it had reassured me. I didn't want Pierre locked up in a strange police station overnight. Of course he wasn't guilty. Anyone could see that. I stood alone in the foyer, staring at the pictures on the walls. Nothing made sense about this case. Surely murder was never random. And yet, who would want to kill an amiable farmer whom nobody had met before? Then I corrected myself. Sir Mordred had met him. Many years ago.

$\mathcal{C}$hapter 31

July 28

**Thank heavens for Agatha Christie. Suddenly everything is
beginning to make sense.**

Mrs. Holbrook and my grandfather managed a passable dinner that
night. Meat pie, new potatoes, and runner beans followed by stewed
plums and custard. Not exactly haute cuisine but certainly tasty
enough. It would have been an enjoyable meal if Fig had not been
present. We had to hear about how hard life had become at Castle
Rannoch, how the new boiler was not working properly and of
course Binky didn't have a clue when it came to dealing with trades-
men. We moved on to her mother's rheumatism, her sister's leaking
roof and no money for Maude to go to a finishing school and God
knows how they'll be able to afford for her to be presented at court
in three years' time.

"Just pray you have sons, Georgie," she said. "That way you'll never have the dreadful expense of coming out. How we'll be able to do it for dear Addy, I don't know. Of course, she's such a difficult child that one would worry she'll ever be able to be groomed enough to curtsy to the king." When I opened my mouth to say something in defense of Addy, who to my mind was wonderfully spirited and inquisitive, she went on. "And this new king—you know him quite well, don't you, Georgie? Binky says he's a decent enough chap, but can he rule? Has he got the backbone for the job?"

"I hope so," I said, not wanting to admit that I also had my doubts. He had been away for weeks on a yacht on the Med with Mrs. Simpson, and I gathered he had refused to check government dispatches the way monarchs were supposed to.

"How are we going to endure two more weeks of Fig ranting on about the state of the world?" I said as Darcy and I wearily climbed into bed.

"She really is a pain, isn't she?" Darcy slid into bed beside me. "I wonder sometimes that Binky has not throttled her in her sleep before now."

"And I can't help thinking about poor Pierre, all alone in a police cell."

"We'll go there first thing in the morning to make sure he's all right and the solicitor has arrived," Darcy said. "Now, stop worrying and go to sleep. You need to think calm thoughts for the baby's sake."

As if in response to this the baby did an enormous kick that even Darcy felt. "Well, that's definitely expressing an opinion," he said. "Going to be a boy, with a kick like that. Another rugby player."

I fell asleep in Darcy's arms although my night was disturbed by strange dreams of giving birth and forgetting where I had left the baby. The morning dawned blustery and with the promise of rain. Maisie brought my tea at the correct hour. "You'll be pleased to hear that Queenie's back at work, my lady," she said as she placed the tray on the bedside table. "She said she couldn't leave you in the lurch no matter how bad she felt."

"Well, good for Queenie." I reached out for the teacup. "Tell her I'm proud of her."

After I had washed and dressed I went downstairs, anticipating a good breakfast. Fig and Binky were already sitting in the dining room. There was a look of extreme disapproval on Fig's face—even more than the usual look of disapproval.

"No kidneys, Georgiana. And not a piece of bacon in sight. Are you economizing?"

"No, Fig. It must be Queenie. She probably couldn't face cooking kidneys."

"You still have that awful girl? You should have dismissed her years ago, Georgiana. An utter disaster, that's what she is."

"Be grateful for her now, Fig. She's all we've got until the police release Pierre. And she's been quite ill. I don't know if you've heard that people were poisoned at the dinner party Pierre cooked. Queenie was one of them."

"I did hear something strange last night. People poisoned?"

I wished I had kept quiet, as I now had to relate the whole story to her. At the end she gave me a pitying sigh. "It's absolutely clear that it must have been your foreign chef. They come over here wanting to make mischief. You may be fond of him, Georgiana, but it was lucky he was found out before he poisoned you."

"I don't think it was he, Fig. Darcy and I are going to the police station after breakfast to make sure our solicitor is with him and he's given a fair hearing. His English is very limited."

Fig gave a dramatic sigh. "Well, given the circumstances, one must make do with scrambled eggs, toast, and porridge, I suppose."

I finished my breakfast and waited impatiently for Darcy to drive into Haywards Heath. On the way the first drops of rain spattered on the windscreen. Once at the police station we were pleased to find that Sir Hubert's solicitor had already sent one of his colleagues to see Pierre. He came over to report to us.

"It's not right, keeping a chap waiting like this," the solicitor said. "They said the damned police inspector was called out on an emergency. And we've got the local French teacher coming soon too."

"I suppose we won't be allowed to see him?" I asked.

The solicitor shook his head. "Definitely not at the moment."

At that moment the door opened, sending in a gust of wet air and Inspector Sturgeon along with it.

"What the . . . ?" He went to say something cutting, remembered who we were, and frowned. "Lady Georgiana, Mr. O'Mara, I thought I told you not to come here," he said, still frowning at Darcy and me.

"We only came to check on our chef and to make sure our solicitor had arrived to represent him," I said. "May we at least speak with him, to let him know we are on his side?"

"He'll need someone on his side, if you ask me," Inspector Sturgeon said. "There's been a second death. The old lady, Miss Ormorod, died last night." He paused. "Of course, in her case age might have been a factor. A weak heart, an upset stomach were too much for her frail constitution."

"Oh dear. How very sad," I said. "Was she still staying with her friend nearby?"

"She was."

"Darcy, we should visit her friend to see if there is anything we could do."

Darcy shot me a strange look but then said, "Yes, of course. Do you have the friend's address, Inspector?"

He also gave me a strange look. "I don't see what . . ."

"Elderly spinster. Probably so flustered that she can't think what to do next."

"Well, she won't be able to do anything until there's been an autopsy," the inspector said, "but here's the address." It was written on a sheet of paper along with some other addresses.

"Just let me get out a notebook," I said, fishing in my purse while I continued to stare at the sheet. I noted Halliday at Oakridge Farm, also Mallowan, staying with the Finlays, at Little Challing near Wivelsfield. I copied Miss Beryl Parson's address and left, feeling rather pleased with myself.

"You want to visit Miss Ormorod's friend to offer sympathy or to be nosy?" Darcy asked me.

"Both. And I have the addresses of Halliday and the Mallowans. It might help to speak to them."

"Georgie, the police are onto this. I know you want to help Pierre but perhaps we should leave this to the police now. It can't be good for you, running around like this right before the baby is due."

"At least let's go and talk to these people. Who knows, they may reveal something we didn't know before."

Darcy sighed as we headed back to the motorcar.

Miss Parsons lived in a picture-perfect cottage with a thatched roof in a small village not far from the main road.

"How very kind of you to come," she said, ushering us into a tiny sitting room decorated with lots of crochet doilies and chair covers. A tabby cat took one look at us and slunk out of the room. "I know who you are, of course. The whole neighborhood was abuzz when you moved here last year. Such an honor to have one related to the king nearby."

She motioned for us to sit and rushed into the kitchen to put on the kettle.

"We were so shocked to hear the news this morning," I said when she returned. "And of course we were at the dinner where the guests ate the poisoned berries."

"What a terrible thing to have happened," Miss Parsons said. "I can't believe that anyone in his right mind would do such a thing. Poor Hettie was horribly sick to start with, then just when she seemed to be getting better her heart gave out. I found her lying there, poor dear." She put her hand up to her mouth.

"Tell us about her," I said. "You two were old friends."

"Since school days," she said. "Hettie was the rolling stone and I gathered the moss, I'm afraid. I taught the top class at the infant's school until I retired. She threw herself into her charity work. She had no children of her own but she worked tirelessly for disadvantaged children around the world. She became quite an important figure with a major charity."

"She went to the banquet because Sir Mordred had chosen her charity, did she?"

Her face clouded. "Oh no, dear. She went to the banquet because she wanted to find out more about his charity. She hadn't come across it before and she wanted to suggest that he donate the funds to her very reputable charity instead."

The kettle screamed from the kitchen. She went through to make the tea. The cat returned with her and brushed against Darcy's leg.

"And did he do as she suggested?" I asked.

"No. Quite refused. He was rather short with her, I gather. She came home upset. She said, 'I believe that man might be a charlatan. He'd give me no details at all of this South African orphanage he supports. In any case the money is not coming to my charity.'"

"That's interesting." I exchanged a glance with Darcy.

"And now she's dead, poor dear."

"As you say, and now she's dead." Darcy repeated the words.

Chapter 32

JULY 28

AT HALLIDAY'S FARM AND WITH THE MALLOWANS

At last some things are beginning to make sense. But I still can't see
how anybody specific could have been killed.

"That's interesting, don't you think?" Darcy said as we drove away.
"She was suspicious of Sir Mordred and now she's dead."

"Except we come back to the first question: how could a specific
tart have been given to anybody? In fact"—I paused, waving my
arms for emphasis—"Miss Ormorod wasn't supposed to get that
tart at all. When I refused mine, it was passed on to Mr. Mallowan.
Miss Ormorod got his, and Mr. Halliday had the extra one."

"And Mr. Halliday is also dead," Darcy said dryly.

"But the servers were sure they just grabbed the nearest tarts
from the table in no order. And besides," I added, "Sir Mordred was
also taken ill."

"Yes, that does complicate things," Darcy said. "I'll be interested to hear what Mrs. Halliday has to say."

After about fifteen minutes we turned off the road and bumped down a farm track, liberally spattered with mud. Oakridge Farm was a classic brick building, comfortable but not fancy. There were ducks and chickens in the yard and two dogs got up to greet us, giving suspicious barks. A laborer appeared from a barn. We told him we were there to offer condolences to Mrs. Halliday and he led us to the front door.

Mrs. Halliday looked smaller and frailer than I remembered her, dressed entirely in black, her face pale.

"It's good of you to come," she said in a cracked voice. "I'm in the process of arranging the funeral and I really haven't a clue how to do this. They haven't returned his body yet. So distressing."

"You don't have family nearby?"

She shook her head. "My parents are gone. Tubby's too. I have one brother in Yorkshire but he has no close relatives. His brothers both were lost in the Great War."

"No children, then?" Darcy asked. I thought this rather tactless of him since I was standing in front of her with a large bulge.

"I'm afraid not. We were not blessed that way. But do come in."

She led us into a well-used sitting room and offered us the obligatory cup of tea. The kettle must have been on the range because she returned with the tea tray very quickly.

"I'm still in a state of shock," she said as she poured for us. "When the police told me that Tubby had been deliberately poisoned, I couldn't believe it. Who would do such a thing? Everybody liked Tubby. He was the life and soul of the party—active in local affairs. Justice of the peace. Master of the local hunt. Got the most out of life."

"We've been asking ourselves the same question," I said. "Of course it seems very much like a random act, that the person did not care whom they killed. But that's hard to believe, isn't it?"

"It is." She sighed. "He was so looking forward to that night too. When he saw that article on Sir Mordred he waved the newspaper at me. 'That must be old Shrimpy,' he said. And then the announcement of the banquet. He couldn't wait. He and Shrimpy Mortimer were thick as thieves at school. Great pals. Tubby had been trying to contact him again for years, not realizing that he'd been in South Africa and then inherited the title." She paused, smoothing down her skirt. "Such larks they used to get up to at school, Tubby told me. Shrimpy was such a fun-loving boy in those days." She looked up and met my eyes. "But look at him now. Not an ounce of fun left in him, is there? It must have been his time in the army. War does that to people, doesn't it? When you've seen too much and had to do things your conscience tells you not to."

She looked at Darcy this time; he nodded.

"Tubby joined up in the Great War," she said, "even though he was midthirties by that time. But his younger brothers went and he didn't like to be left behind. Then they were both killed in the trenches and Tubby came through without a scratch. Such a funny old world, isn't it?"

There was a long silence.

"Mrs. Halliday," I began tentatively, "how was your husband after the dinner? Were there any signs that he was becoming sick?"

"He wasn't himself when we drove home, I realize now," she said, a puzzled frown on her face. "Quite agitated. Face really red. Speech slurred a little but I put that down to his drinking. Tubby did like to drink a lot, I'm afraid. He was muttering to himself on the way home about it not being right."

"What not being right?" Darcy asked.

"I don't know. Tubby was the sort who got a bee in his bonnet about the smallest things."

"You don't happen to have any photographs of Tubby and Shrimpy when they were in school, do you?" I asked.

"Of course. Tubby displayed them on the wall of his study. All the rugby teams. And cricket teams."

She disappeared, then returned with several framed photographs.

"Junior colts," she said, handing us a photo of boys looking impossibly young and innocent.

"I remember those days," Darcy said. "Such knobbly knees."

"There's Tubby," she said, although this was not necessary. I had already picked out the boy in the back row, big for his age, with fair hair, neatly parted in the middle, over a round, hopeful face.

"And Shrimpy?"

"In the front row. Holding the ball."

I thought I could recognize a young Sir Mordred, even though his hair was no longer that dark, unruly mop. He certainly did merit the nickname. A skinny little chap.

"He looks small for a rugby player," Darcy said, having been a good one himself.

"Yes, but such a fast runner, Tubby said. If he got the ball, nobody could catch him."

She passed me the next photographs. The last one was of the first fifteen in their final season, Tubby now meriting the nickname at the back and Shrimpy again holding the ball, sitting center in the front. I stared at him. Again there was something of Sir Mordred I could see in that face. The hair was now slicked down and I could tell he was trying hard not to smile. There was a spark of fun and mischief in that face.

"Thank you." I handed them back. I couldn't think what else to say, or to ask.

"We mustn't take up more of your time," I said. "But we wanted to let you know that you can call on us if you need help. My godfather, Sir Hubert, knows everybody in the area. He can probably help you with undertakers and that sort of thing."

Mrs. Halliday dabbed her handkerchief to her face. "Most kind," she muttered.

We stood up.

"Not the easiest man," she said. "A bit blustering. Thought he knew best. But a good heart. I shall miss him. Actually I don't know what I'm going to do without him."

As we drove away in the motorcar Darcy turned to me. "Did you learn anything? I'm not sure what you wanted there."

"It did cross my mind that she might have killed him. He was quite dismissive of her, wasn't he? But she's so clearly devastated."

"It's funny, isn't it," Darcy said, "that some women with bullying husbands are so attached to them."

"I know how they feel," I said dryly, making him laugh.

"Where now?" he asked.

"I thought we'd visit the Mallowans, if they are still staying with the Finlays."

"Finlays?" Darcy frowned. "Weren't they at the Mountjoys' once? Quiet little fellow who collects old books?"

"Yes, I think so."

"And do you know where they live?"

"I took the trouble of copying down the address when we were at the police station," I said. "It's just past Wivelsfield."

"Wivelsfield. Silly names in this part of the world, aren't there?" Darcy chuckled. Then he became serious. "Look, old thing. I know you want to clear Pierre's name, but I don't want you taking on too much or getting upset right before the birth. We have to assume the police will do a good job and our solicitor will make sure that Pierre is not coerced into a confession. And frankly, if he doesn't confess, there's no way they could prove he did this."

"That's just the point, isn't it?" I said. "We have no way of proving how anybody did it. How easy would it be to shove a random berry into a tart? Anyone could have popped into that serving room while they went to the loo and shoved in a few berries."

We drove through lovely summer countryside. The rain shower had passed over and white clouds raced across a deep blue sky. Honeysuckle spilled over hedgerows. A pheasant flew low in front of us. Fat cows watched us from fields. It was England at its best and I wished I could enjoy it.

The Finlays' house was an attractive Georgian residence, like a large doll's house, set in immaculate grounds. We were shown in by a maid and found the Mallowans taking coffee with their hosts in a charming room overlooking the grounds. The men rose to their feet.

"So sorry to disturb you," Darcy said. "Darcy O'Mara and my wife, Georgiana."

"Oh, we've heard all about you," Mrs. Finlay said, coming forward to shake hands. "Agatha gave us a vivid description of the infamous banquet. Of course it's right up her alley, isn't it? A banquet in a creepy house with a poison garden and then random people are poisoned."

"Only she hasn't managed to solve it yet," Mr. Finlay said. "Buck up, old girl. This isn't like you."

"I admit I'm at a loss." Agatha Christie shook her head. "I've never come across a random poisoner before. The elderberries I could understand. A silly prank. That could easily be Sir Mordred's son. He clearly is at odds with his father. Or the daughter and husband. They are not too fond of her father either. But adding the lethal berries . . . that's something different."

"And we have more news for you," I said. "The elderly lady, Miss Ormorod, has died."

"Well, I suppose that's not so much of a shock," Mr. Mallowan said. "Old lady, rather frail, all the excitement of the evening and then the stomach complaint. It could all have been too much for her heart."

"I suppose so," Agatha said. I found she was looking at me. "Would you care to see the rose garden, Lady Georgiana? The Finlays are famous for it. Dickie tends those roses like his babies, don't you, Dickie?"

"I must admit I get great pleasure from it," he said. "Would you like me to show you around?"

"I thought Lady Georgiana and I might take a little stroll together, if that's all right with you," Agatha Christie said.

I caught Darcy's eye. "You stay here," my gaze said.

"I think we'll let the ladies have their chat," he said.

Agatha and I went out through the French doors, across a terrace, and through an archway of pale yellow roses to the garden beyond. It was indeed a heavenly place.

"I noticed that you are also a keen observer, Lady Georgiana," she said at last. "I wondered what your thoughts were on this now you've had time to consider it?"

"I admit I'm in the dark," I said. "If the killer had wanted to strike a particular person, then the handing around of tarts would be far too risky."

"So who would be your suspects?"

"I'm still inclined to go for Sir Mordred's children, I suppose. They do have a large inheritance coming to them. And there is no love lost in that family. And I had mentioned to you that Edwin sort of hinted to me that he'd thought his father killed his mother."

She nodded. "Yes, that does seem a good motive. And he had the means."

"He was sent to see if everything was ready for the dinner. He would have checked the serving room, wouldn't he?"

"He would indeed. But then wouldn't he have made sure that the lethal berry went to his father?"

"I know. That's the problem. There was no way of making sure anyone got the right pudding."

"But again we know that two lots of elderberries would not have finished anyone off. Just given them a nasty stomachache. It was the deadly nightshade. But it would surely have needed more than one berry. Quite a few to kill someone, in my experience. And how would you make sure the right person got that? We've presumed it was Sir Mordred. But the question might be, who wanted to kill Mr. Halliday?"

I toyed with this theory. "I've just spoken with Tubby Halliday's widow and it seems he was well-liked—an ordinary country farmer. Except . . ."

"Except?" She stared at me expectantly.

"Except he did know Sir Mordred, years and years ago. He was the only one at the banquet with a personal connection, wasn't he?"

I saw Agatha's face as a thought occurred to her. "Not the only one. Didn't the orphanage woman already know him?"

"They'd only corresponded," I said. "She didn't know him in person."

"The only two people with the most tenuous connections and yet they are dead." She paused. "The problem is that Sir Mordred was also poisoned." Those intelligent eyes held mine.

"We still come back to how anybody could have made sure that the right tart went to the right person," I said. "Surely there was no way . . ."

Agatha Christie stopped suddenly, staring at a spectacular yellow rose. "How do we know that Mr. Halliday was fed a deadly nightshade berry or two? There wouldn't have been much of it left in his digestive system by the time they did an autopsy."

"I suppose it was the atropine in his blood," I said.

She looked excited now. "Precisely. And that atropine need not have come from a plant. You can get it at the chemists. It is in eye drops as well as other things."

"So you are saying that the atropine need not have been in a tart at all?"

She nodded, gripping my arm excitedly. "What was there on the table that would have been served to a particular person?"

I thought back to the dinner. "The crab mousse was already put out when we arrived, wasn't it?"

She nodded again. "Crab mousse. A little hard to doctor. But what else?"

I spun to face her. "The wineglasses," I said excitedly. "The mead was already in them when we came to the table!"

"Now we're getting somewhere. A few drops of atropine in the mead would not be noticed because the mead was so horribly sweet."

"Golly," I said.

"So there you are. That's how it was done." She clapped her hands in delight. "You want to kill a particular person, so you put the atropine in the mead. That could have been done well ahead of time, before the guests arrived. But then, as a red herring, you dot a few elderberries around randomly. Sir Mordred went in to inspect that all was in order before dinner, didn't he?"

"But my assistant cook was already in the serving room."

"And I'm sure she'd have been terrified of Sir Mordred. He'd only have had to say something like 'careful those wineglasses aren't too near the edge' and she'd have her back turned while he planted a few elderberries into the tarts. He knows several people will become ill. One will die."

"In this case two will die," I said. "Unless Miss Ormorod's death was more a result of old age."

"Two will die," she repeated. "And I find it interesting that those two were the only ones, apart from his family, with a definite connection to Sir Mordred."

"But Sir Mordred also became ill."

"Another red herring," she said. "He gave himself an elderberry or two to make himself sick. Or he just claimed to have been taken ill. Who would have checked on him?"

I stared at her for a moment, digesting this. "Are you saying that Sir Mordred was not the victim but the mastermind behind this?"

"It seems the most likely answer to me," she replied.

I stared at her in complete admiration.

"Golly," I said again before I reminded myself that I had promised to stop using such girlish exclamations. I considered the implication of this. "So you think that Sir Mordred knew that Halliday and Miss Ormorod were coming to the banquet and decided to finish them off? But why? He hadn't met Tubby Halliday since their school days. I don't think he had ever met Miss Ormorod before."

"They must both have known something that could damage his reputation badly enough that he'd kill for it," Agatha Christie said.

"Tubby Halliday's wife said they were thick as thieves at school, but Sir Mordred denied that, saying he couldn't stand the man."

"Ah." Agatha Christie gave me a knowing smile. "That itself is telling, isn't it? What if they were good friends at school, I mean really close friends, as in an intimate relationship?"

I shook my head. "I don't think that sort of thing would worry Sir Mordred. It's not uncommon in the world of the arts, is it? Look at Noël Coward. Everyone knows about him. Everyone adores him."

"That's true," she agreed. "Then it was something else. Something about him that Mr. Halliday knew that could ruin him. Something he did at school, maybe?"

"Lots of people do silly things at school, don't they?"

We walked on, the scent of roses all around us. I was conscious of the stillness of the day, the humming of bees, and was struck by the contrast—the idyllic peace of an English countryside and yet two people had been killed in this same beautiful and peaceful setting.

"Well, what about Miss Ormorod?" Agatha asked.

"I don't think he'd met her before. She represented some charity, and I gather she expected the proceeds of the event to go to her charity. But the woman she was staying with said that he planned to send the money directly to some orphanage in South Africa. Miss Ormorod was suspicious."

"She felt everything wasn't quite aboveboard?"

"I gather so. She said the man was a charlatan."

"And was keeping the money for himself, maybe?"

"Maybe."

"But would that make you want to kill somebody? To hush them up?" Agatha shook her head. "I don't think so. Look how many politicians are happy to pocket money they shouldn't keep."

"And it doesn't make sense. Sir Mordred is a rich man. He makes a lot of money from his books and he married a rich wife. He's also rather stingy, I suspect."

"Stingy?"

I nodded. "He keeps a minimum of servants. He used his son's friends as servers. And the house—well, the house didn't look quite up to snuff, did it? Not lovingly cared for."

"That's what happens when a man lives alone, I suppose," she said. She gave a little sigh. "Well, Georgiana"—she broke off, giving an embarrassed grin—"I may call you by your first name, mayn't I, seeing that we are in this together?"

"Of course."

"And you must call me Agatha. As I was saying, we seem to have given ourselves quite a challenge. We have come up with a man who had the means to carry out the deed, but we haven't come up with a real motive. Neither of these people could have done him real harm, could they?"

"Should we mention our theory to the police, do you think?"

"I can't see what good it could do at this stage," she said. "Those glasses containing the mead would have been washed long ago. There would be no proof. But you notice how cleverly Sir Mordred excluded himself as a suspect. There were no berries on his deadly nightshade. A clever man, although he does write the most horrible books, and he cheats too—he has used supernatural means on several occasions to solve a crime."

I tried not to smile. Literary rivalry.

Chapter 33

I am excited that we might be getting somewhere. Was Agatha
  right? Was this all carefully planned? I remembered how Sir
  Mordred had suddenly come up with the idea of hiring my chef.
  Was that after he learned that Pierre not only spoke little
  English but was also an avowed communist? The perfect person
  to be the scapegoat. What we had to do was to find out why
  these two apparently harmless people represented a threat to a
  successful novelist.

"So did you and Mrs. Mallowan have a good chin-wag?" Darcy
asked as we drove home. "Did you solve the crime between you?"
he asked in a joking manner.

"Actually yes, I think so," I said. "It's just that we can't come up
with a good motive."

Then I related how we had worked it out. He looked rather impressed.

"Good God," he said. "It does all make sense. He mentioned he had a laboratory, didn't he? He could easily have brewed a concoction of deadly nightshade when there were berries on it. And then put random elderberries onto the tarts to throw us off the scent. But the question is why?"

"You know people in London," I said. "You could ask around about Sir Mordred. See if he is likely to have any deep, dark secrets he wouldn't want made public."

"I could do that," he said. "And you, I think, should rest, not keep running around at this stage. You'll need all your energy in a week or so."

"You may be right," I said. "My back has been aching all day. But I'd dearly love to go to that inspector and tell him we've solved his case. He was so smug and condescending, wasn't he?"

"He was, a little," Darcy agreed. "Let's hope the solicitor has managed to extricate Pierre. I don't think I'm ready to go back to Queenie's cooking."

We arrived home to find a message that the solicitor had managed to gain Pierre's release but that he was not to leave our house until the case was solved. We sent Phipps to retrieve him from the police station.

"All this running around is not good for you, Georgiana," Fig said as I entered the sitting room. "You need to put your feet up. Save your strength for all that pushing and straining you're going to have to do. Now, I went up and checked on your nursery this morning and I've made a list of things you don't have and are going to need. And I've also had some thoughts on a suitable nanny. I remember that my mother said that the youngest of the Fraser-

Huntingdon sons had gone off to school. That might mean that their nanny is now available. And you know the Fraser-Huntingdons, don't you? Such a proud military family. Generation after generation of generals. The boys all go to Gordonstoun. You know, that outdoor school where they have cross-country runs at six in the morning and cold showers?"

I shuddered, imagining my darling baby being ducked into cold water to harden him up and spanked if he cried.

"Thanks, Fig, but I'm not even sure I want a nanny," I said. "I'll have a nursemaid who is good with children and I want to look after the baby myself."

"Yourself?" That perpetually haughty look became even haughtier. "As in change nappies? Get up in the night to feed the little monster? You can't mean that, Georgiana."

"Oh, I think so," I said. "At least I want to give it a try."

"But what about when you want to travel? You'll surely go over to Ireland to see Darcy's father. And you always seem to be popping across to the Continent."

"Then we'll take the baby with us."

She stared at me as if I'd said that I was going to be taking along a circus, complete with lions and fire-eaters. "Take it with you? Are you mad? Babies demand attention. It will spit up over your nice dress and cry at the wrong moment. No, Georgiana, absolutely no. Babies are a horrid inconvenience. One has to have them, to carry on the line, but the less you see of them, the better."

"I think I'll go and take that nap you recommended," I said and beat a hasty retreat. In truth I had been feeling rather washed out and my back was now most uncomfortable. I felt better after a rest, ate some cold ham and salad for lunch, then greeted Pierre warmly when he arrived home. He took my hands and thanked me profusely for believing in him and helping him. Off he went to the kitchen, promising to make us the best meal we had ever eaten.

After lunch I took a deck chair into the garden and would have passed a relaxing afternoon if Fig had not drawn up a chair beside me and given me a lecture on child raising. In her case I could see the wisdom of a nanny. She had raised two delightful children who were nothing like their mother.

"And the moment they are seven," Fig was saying, "you pack them off to boarding school. Podge is coming up soon. I told Binky we should consider Hyland House for him."

"Because it's close to home?" I asked. "That's nice. You can go and visit him a lot."

"No. Because it's a feeder school for Gordonstoun. Tough. Outdoorsy."

One thing she was not going to do was to subject my nephew to that sort of regime. I sat up. "Absolutely no, Fig. He is a sensitive little boy. It would be quite wrong for him."

"It's precisely because he's sensitive, Georgiana. He needs to toughen up. Be a man. It's a hard world and he'll be a duke someday."

"I don't think dukes are any longer required to lead the charge into battle, Fig," I replied. "He might want to be a poet or a farmer like Binky."

"Oh, Binky is absolutely useless. You know that. If it weren't for the income from the tenants we'd starve."

At that moment the dogs came bounding up to us, ahead of Sir Hubert and the explorer, and I was mercifully saved.

Darcy spent the afternoon making telephone calls to London. We ended the day with a fabulous dinner of shrimp soufflé, followed by what Queenie had called the cocky-van, and then a floating island of meringue and spun sugar, finished with a slab of ripe

Stilton and peaches. I went to bed feeling quite content, Fig and Sir Mordred banished to the back of my mind for the moment, only to be awoken in the darkness by the strangest sensation. I must have groaned because Darcy woke up.

"What's the matter?" he asked.

"I feel terrible," I said. "I have the most awful stomach cramps and I feel sick." Then I realized what I had just said. "Do you think we have got it wrong? It was Pierre after all and now he's trying to poison us?"

Darcy sat up. "I'm calling the doctor right away." He switched on the bedside lamp and reached for his dressing gown.

"Maybe that's a bit hasty," I said. "I'm not feeling quite as bad at the moment. And the food was very rich."

"I'm not taking any chances," Darcy said. "Remember we also drank tea at Mrs. Halliday's. Until we know definitely who killed Mr. Halliday we can't be too careful, especially with you in such a delicate condition."

He left me and I heard his slippers on the stairs then his voice floating up from the foyer. Then another wave of stomach cramps shook me and I was glad the doctor was coming. Darcy reappeared. "He wasn't too pleased to be called out at four o'clock in the morning, but he's on his way," he said. "Is there anything I can get you?"

I shook my head. He sat beside me and held my hand. "My God, if anything happens to you, Georgie . . ."

The warmth of his hand in mine was comforting and I relaxed a little. Everything was going to be all right, I told myself. But then there was another round of intense cramping. Darcy went downstairs to watch for the doctor. I lay there, feeling miserable, until I heard a motorcar pull up, hushed voices below, and then feet on the stairs.

"So, young lady, you think you've eaten something that doesn't agree with you?" he said. "Any vomiting? Diarrhea?"

"Not yet. I do feel sick."

"Let's take a look at you." He pulled back the bedclothes, started to examine me, then glared at me. "You don't have a stomach upset, my dear. You're in labor."

"That can't be right," Darcy said. "The baby's not due for another week at least."

"First babies can be unpredictable," the doctor said, "and the timing is not always that accurate. Were your periods always regular?"

"Not exactly," I said.

"There you are, then. We can only make a prediction based on what you tell us, and that also isn't always accurate. Anyway, no point in debating it. The young woman is in labor, and if you'll leave the room, sir, I'll examine her to find out how far along she is."

"If she's in labor we must get her to the nursing home right away," Darcy said.

The doctor looked up. "No time for that, Mr. O'Mara. Her water just broke. That baby is well on its way."

Suddenly it was all hands on deck. Darcy woke the servants. The bed was stripped. A rubber sheet added. Hot water and towels brought. I lay there watching it as if it was a film, feeling excited but frightened at the same time. Outside the window daylight appeared in the sky. The dawn chorus was deafening. I went from feeling quite normal to being consumed with a round of pain.

"How long will this go on?" I asked when Maisie wiped sweat from my forehead.

"With first babies it could be a few more hours," the doctor said. "We must just let nature take its course."

Not the news I wanted to hear. I began to think about stories I'd heard. Women who had died in childbirth. Babies born with the cord around their neck. "It's going to be all right," I told myself.

Sir Hubert was informed. Apparently he telephoned Zou Zou, who said she was on her way. I wasn't sure how much time passed, but the interval between the contractions was getting narrower. Then I was conscious of a commotion in the doorway. In burst Fig.

"Georgiana, my dear girl, why didn't you call me? I'd have come immediately. You need a woman by your side. Not these heartless men. Do you want some barley water? Brandy? Let me massage your back. That sometimes helps with the agony, so I'm told. Not that I ever experienced it. Binky wouldn't come near the room when I gave birth. Frightened he'd faint dead away, stupid man. And you know what Dr. Mackintosh was like. Not exactly the most kindly of men. Told me to lie there and push."

"Should I be pushing?" I asked, giving my doctor a worried look.

"Not yet. You'll know when you have to," he said, glaring at Fig. "I think Lady Georgiana might feel more comfortable if she was alone at this moment."

"Not at all. She needs a woman. A close relative," Fig said and pulled up a chair beside my bed to emphasize this point.

It must have been midmorning when there was a ring at the doorbell. I heard Mrs. Holbrook's voice. It sounded pleased. A female voice. Light feet on the stairs. It must be Zou Zou, I thought and felt comforted that she was here.

Then someone came into the room.

"Darling. Don't worry. Mummy's here now," said my mother, enveloping me in a cloying wave of perfume.

Chapter 34

JULY 29

EYNSLEIGH

No time to write my diary. Rather busy. Too many things happening. Some good. Some bad.

"I came as soon as I heard the news," Mummy said, perching herself on the bed beside me. "I was in London anyway. I told Max I had to be ready to greet my grandchild so I'd just arrived at Claridge's when I ran into Zou Zou at dinner last night. Then she telephoned me first thing this morning with the news and we drove down together. She's coming up when she's put her motorcar away. So now you are in the good hands of the women who love you." She looked up, looked around. "Oh hello, Fig," she said. "What are you doing here?"

If I hadn't been in so much pain I'd have smiled.

"Madame, I think there are now too many people in this room," the doctor said.

"I quite agree," Mummy replied. "And for your information I am 'Your Grace' and not 'madame.' But as her mother I think I have a right . . ." She looked around. "Darcy, why don't you take Fig downstairs and get her brandy. She looks a bit pale. We don't want her fainting in here."

"I'm perfectly fine, thank you," Fig said in an icy voice. "I wouldn't have thought you'd know how to assist and comfort a woman in labor, having only had one child and then deserting it. I have produced two wonderful children who are the light of my life."

"As long as you only see them for an hour a day at teatime," Mummy replied sweetly.

"I resent that." Fig's voice was rising dangerously.

"Oh, come on, Fig. I've seen you with your children. You don't have one maternal bone in your body."

"Enough not to run away with a succession of men!"

"That's because no man ever asked you . . ."

I sat up, grimacing. "All of you. Out of this room! Now!" I yelled. "Leave me in peace to have my baby."

There was a stunned silence. I didn't often yell.

"Well, if that's what you want, I suppose we should leave you to get on with it," Mummy said in a huffy voice. "Come on, Fig. Let's go."

"Not you, Darcy," I said as he hesitated at the door. "I want you here, with me."

He came over to the bed. "You're doing splendidly, old thing," he said. "It won't be long now, will it, Doctor?"

The doctor gave a noncommittal grunt. "You can never tell with first babies," he said. "They take their own good time."

Midday passed. They brought me up some broth but I didn't want it. Darcy went down to get a bite to eat. Zou Zou came in and said some encouraging words. "And wait until you see the divine stuffed elephant I've brought with me," she said. "The little darling will love it."

But I didn't even want Zou Zou anywhere near me at this moment. I couldn't be bright and cheerful and polite. I wanted to scream and a lady does not scream in public. I gripped Darcy's hand when a wave of pain came over me. He looked at me. "It's all right. Go ahead and yell if you want to."

Then suddenly I said, in a surprised voice, "I have to push. Something's happening."

"Good girl," the doctor said. "Wait for the contraction, then push with all your might."

I waited. I pushed. I waited again and pushed again.

"Why isn't it coming?" I asked.

"It is coming. Very nicely. I can see the top of the head. Lots of dark hair. Just like the daddy. Now, one more big push . . ."

And suddenly a loud and lusty cry filled the room. I looked at Darcy in amazement. The doctor wrapped the baby in a towel. "You have a fine son," he said.

"A little boy," Darcy said, his voice cracking with emotion.

"I have a little boy," I repeated and burst into tears.

The doctor cut the cord, cleaned up the baby and put him into my arms. Little dark eyes frowned up at me. "I think I know you," they seemed to be saying. A tiny hand reached out and touched my cheek. It was all too amazing to be real.

"He's got good big hands," Darcy said. "Going to be a rugby player."

※

WHEN I WAS spruced up and ready to receive visitors, the rest of the household was allowed into the room.

"You've a boy. An heir. A future Lord Kilhenny," Sir Hubert said, patting Darcy on the back. "You must be very proud."

"I was hoping for a little girl," Mummy said. "Weren't you, Zou Zou? Not much fun dressing a boy. They get everything dirty."

"But he is a lovely baby." Zou Zou reached forward to stroke that dark hair. "Handsome. Going to be a heartbreaker like his father." She gave Darcy a knowing wink. Those two had been rather too close at some stage, I suspected.

I looked around and saw my grandfather hovering in the doorway. "Come and see your great-grandson, Granddad," I called.

The others parted to let him forward. He stared down at the baby with a look of such tenderness that it melted my heart. "He looks a lot like your uncle Jimmy did," he said. "He was a handsome baby too, I remember."

"You have an Uncle Jimmy?" Fig asked.

"He was killed in the Great War," Granddad said.

"Have you decided on the name?" Fig asked. "Is he to be Darcy? A rather strange name, I've always felt. Not quite normal." And this from one who was called Hilda.

"We've discussed it," Darcy said, "but haven't quite decided."

"You'll have to come up with a name for the birth certificate," Fig said sharply.

Darcy caught my expression. "Georgie needs to rest now," he said. "Let's give her some time to sleep."

They tiptoed out, one by one.

"What do you think we should call him?" he asked me. "Definitely not Darcy as his first name. Two in one family is too much. And my baptismal first name is William because the priest told my parents that Darcy wasn't a true saint's name. So he could be William. Or Thaddeus Alexander like my father?"

"Oh golly, no," I said.

"Or Albert after his grandfather and great-grandfather?"

"That should probably be in there somewhere," I agreed. "But Albert is such an old man's name."

"William, then?" Darcy studied his son's sleeping face.

I looked too. Billy? Will? "He doesn't really look like a William to me, no more than you do," I said. "You know, I just had an idea. Granddad said he reminded him a lot of Uncle Jimmy. Would you mind if we called him James?"

"James O'Mara. Has a nice ring to it," Darcy said. "James Albert Darcy, Eighteenth Baron Kilhenny. Yes, I think we can go with that."

"That's perfect." I beamed at him.

"Right. I'll spread the news," Darcy said, "and leave you to sleep. Is there anything you want?"

"You know what I want?" I replied. "I'm starving. I've missed several meals. Right now I could do with scrambled eggs and bacon."

THE NAME WAS universally approved of, except that Binky wondered if we should add a Fergus, Bruce or Hamish to it, to honor my side of the family. I pointed out we'd got Albert and you couldn't get much more of an honor than that. Granddad actually wiped away a tear when I told him we'd called the baby after Uncle Jimmy—and him, of course. Another Albert. So we were honoring both sides of my family.

James Albert Darcy slept peacefully, woke up to feed and slept again. Mummy, Fig and Zou Zou amused themselves by annoying each other, in between trying to outdo each other in giving lavish gifts to the baby. The explorer, annoyed at not being the center of attention, I suspect, went home, having promised to send us one of his priceless artifacts as a christening present. I didn't think a baby would be thrilled with a shrunken head or war club but was gracious.

And two days later Darcy got a telephone call from London. He came into my room when I was nursing James. "Sorry to interrupt," he said, gazing down at us tenderly, "but my man in London has reported back to me. About Sir Mordred. It seems his financial state is not that wonderful. His publisher confided that his books are no longer selling well. His sort of stuff is a fad that people tire of and he tends to churn out the same story each time."

"But he married money," I said.

"He spent her money buying the manor, and the house he inherited needs lots of repairs," Darcy said. "Moreover, his wife left him an income for life but the bulk of her fortune goes to the two children, so he doesn't have that much disposable cash, which he needs right now to fund this film with Laurence Olivier."

"He has to fund his own film?"

"He has to come up with the bulk of the cash, and he's desperate to do it because it will put his name back in front of the public."

I thought about this. "So you are saying that he held the open house and the banquet to make money for himself?"

"It appears that way."

"And the old lady smelled a rat. She was going to check up on his South African orphans."

Darcy nodded again.

"But would that make you want to kill, Darcy?" I asked. "It would be an embarrassment, that's all. How many public figures have misused money, after all?"

He nodded. "But he is a vain man, isn't he? He'd hate to be scorned."

"And that doesn't explain why he wanted Mr. Halliday out of the way."

"No, it doesn't."

"You'll share this information with Inspector Sturgeon, will you?" I asked.

"Oh, definitely. It's up to him what he does with it."

AFTER DARCY HAD gone and James Albert was lying in his bassinet, awake and alert, I thought about what he had just told me. So Sir Mordred was a shifty character, but surely people did not kill because they were mishandling money, unless it would mean their utter ruin, which this wouldn't. In fact it might work the other way around. His name would be in the public eye again if there was a scandal. And scandals sell books.

Inspector Sturgeon did not seem to agree with me when Darcy told him this. He was inclined to believe that the old lady's death was of a weak heart, not from anything sinister. And he couldn't come up with any good reason for wanting to bump off Mr. Halliday.

And so, it seemed, we were at a stalemate. Mummy, Zou Zou

and Fig flitted in and out with advice, presents, and complaints about each other (not Zou Zou; she never complained, but instead told stories about the other two locked in combat). I lay in bed, feeling bored and wanting something to do. This two weeks of lying in was stupid, I told myself. I felt perfectly fit and ready to get on with life again.

On a fine afternoon I was sitting in the armchair by the open window with James on my lap. His eyes were open and he was focused intently on my face, reacting as I smiled and talked to him. I, in turn, gazed at him in utter adoration. I couldn't believe I had produced something so absolutely perfect. His little hand grasped my finger so strongly that I was surprised. I examined those little hands, those perfect tiny fingers. . . . And then I froze. It was almost as if I was having a vision. I was seeing those photographs of the rugby team at Harrow. Shrimpy Mortimer sitting in the middle, holding the ball. And in the final photo, the first fifteen, the finger on one of his hands was misshapen, with the joint swollen.

I stood up and put James back in his bassinet, much to his annoyance, then rang the bell. Maisie appeared, out of breath from running. "You wanted something, my lady?"

"Yes, Maisie. Please tell Mr. Darcy I have to see him immediately."

I waited impatiently, and it seemed to take ages to find him. I was worried that he had gone off to London or somewhere without telling me. But then I heard his feet, hurrying along the hall.

"What's up, old thing?" he asked. "Everything all right?"

"He's not the same person," I blurted out.

"What? You think they switched babies? I call tell you they didn't. I watched him being born."

"No, not babies. Sir Mordred!" I started pacing excitedly.

"Shouldn't you be lying down?" Darcy took my arm to slow me.

"I feel perfectly fine. Listen to this, Darcy. I was looking at James's fingers, thinking how perfect they were, and then I remembered the rugby photographs that Mrs. Halliday showed us. In the last one Mordred's finger was deformed."

"Yes, I remember Mr. Halliday reminded him that he'd broken his finger and they were worried he wouldn't be able to play anymore but he battled through with his hand strapped up."

"Broken limbs never heal absolutely perfectly," I said. "Always a little crooked or deformed. Sir Mordred's fingers are long, straight, and perfect. Mr. Halliday noticed them. He was going to say something. I saw him. Perhaps he was coming to the conclusion that this Sir Mordred was not the same person he knew."

"But why lie about it? Why not say, 'No, I'm not that Mordred'?"

I was moving my arms excitedly again. "Because that Mordred inherited the house and the title."

"So who is he?"

"Remember what he told us about South Africa? He and a friend were prospecting for diamonds and the hole collapsed on them and he was dug out but his friend wasn't so lucky. What if the one who wasn't so lucky was the real Mordred? What if the man we know was the friend—the penniless friend who knew that Mordred had just inherited a title and estate? Perhaps they looked similar enough that he could claim to be Mordred (who had told him he'd never met the cousin from whom he'd inherited), go back to England, and start a new and comfortable life."

Darcy was just staring at me. I went on. "Perhaps he'd always wanted to be a writer but never had the time or funds to do so. And in case anyone might recognize him, he adopted this extreme persona—the long silver hair, the round wire glasses, the ridiculous outfits."

"And he's got away with it, until Tubby Halliday, a former close friend, wanted to come back into his life. And a close friend would know—already began to suspect that night that something wasn't right."

"And when he saw Sir Mordred's hands he knew," I finished for Darcy.

"So he had to die," Darcy said.

We looked at each other, digesting the enormity of what we were thinking.

"How do we prove this?"

"There must be old newspapers on file at the South African High Commission," he said. "Surely a dramatic event like two young men in a mining accident might make the papers?"

He went down to telephone the High Commission and the next day he set off for London, returning triumphant. "Here's a copy of the article in the newspaper," he said. He showed me the grainy photograph of two young men, bare chested, sitting together on a rock, holding shovels, smiling at the camera. One of them was Sir Mordred. And the other . . . "That's Shrimpy Mortimer," I said.

Chapter 35

AUGUST 4
EYNSLEIGH

Now I have plenty of time to write a diary. All is well with the
world. I have an adorable baby, the most beautiful and
intelligent child ever born. And a proud husband. And too
many relatives around me. But Sir Mordred Mortimer has been
arrested for the murders. When they searched his laboratory
they found he had distilled atropine from deadly nightshade. It
would only have taken a couple of drops. The elderberries were
only added to confuse, to make Sir Mordred seem a victim and
to pin the crime on Pierre.

It turned out that the man we knew as Sir Mordred was in fact a
South African called Jack Wheeler. He was raised in an orphanage
in Cape Town, which might explain his desire to help South African orphans, if he truly intended to do so and not keep the money

for himself. It would also explain why he couldn't speak French. Any English public school boy would have had French drummed into him for years, even if he spoke it badly. He and Bobby Mortimer became friends while working together on a ranch after the war ended and Mortimer decided not to go back to England because there was nothing there for him. They decided to try their luck together at diamond mining. What we would never know was whether there really was a cave-in at the spot they were digging. Was Jack Wheeler always opportunistic? Had he just learned about his friend's good luck? Mortimer was about to go off to England to claim a title. Was it just too tempting to make sure the soil gave way? Did he kill his friend first and then stage the cave-in? We'd never know.

Then there was poor old Miss Ormorod. Once he knew she'd be checking out South African orphanages, he couldn't take a chance with her. Also we would never know if Sir Mordred killed his wife, as Edwin had hinted. Since he did not seem to gain financially from this, the answer was probably no. But then perhaps he didn't like her controlling the purse strings. Perhaps she grew tired of him and wanted a divorce. They say that when you have killed once, the subsequent murders are easy.

And so life returned to normal at Eynsleigh—or as normal as life can get with a prima donna like my mother, a poisonous woman like Fig, and a fun-loving beauty like Zou Zou under one roof. Granddad and Binky formed an unlikely alliance and spent a lot of time with Sir Hubert making plans in the grounds. It seemed we were going to get the home farm going again, perhaps have pigs and sheep and to extend the orchard.

I wondered what Mummy would think when she saw that Sir Hubert was keen on Zou Zou.

"That woman," she confided to me as she perched on the side of my bed. "Making cow eyes at Hubert. Quite sickening to the stomach."

"They'd be perfect for each other," I said. "And you didn't want him, remember?"

"I know." She sighed dramatically, the way only an actress can sigh. "Biggest mistake of my life, as it turned out." Then she paused. "No, perhaps the biggest mistake was leaving you. Not being part of your life, watching you grow up."

This took me by surprise. "Again, that was your choice."

"Not exactly." She paused, her delicate hand stroking the white sheet. "It turned out that Bertie had a second family in the South of France. A mistress he adored. He was spending more and more time there. And you know I can never take second billing . . ."

"I met her, you know," I said to Mummy as the memory returned sharply. "I met Janine. My sister. She looked just like me."

"You did. And?"

"She was killed. I didn't have a chance to get to know her."

Mummy sighed again. "So many tragedies and missteps in the past."

I looked up, my eyes holding hers. "Don't make another one, Mummy. Think very carefully before going back to Germany, won't you?"

"But Max adores me," she said. "My life there is most pleasant."

"When you marry him, you'll be a German citizen. You won't be able to leave."

"Why should I want to leave, silly?"

"You've seen the way things are going, Mummy. The Nazis control everything."

"But look at what they've done for the roads. The railways. Darling, you should see the stadium they've built for the Olympics. They started on the first of August, by the way. I have to get back for at least some of it. Max insisted. We have a special box, and those men in their tiny singlets—so invigorating."

"Will you come back here soon?" I asked. I heard the longing in my own voice. I had always wanted a mother like other girls. One who shared secrets with me and helped me choose clothes and told me stories. I had come to accept that this one would never be like that. She stood up from my bed.

"I'll try. Life is so hectic, you know. And guess what? Herr Goebbels suggested that I should be in a film they want to make. Imagine me as a German film star. The perfect blond beauty— that's what he said. Wasn't that sweet of him? I've still got it, even if I am a grandmother now."

Then she made her grand exit, sweeping from the room, probably hearing the applause in her head. I stared after her wondering if she really did not know the way things were heading in Germany and that the film would probably be some kind of propaganda. Or perhaps she knew and just did not care.

Later that day we had another visitor. It was Edwin Mortimer.

"I came to say good-bye," he said. "I wanted you to know that I'm going to America. To my mother's people."

It was just dawning on me that by solving a murder I might have helped to ruin two other lives. "I'm so sorry, Edwin," I said. "But we had to get to the truth, didn't we? Your father killed two people. Maybe more. Maybe he killed the real Mortimer."

Edwin nodded. "Quite possibly. He was a heartless person. He never showed us any affection." He ran his hand along the back of a chair. "It's rather strange coming to terms with the fact that my name is not Mortimer. It's Wheeler. Edwin Wheeler. I think I might get it changed to my mother's last name. Van Oster. Edwin Van Oster. That's sounds all right, doesn't it?"

I nodded. "I think it's good to get away and make a new start," I said. "Won't you sit down? We're about to have lunch if you'd like to join us."

He shook his head. "No, thank you. I just came to tell you what's happening to us. Sylvia and Stanley are going to the South of France and buying a villa where he can write his poetry. We've actually become rather rich. How ironic, don't you think?"

"And Blackheart Manor?" I asked.

"We're selling it. We always hated the place. I wonder who'll want a poison garden."

He left then. I noticed that the worried look had gone from his face.

BY THE END of the week Zou Zou decided she should be going home, Granddad announced that he missed his little garden, and Sir Hubert started making plans for a mountain he hadn't yet climbed. Darcy said that he should be getting back to some sort of work and he couldn't keep turning down assignments. Only Fig and Binky showed no desire to leave.

"It really is pleasant down here, Georgiana," Fig said, stretched out in my deck chair and now looking as red as a lobster in a bright orange swimsuit. "I think we might make this an annual thing. Scotland is never warm in summer."

Darcy was sitting beside me. He sat up, leaning forward. "You'd be welcome to stay on, of course," he said, "but Georgie and I will have to go to Ireland soon to present the baby to his grandfather.

We'll probably take Pierre with us, and Maisie. But Queenie can stay to look after you if you'd like."

As soon as we were alone I burst out laughing. "You were brilliant," I said. "Her face when you said that Queenie could look after them!" I paused. "Were you serious about going to see your father?"

"I was. The stubborn old fool won't do anything about Zou Zou, so I'm going to make sure he knows he's got a rival and had better act fast. And a trip to Ireland will do us good, don't you think? Just the two of us. Plus the future Lord Kilhenny, of course."

"Perfect," I said.

Epilogue

James Albert Darcy was baptized at the nearest Catholic church in Haywards Heath on August 15. The godparents were Zou Zou and Sir Hubert. Mummy had already gone back to Germany and I saw her photograph at the Olympic games, standing between Max and some German Adonis. James wore family christening robes sent down from Scotland at Fig's request. He looked utterly adorable, asleep amid that sea of white lace with a silly little lace cap on his head.

As we came out of the church I was surprised to see faces I knew. Mr. and Mrs. Mallowan were there.

"We were on our way to the station to go back to London," Agatha said, "then we heard that the baptism was to be held and felt we should come along to show support."

"Many congratulations," Max said. "You have a fine son, I see. The heir. Now all you need is the spare."

Agatha moved closer to me as people surrounded Darcy, with baby James in his arms. "Just a word from an old hand," she said.

"Don't let motherhood become all-consuming. You have a fine brain. I was impressed at the way you solved that murder."

"Oh no," I said. "You were the one who realized that the poison need not have been in the tarts."

"But I understand you were the one who noticed the fingers. Very astute of you." She took my hand. "So don't waste your talents, my dear. And come and stay at our house in Torquay sometime. It's delightful. On the water. You'd love it. And you can help me plot my next book. I'm getting a bit stuck with Hercule Poirot. He's been rather pompous as usual but he won't tell me who did it!"

She patted me on the arm as I was swept up into the crowd.

Acknowledgments

As always my heartfelt thanks to my team at Berkley, and my agents at Jane Rotrosen—Meg Ruley and Christina Hogrebe—who make working with them such a joy. Thanks to John and Clare who are the first eyes on my books.

Also thanks to my college friend Christine Hodgson who took me around the poison garden at the Chelsea Physic garden, and my friend Louise Penny with whom I explore it when we are both in England (it has the best restaurant).